WELL-HEELED AND WELL-ARMED

The door to the prefab opened and Dugger stepped out onto the porch. He was holding a baby flame-thrower, made especially for the mercenary market. Dugger's coat was off and he'd left his tie somewhere. The tails of his shirt were not tucked in. I looked around for a weapon and didn't see anything. Burning is not a good way to die.

The front gate was closed. No escape there. I edged toward the door of Building #1 while Dugger tracked me with the nozzle on the flamethrower. "Ever smell burning butt, Murdock?" And then he chuckled and pressed the trigger. A bright tongue of flame sliced through the cold air . . .

"A COMPLEX AND GRITTY STORY HIGH-LIGHTED BY THE AUTHOR'S ABILITY TO WRITE ABOUT CREDIBLE CHARACTERS IN REALISTIC RELATIONSHIPS . . . WILL LEAVE READERS EAGER FOR THE NEXT MURDOCK ADVENTURE." —*Publishers Weekly*

"AN AUTHOR WHOSE CANNY EAR CAN TRANSLATE ACTIONS INTO WORDS THAT ARE THRILLING READERS EVERYWHERE." —*Ocala Star-Banner* (Florida)

BY ROBERT J. RAY:

Matt Murdock Mysteries:
Bloody Murdock
Murdock for Hire
Dial "M" for Murdock

Other Novels:
Heart of the Game
Cage of Mirrors
The Hit Man Cometh

DIAL "M" FOR MURDOCK

A MATT MURDOCK MYSTERY

Robert J. Ray

A DELL BOOK

Published by
Dell Publishing
a division of
Bantam Doubleday Dell Publishing Group, Inc.
666 Fifth Avenue
New York, New York 10103

Reprinted by arrangement with St. Martin's Press

Printed in the United States of America

Published simultaneously in Canada

May 1990

10 9 8 7 6 5 4 3 2 1

OPM

For Marjorie Luesebrink, M.F.A., whose mind
brims and brims with electric ideas

# Acknowledgments

Several people helped in the writing of *Dial "M" for Murdock* and I'd like to thank them here. Frank B. Ray and Tony Troianello gave me sage advice on the mysteries of refrigeration and meat lockers. Ed Waale and Phil Simone proffered valuable insurance industry data. Bruce Greenfield, M.D., guided me through the medical maze that surrounds a death in civilization, and, along with Scott Taylor, Marjorie Luesebrink, Doris Odion, and Chris Eyre, read the manuscript with depth and critical understanding. I got valuable early feedback from Don Stanwood, Jean Femling, Maxine O'Callaghan, Cynthia Farley, Joann Mapson, and Kaye Klem, members of Fictionaires. Jared Kieling, my editor at St. Martin's, tightened the manuscript with his keen eye for plotting. And Jesse Cohen, Assistant Editor, created his usual masterpiece with the Murdock jacket copy.

Friends and experts—they make the book better, every time.

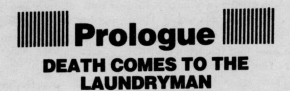

Prologue

DEATH COMES TO THE
LAUNDRYMAN

On the morning of *La Muerte*, Emiliano woke from a nasty, sweaty, champagne-fizz sleep to find an animal crouched on his naked belly.

Emiliano screamed—"*Aiyee, pendejo!*"—and slapped blindly at the beast with his open hand.

The animal, a huge blue furry blur at the edge of the dark, dug its claws into soft flesh and plunged hissing off the bed. Pain knifed through Emiliano—belly, crotch, thighs, *cojones*—and he reared up in the tangle of black silk sheets, groping for a light to brighten this eerie March dawn. This could not be happening. He was still asleep, that was it, mired in a deep blue dream. He was not a grown man, snatched awake in California. He was instead a child asleep in Mexico, and the great gray cats were coming, the terrible dream-tigers with the sharp claws, the long gnashing teeth.

When he woke up, the dream would vanish.

He reached to switch on the light, to end the terrible

1

dream, and knocked over the chrome bedlamp from Tiffany's. The lamp toppled with a muffled crash onto the deep pile carpet. The bulb exploded in the dark with a soft pop. He was awake. *Mierda.*

The pain licked at him now, and he knew he was wounded, bleeding. Cupping himself gently, he swung his legs off the bed. Except for one thin silk sock and his gold Rolex, he was naked. He turned his head and there the damnable beast sat, purring, licking its belly fur, mocking him from the doorway.

El Gato!

The cat, a blue Manx bloated from overfeeding, stopped licking itself and cocked its head, its eyes glowing like the dead orbs of an Egyptian demon-god from a dank Pharoah's tomb.

Emiliano growled his standard challenge. *"Pinche pendejo maricon!"*

He went to his knees, cursing, groping furiously beneath the huge bed until his fingers found the silver handle of the Austrian riding crop.

He brandished the riding crop in his left hand and charged. The cat bounded away. Emiliano hesitated at the bedroom door, breathing hard, listening for sounds of his wife. Nothing. She was out of the house on her morning run. Three miles. Four. Five. Each morning, she ran into the dawn, trying to escape.

El Gato slipped around a corner into the upstairs study. Emiliano followed, slamming the door behind him and locking it.

This was his lair, the cave of the stockbroker. Records. Books. His own compact disk player. Two shelves of the Russians: Stravinsky, Borodin, Rimsky-Korsakov, Rachmaninoff. Three filing cabinets. The AST computer terminal was linked to a mainframe in his brokerage house in Newport Center. Emiliano was a scholar and a thinker. He would miss this room.

Time for sweet revenge.

He sank to his knees to probe beneath the desk with the riding crop. He jabbed. El Gato hissed. Grunting with effort, Emiliano tried to move the desk, but the carpet was thick and the oversize desk was heavy. Sweat streamed from him, stinking of yellow champagne. There was a time, not so long ago, when he could have moved that desk. Marriage had made him weak.

Gripping the riding crop, he tried again for the cat, thrusting, his head deep into the dark recess beneath his desk. He was Scaramouche, the legendary French lover, carving his enemies with a silver rapier. He was El Condor, the famous Mexican torero, wielding the bullfighter's vengeful sword.

He stabbed, and the cat snarled, a wild, wailing sound. As a youth, Emiliano had dreamed of training to become a bullfighter, a toreador in the bullrings of Mexico, South America, Spain.

"Gato!" he cried. "Gato, you *cabron!*"

The dream of glory in the bullring faded as a wave of sickness rocked Emiliano, forcing him to retreat, butt first, like a scuttling crab. He dropped the riding crop and crawled feebly to the door, tears in his eyes, his gorge rising. Unlocking the door took an eternity. He dragged himself to his feet and stumbled toward the bedroom, his stomach reeling. Only twenty feet to the toilet. Only—

No use.

He vomited just inside the bedroom door, splashing party puke on the deep red carpet. He lay there, naked and gasping, his face inches from the pool of vomit that settled slowly out of sight. It had a sweetish, sickly, complex smell, the sourness of last night's alcohol mixed with

3

bitter green bile. The clock ticked, drawing him closer to *La Muerte*. For a moment, he passed out.

The phone rang. Three soft buzzes and then nothing. Who was calling at this hour? Had the caller hung up? Had his wife answered downstairs? The phone rang again, twice, then stopped.

He lay for a moment staring at the phone, then crawled to the lavatory to wash off his face and rinse his sour mouth. In the medicine cabinet, he found the pink pastilles from Dr. Ames. His hand shook as he wrenched off the cap and tossed two onto his tongue. Their bitter taste made him gag and he sloshed water into his mouth from the silver Italian carafe, handmade by silversmiths in Florence. A love gift from his wife, on their honeymoon.

In the mirror his face was green beneath the coat of winter tan. There were dark circles under his eyes. He was forty-eight years old, tall for a Mexican, and rich. So why did he look like death? A close examination revealed red claw marks on his stomach, and spots of dried blood. His precious *cojones,* thank God, were intact.

Leaning into the pink lavatory, he read the label from the pharmacy. Physician: Dr. Sylvan Ames. Patient: Emiliano Mendez-Madrid. Address: 17 Spyglass Rim Drive, Newport Beach, CA. Dose: Two every two hours for stress.

"Take a couple for the heebie-jeebies," Dr. Ames had said. "Or if your bones start to quiver and shake. You could be edgy prior to the big event. Stay off the booze and keep your mind on the future. You're a lucky man, Mendez. It's not every fellow who can get himself reborn on Sunday on a tennis court in California."

He locked the bathroom door and pulled on the edge of the striated pink marble lavatory. It had been custommade by workmen from Marfil, near Guanajuato in cen-

4

tral Mexico. As he pulled, a section of the wall swung out on oiled hinges to reveal a shallow hiding place measuring two feet square. In the secret space was a rectangular package, wrapped in plastic. He opened the plastic and thumbed its contents, $210,000 in used fifties and twenties. Emiliano had $6.5 million in a bank in Zurich. When the insurance was paid, he would receive $3.5 million more. He did not plan to return to California. This secret money was for unforseen events, just in case.

The time was 7:38 as he belted his silk robe and walked downstairs for morning coffee. He was feeling better now, more himself. He peered over the railing of the balcony that ran the length of the second story. El Gato, the coward, was nowhere in sight.

The party mess had been cleaned up, the room straightened. Chavella, the maid, was in Durango tending a sick brother. That meant his wife had been up for some time, silently busying herself. The ashtrays had been wiped clean, but the lingering smell of marijuana sickened him. The papers and streamers were gone. Near the kitchen door, three oversized trash sacks bulged with waste from the Saturday night fiesta. There was a dark burn spot on the orange sofa where beautiful Terri Wentworth, the Hot One, had dropped her marijuana cigarette while laughing at one of Emiliano's jokes.

His wife stood leaning against the kitchen cabinet, facing the Pacific as she talked on the phone. Her long black hair was piled on top of her head, and she wore soft white running shorts and a sleeveless white tank top that outlined her breasts. On her legs were fuzzy white leg warmers. She was barefoot. His wife was thirty-four, five-ten, intelligent, and very beautiful. Alas, despite the other women, the buttery beach girls, he wanted her. What would she say if she knew today was the day for *La Muerte*?

As he came into the kitchen, his wife handed him the phone.

"It's Rudolfo," she said.

The taste of vomit rose again in his gorge as he took the phone. His wife padded to the Mr. Coffee machine and poured him a cup of black coffee. Then she left the room.

"Rudolfo," he said heartily. "You *cabrito*. Where are you?"

"At the Côte d'Azur, *maricon*. Where else?"

He sipped the steaming coffee and tried to organize his thoughts. "You missed a big party, my friend," Emiliano said, in Spanish. "Why did you not inform us of your arrival?"

Rudolfo evaded his question. Instead he said: "I will buy your breakfast this morning, Emiliano. We have much business to discuss. Eight statues arrive Tuesday."

"From Europe?" Emiliano asked.

"From Argentina, a private collection. Their condition is excellent. Is there space available?"

"Oh, yes. There is ample space. Always."

It was the usual code. One statue from Argentina meant $1 million in U.S. currency. Eight statues meant $8 million, which brought the year's total up to $47 million. On Tuesday Rudolfo's couriers would hand over $8 million in cash. Emiliano's job—through his stockbrokerage house of Gebhardt, Wingo, and Mendez-Madrid, Inc.— was to turn the cash into financial instruments: stocks, bonds, letters of credit, money market funds, even some treasuries. Emiliano was a money-launderer. He turned dirty money into clean money. The dirty money came from drugs, mostly cocaine from Colombia, brought by Rudolfo's syndicate through Mexico, then smuggled into the United States. The laundered money went back to circulate in the world's economic system. Rudolfo and his crowd were buying up large chunks of Mexican real estate, working off the hard-pressed peso. As he laundered, Emiliano skimmed.

Did Rudolfo know? Could he guess how much?

"Ten o'clock, *amigo*," Rudolfo said. "The trip was wearisome. I need an hour for a quick siesta, to revive these old bones."

"The warehouse is crowded, *amigo*."

"We shall discuss it over food."

"We are twenty percent over." That meant a loss of 20 percent on the $8 million as it passed from hand to hand.

"I should take my business elsewhere, Emiliano."

"That, of course, is your decision."

There was a pause while Rudolfo covered the phone and spoke to someone in his hotel room. "Ten o'clock," Rudolfo said. "At Las Brisas. Come alone."

"Why not meet us at the club?" Emiliano said. "I have a match. You can watch the ladies."

"Is your memorable wife playing?"

"Of course."

"Then I consider it my duty. What time?"

"The match is at ten-thirty," Emiliano lied.

"Have you spoken to your wife about that other matter?"

Rudolfo wanted a threesome, a *ménage à trois* with Roxanne. "Yes. And she agrees."

"Ten-thirty, *amigo*." Rudolfo hung up.

Sweating heavily, Emiliano hung up and stumbled out of the kitchen. He found his wife in her study, editing an essay on one of her damnable South Americans. The bitch was always editing, reading, writing, pretending to be a scholar. *La profesora*.

"What did Rudolfo say? What were you two whispering about?"

She looked up. "I wasn't whispering, Emmy."

"You bitch."

His wife stood up and brushed past him. He smelled faint perfume, mixed with athlete's sweat. He had the desire to grab her, strike her, club her to her knees. But she was tall, strong as an Amazon queen. At the stairway she stopped.

"Claude Belker called."

"What did he want?"

"He didn't say. Claude never does. You look terrible, Emmy. Are you sure you feel up to the match?"

"It's only mixed."

His wife smiled. As she walked upstairs, he admired her brown legs and her tight buttocks. He phoned Claude Belker at his home in China Gate, but there was no answer.

At 9:07 they drove in the brown Mercedes off fashionable Spyglass Hill and down through the winding streets of Newport Beach. It was a beautiful morning, the air swept fresh by spring rain. *La Muerte* was set for 10:02. With Rudolfo lurking, there was no turning back.

His wife was driving, and he sat slumped in the passenger seat, blinking back at the dashboard clock. He had on his Lacoste tennis whites and his new tennis shoes. The shoes retailed for $190. In his tennis bag on the back seat was his new Sahara Defender racquet that cost $750. His wife was a smooth driver. When they passed Jamboree Road, he saw the silver gray ambulance with the logo of Esprit Ambulance Service painted on the side. His wife did not notice.

Their opponents for the tennis match, Bob and Betsy Maclean, were waiting in a knot of colorfully dressed people in the stands overlooking Centre Court. Bob Maclean was the ex-mayor of Newport Beach. Betsy was the owner of Sandcastle Real Estate. Bob was on the list for June and therefore part of today's events.

There was much hand shaking and replaying of the party the night before. His wife did not participate, but walked instead to the pro shop. Emiliano watched her go with a measure of sadness. He turned to speak with Betsy about the market, inflation, the Fed, Ginnie Mae's, and Eleventh District indices. Her melon breasts were lightly dusted with freckles. Their court came up at 9:31, a minute off schedule.

Dr. Ames appeared briefly at 9:59, with Señor Robertson, the insurance agent from Heartland. The doctor wore gray slacks, a pink shirt, and a conservative gray blazer. Señor Robertson wore a pale blue track suit, with yellow stripes. They stood for a moment, watching the tennis through the windscreen. Dr. Ames lit a cigar. That was the signal. *La Muerte* would proceed on schedule.

"What is the damnable score?" he asked his wife.

"Love-three."

"First set?"

His wife stared at him. "No, Emmy. Second set. Did you leave your serve in San Francisco?"

"Don't rub it in, *querida*."

"I hate losing," his wife said. "Especially to her."

In the next game, his wife sliced a low backhand sharply cross court, pulling Bob Maclean wide, forcing him to loft a lob.

"Mine!" Emiliano called. He dashed back, the California sun an orange wafer against the bright spring sky, pivoting the way he had as a young student at UCLA, a horny Mexicano from Guadalajara. Where had the good times gone?

He slashed at the ball with his black Defender, uttered a cry loud enough to be heard on the adjacent court, and collapsed. He skinned his knee as he went down and cursed himself for that kind of stupidity. The ball sailed through the air for a perfect winner. Good. Take that. Make his parting shot at Le Club one to remember. Lying on the green court, the heat rising, he saw his wife's stricken face as he grabbed his chest and cried out: "Ahhh!"

"What is it, Emmy?" She ran toward him. "Emiliano?"

"Doctor," he called, his voice grating. "Get a doctor!"

"Call a doctor, Bob, Betsy. *Do* something." His wife dropped her racquet and went to her knees. "Emmy, what is it? Are you all right?"

"It hurts," he grated. "There is much pain."

"Dear God," she whispered. "Can I do something? Emmy? Can I do anything?"

"It hurts," he said in Spanish.

She bit her lip and called again for a doctor. The green laykold surface was toasty from the sun. In the arms of *La Muerte* he still felt apprehensive. This was a new journey, one he had never taken before. How many others had preceded him? Strich. Logan. Barrymore. "Ahhhh!" he moaned.

The court filled with people, staring down at him. Someone gave him first aid, blowing air into his mouth. The breath tasted of fried eggs, sulphurous, and stale marijuana smoke.

At last there were murmurs from the crowd, and then a voice Emiliano recognized, a British voice, that blurred London accent. It belonged to Señor Jerome, a sour, surly man with bad teeth and the white hair of the albino. Señor Jerome worked for Señor Robertson. Whom did Robertson work for?

Strong arms lifted him up.

"Start a bloody IV," said Señor Jerome.

"Got it," another voice said.

A blanket went over him.

"Where are you taking him?" his wife demanded.

"St. Boniface, missus. We'd better get going now. Would you clear the way, please. That's right. Everything will be just fine now, missus."

They rolled him along the walkway between the tennis courts, where people were still playing tennis. The stands above Centre Court were half-full with spectators. In a moment life at Le Club would be back to normal, with no memory of his passing. At the ambulance his wife tried to get in with him but was stopped by Señor Jerome.

"Sorry, missus. It's against the rules, you see."

"But—"

"You can follow along in your car, missus. It's just up the hill."

"But I—"

He heard Bob Maclean's voice. "It's okay, Rox. You can ride with us."

"Thank you, Robert. Where is your car?"

"This way, Rox. We're ready when you are."

Emiliano was inside the ambulance now, the needle of the IV stabbing his left arm. The wide rear door stood open, framing the world in a square of California sunlight. A good way, Emiliano thought, to start a new life. He had the sudden insane urge to sit up and wave goodbye. Señor Jerome towered over him, holding a hypodermic in his right hand. Fear gripped Emiliano. No one had mentioned shots. This was not part of the plan.

"Emmy?" his wife called. "We're leaving now."

The ambulance started, and he felt the jab of a needle.

"There," Señor Jerome breathed. "Now that's done."

His wife was framed in the square of light, white dress, tanned arms and legs, dark shining hair, close but still very far away, dwindling into the distance. Would he ever see her again? A man stood beside her, a dark man with a heavy mestizo face. He wore a white suit and white shoes, and he was staring at the ambulance as he gripped the woman's bare arm. A pity that Rudolfo had come too late to watch the tennis.

Now Emiliano thought of his wife. He did not forgive her for wanting a divorce, the first in his family. He did not forgive her for being a bitch, a witch, a *bruja*. After *La Muerte* what would she do? Would she return to her beloved East Coast? Would she trap some balding professor into marriage? What would she do when she discovered he had changed beneficiaries? What would she do when the bank took back the house? Let her wait tables. Let her throw her body on the mercy of the marketplace. Let her compete with beach girls for tips. Ah, how he would miss those beach girls. How . . .

The door of the ambulance closed and Señor Jerome covered his face with one corner of the winding sheet. Now Emiliano was afraid. Sweat poured from him, soaking his clothes. In Zurich it would be snowing.

Think of the money. $6.5 million skimmed into his Swiss account. $3.5 million from the insurance. Some $10 million, a tidy sum, and quite tax-free. Think of sun-skinned beach girls. Think of Rudolfo's rage. Think of the good times to come after *La Muerte*.

He heard a squeak of rubber as the ambulance pulled away.

After that Emiliano knew only the terrible white silence of the shroud.

He assured himself it was only temporary.

1

The temperature was 86 degrees in the shade when I finished my run along the edge of the Pacific. The season was early June, time for schools to be letting out in California, and the beaches were already clotted with eager sun-people. My place overlooks a slice of beach near the Newport Pier, an area known locally as Punker's Strip.

Punker's Strip includes the pier, the quad, the parking triangle, the dory fishermen, a row of dark bars for tourists masquerading as locals, three snappy restaurants, an upscale bed and breakfast place, lots of sand and seagull crap, a public toilet, and a population of skinheads and bikers and cops and assorted teenage punkers. It's an interesting area, sort of a symbol for California. Everyone can drive. Everyone has a tan. No one can read. Most summers, I call the tow truck at least once on weekdays and five times on the weekend.

Sweating from my run, I climbed the stairs to my deck to find a guy in a business suit waiting. Behind the expensive tinted glasses he looked like any corporate suit. When he moved, he seemed familiar, a shadow against the jungle, a shape from the past. He had sandy hair and a neat mustache. When he grinned and held out his hand, I knew him. It was Bruce Halliburton, Harvard, Annapolis, Langley, Saigon. A snappy attaché case with gold initials rested on the boards of my deck.

"Captain Murdock, I presume? The man behind the gray-streaked facial hair?"

"Goddam," I said. "If it isn't Superagent Halliburton."

He took off the dark glasses, and we shook. The eyes still had their shrewd scholarly look, as if he peered into the test tube of life like a scientist, knowing before he looked what would be there, writhing inside the glass, waiting to be measured, weighed, scoped, analyzed.

"Want a beer?"

"Is there gin?"

"Yeah." I remembered Bruce was a martini drinker. "We got ice, vermouth, bitters."

"I am impressed."

He picked up the attaché case, and I unlocked my door. Once inside, I walked across the room to turn off the alarm. It has push buttons like a telephone. The code word is UNICORN, a suggestion from Wally St. Moritz, who runs the Saintly Silver Surfer, down below. Unicorn, in numbers, is 8642676. You have forty-five seconds to code in the word before the alarm goes bananas. I punched in the cutoff code, but nothing happened. My alarm is Econo-Alert, the economy model, made by Aries Security. Sometimes you have to recode. And recode. And recode.

Today, the third time was a charm. Gotcha. The red light stopped blinking. I hauled out gin and ice and vermouth. While Bruce mixed his martini, I popped open a Bud. The first sip is always the best.

My place on the Newport Pier was built back in the forties by Uncle Walt Wieland, my mother's oldest brother. He taught me about woodworking and carpentry. When he died, Uncle Walt left me the place in his will. It's a super pad. A cooking island separates the kitchen from the living room. I've got built-ins and gadgets from Sears to make life easy. The fridge is old but roomy. The place has a homey feel.

With the shades up, you can stand in the living room and see 180 degrees, from the end of the pier out along the beach to Palos Verdes and then across the quad to Balboa Boulevard. Last year I built an entertainment center out of smooth white pine. My ancient stereo is there, and my old RCA video player, and my second-hand TV. As a kid my dream was to play pro baseball. Now, after a stint in the Army and some cop-time and a try at the construction game, I record the baseball games and watch them into the night.

My old man's club was the Dodgers. Mine is the Braves.

To the left of the entertainment center I left a narrow strip of wall for photographs of my parents, a couple of Army buddies, and a few ladies worth remembering. From time to time the photos of the ladies get replaced, usually by a lady who comes on the scene with a fresh sense of design and appropriateness. I don't mind. I care about people, not photos.

The bedroom is roomy. The bathroom is huge. There's a shower and a large tub and a commode imported from Sweden. I installed twin lavatories and a wall-length mirror along the pathway leading to the bathroom. Sometimes guests stay over. There's space in the bathroom for a Jacuzzi, but I'm waiting until I get ahead on money.

My workroom is on the other side of the bathroom. At least half a dozen women wanted that space turned into a bedroom, or a sitting room, or a family room. Use that space, they say. Make it pretty. Dress it up. Jacqueline Dumont, an architect from Grosse Point, actually drew up plans, blueprints for Murdock, that included a cute guest bedroom and a private bath. Jacqueline married a city planner, and they produced two kids.

Bruce looked around at my house and nodded in appreciation as he held out his martini glass in a toast. "To la Bohème."

"That's an opera. Don't tell me. That German guy. Wagner."

Bruce laughed, the Harvard lad smirking gleefully at the high school dropout. "Puccini, Captain. The bohemian life." He indicated the scene down below. "This feels like an opera. All this scenery, all this gritty atmosphere. How do you stand it?"

"I'm eking by, Bruce. Summers are better than winters." Eking was about right. My bank balance at Wells Fargo was $84.57. While the money dwindled, I was waiting for a check to clear on a bank in the Bay Area. The check was for $5,000, payment for helping a Cadillac dealer from San Jose find his estranged wife. I found her in Vegas, playing blackjack with a cowboy from Muskogee and two Iranians. I brought her home to San Jose. Rumors around the Silicon Valley said her husband was about to declare bankruptcy. If that happened, I would become a creditor in a long line of creditors. I had two grand tucked away in my secret cache behind the fridge. Mad money, not to be touched. The sacred hidey-hole. Bruce Halliburton looked corporate prosperous. I hoped he needed some work done.

We sat on the deck, reminiscing about the old days, the girls, the battles, the guys. Sergeant Dave Kellogg was dead, a heart attack in Dallas. Lieutenant Wilbur Aiken was a police captain in Milwaukee. No one knew the whereabouts of Captain Doug Blaisdell, a southern boy who'd gone over from Special Forces to the Company.

"Didn't Blaisdell work with you on that college thing for the Company?" Bruce asked.

"No. That was Jack Tully."

"They're about the same size and build. And they were both at Harvard, before my time. I always mix them up."

I finished the beer. It was time to find out why he was here. "You in town on business, Bruce?"

He produced a shining white business card that identified him as a vice president at Heartland Mutual Life, headquarters in Lincoln, Nebraska. The California office was in Century City, a snazzy corporate stronghold in Los Angeles. There were two phone numbers, both with the 213 area code. I'd seen the Heartland ads on television, a suburban scene with Mom and Dad and two tow-headed kids biking along, and a red, white, and blue farmhouse rising like the American flag in the background. The business card was embossed in black letters.

"What do you do at Heartland?"

"I'm in charge of investigating claims. Clearing them."

"All claims?"

"No. Just the ones with a significant odor."

"Not in Orange County. No bad smells here."

Bruce grinned at me and stood up. "Mind if I have another?"

"Hey. It's Wednesday. Go for it. Another Bud for me."

He walked into the house and came back in a minute with fresh drinks. "What was your per diem back in the seventies? When you went undercover for us?" He removed his gray suit coat and draped it carefully the back of a deck chair.

"Thirty a day, and you guys paid for room, board, and schoolbooks."

17

"And today?"

"Sixty an hour. If the work gets into days, three hundred a day."

"Who covers expenses?"

"The client."

Bruce smiled at my numbers. "You're certainly keeping pace with inflation."

"Yeah. Me and the Department of Defense. Do I smell a job here?"

He nodded and shifted in his chair so he could pick up the attaché case. He opened it and took out a manila file folder and handed it over. The name on the tab was Belker, Claude A. Before he closed the case, I caught sight of a second folder. It had a Spanish name, hyphenated. Mendez-Madrid. Very fancy. Tucked away beside the stack of folders was a small pistol. It looked like a five shot .32. What they call an Airweight.

I opened the Belker file and flipped through the pages. There were three photographs of a heavyset man in his early fifties. Two of the photos were posed for the CEO look, shrewd entrepreneurial eyes, the power suit, the world-beater smile. The third photo showed the same man in a family shot, with a blond woman and two teenage kids. The woman had frizzy hair and dark circles under both eyes.

There were newspaper clippings, with little yellow stick-ons attached to form a chronology. On April 13 of this year Claude Belker's car had crashed into a truck on Pacific Coast Highway. The truck had been carrying half a load of something flammable and Claude Belker had burned to death.

A single, handwritten, yellow, legal size sheet contained information about Belker's insurance. There were four companies involved. Heartland was in for the most coverage at $5.1 million. Dates told the story. On December 1 of last year Claude Belker had beefed up his Heartland insurance—he'd been covered for $1 million—with a second policy for $2.2 million. In January he'd taken out a third Heartland policy for $1.9 million. From January through March 30 he added six policies with three other companies to bring his total insurance coverage up to $14.5 million. In April Belker had died when his car had smacked the gas truck.

A bad way to go, burning.

The death certificate was signed with a scrawled signature with the letters "M.D." after the scrawl. The script was slanted and gothic. It looked like James. Or perhaps Raines. I could not make it out.

Before his death, Claude Belker had been president of Golden bear Savings and Loan, a California thrift institution. Golden Bear had seventeen branches in Orange County, twelve more in Riverside County, and ten others dotting the landscape from San Bernardino up to Lake Tahoe and Sacramento. The headquarters were in Newport Beach.

There was a single computer sheet giving a few facts about Claude Belker. Age: fifty-two. Birthplace: Omaha, Nebraska. Married to Wanda Kilgallen. Two kids: Randy, fourteen; Belinda, sixteen. His house in China Gate was worth $3.5 million. His cars—a Lincoln town car, a Mercedes wagon, and a Porsche—were leased by the corporation. The Porsche had burnt up with Belker. At the time of his death Belker's debt-load had totalled $17.1 million.

"Tidy little sum," I said. "Fourteen mil point five hundred thousand."

"There were four companies involved. Heartland was in for five point one million."

"The lion's share."

"In reverse," Bruce said.

"Who gets the money?"

Bruce leaned toward me, his face CIA intense. "We've found some irregularities in Belker's aps, the ones he filled out in December, January. Our attorneys are stalling on payment—the bulk of the money is slated for a trust, to retire the debt—but if we had more to go into court with, more hard evidence, we could refuse payment altogether."

"What about the poor widow, the starving kids?"

Bruce shrugged. "Personally, they have my sympathy. Professionally, it's not my problem. As a matter of fact, she does have equity in the home in China Gate. Hand me that jacket, will you?"

I handed him the file, and he riffled through the papers with practiced skill, a man totally at home with reports, numbers, spread sheets, actuarial tables, and the patterns of demography. He pulled out a single sheet and showed it to me.

"Four months before he died Claude Belker tripled his insurance. He was carrying just under four million. When he finished, he had over fourteen. Our agent was remiss. Heartland standard procedure clearly states that you list the other policies held, along with the issuing firms and the policy amounts. But our form has only four slots for other insurance, so the standard practice in the industry is to list a couple, three at the most, and let it go at that. Belker had a million with us and had never missed a payment. The three items listed on the Heartland ap brought our man Belker up to one million six with three other companies. Our agent wrote up the two-point-two. In February Belker ran up more debt and took out that second policy. We had no idea what the total was until he died and the claims rolled in."

"Who was the agent?"

"A local man. Bob Robertson."

"What's his story?"

"Bob knew Belker. He saw the debt load and cash flow statement from Golden Bear. Belker passed his physical. He kept in shape, running, racquetball, hiking."

"What am I looking for, Bruce?"

"As I said, irregularities."

"The paper trail?"

"You're the detective. This is your territory." He leaned closer. "It's my opinion that Belker's out there, walking around."

"Alive?"

Bruce nodded. "Very much."

"Who burnt up in the Porsche?"

"Someone else."

"What about the autopsy? The teeth? All that fancy forensic matching?"

"The teeth exploded. A forensic team studied what was left, and determined it was Belker." Bruce drained the last of his martini. "May I?"

"Sure."

We walked inside. Bruce freshened his martini. I still had half a beer. I'd heard about guys faking their deaths, to get the insurance. But nothing this big or this elaborate. Belker must have wanted out bad. And I had the feeling Bruce wasn't briefing me on the whole picture. He had gone through a door and closed it behind him, leaving Murdock outside, in the dark.

"So I'm looking for Belker?"

"Yes."

"How much time have I got?"

Bruce waited before answering. He loosened his tie, a shade of gray that matched the summer-weight suit. The white shirt looked fresh as a Hathaway ad. The shoes had a high gleaming polish.

"We go to court on Monday."

"Terrific." I saluted him with the beer. "Tell me about the autopsy."

"The forensics people didn't have much to work with. The body had been badly burned. All but two of the teeth exploded. Those matched with Belker's dental records. The bones that did remain belonged to the same body-type as Belker. There was a class ring from his college in the Midwest, along with other jewelry. The gold melted, but the stones were identified by the wife. There's something else that goes on in these cases. If a person is seen entering a car at point A, and then if the car has an accident at point B, the person who entered at point A is presumed to be in the car at point B."

"Who saw him at point A?"

"Employees at Golden Bear."

"Two of the teeth matched?"

"Yes."

"But your theory is they switched bodies?"

"That's the only way."

"They didn't have much time."

"That makes it professional."

"So I start today?"

He reached into his jacket pocket and came out with a handsome eelskin wallet. "How about a thousand for a retainer. Three hundred a day comes to nine hundred. An extra hundred for unforseen expenses. We'll pay twenty cents a mile for the vehicle. If you have to fly someplace, keep the paper work clean so you can be reimbursed. Keep receipts for meals on the job, long distance calls, any entertainment. On the expense scale Heartland is about a six."

"The Company was about a two."

"Well, insurance companies do have those corporate tax breaks."

He counted out ten one-hundred-dollar bills. They

were crisp and new. As each one dropped into my palm, I felt better. Monday was four days away, which didn't give me much time. Life was short, and Murdock was getting older. I wondered if Heartland had other work, something steady for my declining years. Maybe I could have some cards printed up, Matt Murdock, Vice President. With two phones.

"What are you working on, Bruce?"

"Another case."

"Related?"

"I'm not sure."

"Local?"

"Yes."

Bruce handed me the manila folder. "This jacket is yours. We have duplicates of everything, but it would be nice if you could return this material intact. You've got both my numbers there, on the card. My secretary is Jennifer Bailey. She'll know where I can be reached. My Number One is Ken Trager. He's a trifle over-eager, but he can be forgiven because he used to play varsity baseball at Michigan."

"What position?"

"Pitcher."

"You've got to be over-eager on the mound."

Bruce stood and picked up his gray coat, which he slung over his shoulder. Standing there, he looked like a male model for a billboard ad for Brooks Brothers. He held out his hand, and we shook, and then he turned and walked down the stairs. As he crossed the quad and unlocked the door to a gray Volvo, he seemed to be carrying his martinis just fine.

I waited a couple of minutes, thumbing through the Belker dossier, and then I made some phone calls. The first was to Golden Bear S & L. They were open until four on Wednesdays. I said I had a large deposit and made an appointment with a vice president named S. Jaspers for three o'clock. The second call was to Josephine August, a real estate broker who owed me a favor. Yes, Josephine said, the Belker home in China Gate was for sale. The asking price was $3.8 million, but she thought the value was closer to $2.9 million. I told her I represented a client with money to burn. That was true. She said I could see the property at 3:45.

The third call was to Kristi Flamingo, at her barbershop on Coast Highway. There were four rings, and then the recorded message began with a couple of lines of poetry: "Wild, wild the storm, and the sea high running,/ Steady the roar of the gale, with incessant undertone muttering,/ Shouts of demoniac laughter fitfully piercing and pealing,/ Waves, air, midnight—"

And then Kristi's voice, stagey, yet feminine: "Hi. This is Kristi and that was Walt Whitman. I can't come to the phone right now, but if you'll leave your name and your number and your message, I'll get back to you. Bye."

I left my name and number and said I wanted an appointment for this afternoon. Around 4:30, I said.

I hung up and took my shower. I always get ideas in the shower. The experts say it's the negative ions. I wouldn't know about that. The water felt terrific, pounding down, and I kept wondering what Bruce Halliburton was not telling me.

2

At 3:04 I was sitting in the sumptuous waiting room on the second floor of the corporate headquarters of Golden Bear Savings and Loan. The offices were in Newport Center, near the big Pacifica Building, the heart of Orange County's financial district. The Pacifica Building is the one that looks like it's about to fly away to Condorland. Downstairs, people stood in line at tellers' windows, doing their part to keep the economy going. I was dressed for the occasion in my new bush jacket, pressed jeans, and cowboy boots. My pistol, a Walther PPK, was locked in the Ford pickup.

It was a suite of golden offices, connected by white corridors with gold-painted trim. The carpet was a deep golden-brown plush, bear color. The chairs were a matching shade, with shimmery brass legs. There was art on the walls and a statue on a fake gold pedestal. The receptionist was a brunette with teeth like Miss Universe, honey-gold skin, and eyes like a young Medusa. My business card said Wallace St. Moritz, Ph.D.

"Mr. St. Moritz?" said the Medusa.

"Doctor," I said, correcting her. "Doctor St. Moritz."

"Mrs. Jaspers will be right out."

I stood up as Mrs. Jaspers entered the waiting room to shake my hand. Her face wore a money lender's smile. Her body wore a four-hundred-dollar suit, dove gray, highlighted by a blue silk necktie. She was five-five, 130, and very buttoned up, like a bank manager or a prison warden. Mrs. Jaspers led the way back to an office, hips doing a nice rum-tum, rum-tum. She was in her late thirties and probably Jacuzzied nude to get her kicks.

Seated behind her executive special desk, Mrs. Jaspers scrutinized my card and gave me a half-smile. "So, Doctor St. Moritz, how can we help you?"

"Interest," I said and reclaimed the card.

"I beg your pardon."

I got up and closed the door to the outer office, shutting out the Medusa. "My organization acquires bits of money. We want to park it, overnight, for a weekend, maybe for a work week, here in California. They sent me to get some bids."

She didn't look interested. "We pay standard rates, Doctor. Today it's seven-point-five. Yesterday it was seven. In today's market there are no guarantees."

"What's the jumbo CD pay?"

She spread her hands, giving me the signal I was wasting her time. "The jumbo requires a minimum of a hundred thousand."

"I know. What's the rate?"

"Today?"

"Yes."

"Seven and three-quarters." Mrs. Jaspers looked puzzled. "Now, I am quite busy, and—"

"This week, Mrs. Jaspers, we've got eight million sitting in a bank in Tulsa."

"Eight million?" She leaned toward me, her face flushed. "Tulsa?"

"Oklahoma."

"Eight million," she mused.

I grinned. "I assume you do wire transfers."

"Oh, yes." She sat back, the bright flush of blood hot in her cheeks and throat. "Is this the normal . . . ah . . . amount?"

"Sometimes less. Sometimes more."

"Where does it come from?"

I grinned. "That's my business, ma'am. What's the rate?"

She rested her elbows carefully on the desk and made her fingers into a tent. "I presume, Doctor, you have other bids."

"Yes."

"Might I ask what we have to top?"

"Nine and a half."

Bleak paleness replaced the color in her face. She reached for her telephone and jabbed some buttons. I heard a voice answer at the other end. Mrs. Jaspers opened her mouth to say something, then remembered she wasn't alone. She covered the mouthpiece with her hand. "Would you mind waiting outside, Doctor?"

"Not a bit."

In the outer office, I asked the Medusa for directions to the men's room. When she answered, pointing the way with barbaric fingernails, her eyes glittered. Belker's office was at the end of an empty corridor, next to a conference room with double doors. "Claude A. Belker," it said. "President." The lock on Belker's office door was easy, eleven seconds with the German picks. It had been two months since he'd died. I didn't expect to find anything.

The carpet in here was the same golden bear brown. The top of the desk was clean. The drawers of the desk were locked. Sweating, the seconds ticking away, I used the picks to unlock each drawer. Papers, file folders, paper clips. Nothing personal. No date book. No photos. I ran my fingers along the rough wood of the underside of the desktop. Bingo. At the far corner on the right side I found something taped to the wood. It had the sharp edges of a photograph. I tugged and the photo came loose. Two people, a girl, long blond hair. And a guy in hunting clothes. No time to study it now. I put the photo in my pocket and eased out of the empty office and zipped around the corner.

Just in time.

From the direction of Mrs. Jaspers' office came voices, the boss-lady asking the Medusa where I was.

"Are you sure you said the men's room?"

"Yes, Mrs. Jaspers. I'm—"

I let them haggle about it for another sentence or two. Then I stepped around the corner, into view, and walked toward them, hands in my pockets to suggest male self-consciousness.

"Doctor?" Her face was contorted with suspicion.

"Coming right along, Mrs. Jaspers." I walked up to her and spread my hands in a gesture I had copied from a hack actor in an old movie about biblical times. Elbows tucked in, palms out, head cocked to the side, like a medieval angel on a wall. "Any luck?"

Mrs. Jaspers nodded, the suspicion fading in the face of her greed. "I think we can do business, doctor."

"Wonderful."

"This is not cash, I presume."

"No. The money is electric. Wire transfers, like I said. It's legal."

"Very good." She looked over her shoulder to make sure we would not be overheard and brought her mouth close to my ear. "On the figure you mentioned, eight million, we'll top your other offer by a quarter of a point. If you can go to a deposit of ten million, we'll go a half point higher."

I stuck out my hand. "Sounds like a deal. How late are you folks open?"

"Today is Wednesday. So it's four o'clock. But I naturally assumed you'd be depositing today."

I made a show of checking my watch. "Can do, Mrs. J. Got to make two calls to Dallas, is all."

Her face was tight again. She wanted my mythical money. "Use my phone."

"Hey," I said. "Great."

I used her phone to punch in a ten-digit number that did not answer. The light was fading from her money-lender's eye as I shook her hand and hurried out of there. The time was 3:25 and I had a ten-minute drive to China Gate.

The guard at the entrance to China Gate wouldn't let me through until Josephine August arrived, so I sat at the curb outside and studied the photo from under Claude Belker's desk.

It showed two people in hiking clothes, a man and a girl, posed together on a gray rock in a mountain setting. The surrounding earth was coppery. Pine trees dotted the landscape behind them. The girl was blonde, trim, and curvy. She wore hiking shorts with flap pockets, a short-sleeve shirt, and boots with gray socks. Over one shoulder was a red daypack. Her head came up to the man's brow. The man was solid, maybe five-ten, with the gut and beefy shoulders that go with a desk job. His pants were full-length. He wore a plaid shirt and laceup boots. I figured his age at fifty. The floppy hat hid his hair, but not the suntanned face. I didn't know the girl but the man was Claude Belker.

They were holding hands and smiling.

Who had taken the photo?

Josephine drove up and tooted and waved. She loved cars. Last time I'd seen her, she was driving a bottle-green Jaguar. Today, she was piloting a silver Cadillac Biarritz.

I climbed in, and we headed past the guard and into the exclusive coastal community of China Gate. The ride of the Cadillac felt squishy and liquified, like the *Q.E.II* on a mirror ocean. You sit way down inside these puffy cars. The seats are too soft. The dashboard is right out of Star Wars. I like to be up above the traffic, where I can see. I like my Ford.

Josephine is about my age and about my weight. At five-seven, she's tall enough to carry it well, and she buys the right clothes at Nordstrom's and Nieman-Marcus and Gump's. Ever since I've known her, she's smoked to keep from eating more than she already eats. A half-smoked filter-tip cigarette smoldered in the ashtray and a pack of Virginia Slims sat on the seat beside her. Where cigs were concerned, Josephine left nothing to chance.

Today she wore a cream-colored dress and a soft blue jacket with big shoulder pads and lots of jewelry. She'd been married three times and was hunting for husband number four.

"Who's your client, Matthew?"

"Confidential."

"You rascal. It's a case, isn't it? Something dangerous and terribly hush-hush?"

"Always."

"Have you changed your mind about that property on the beach, dear? I could get you three hundred thousand tomorrow, if you'd just let me."

"Who wants it? The Trane Company? Or maybe the Duke Corporation?"

Josephine blew smoke at me. "You're holding up progress, dear. Remember, after this afternoon our little slate is clean."

I patted her arm, at the same time moving the smoldering cigarette away from my nose. "I owe you, okay?"

She nodded, sighed, and switched into her real estate spiel. "The properties in here start at number one," Josephine said, pointing at a green and white signpost, "and go to two-twenty. The property you're interested in—pardon me while I snicker—has five bathrooms, each one with a separate bath. There's a maid's room downstairs, a powder room, a bonus room, a library with wet bar, a formal dining room, a brick herringbone fireplace in the living room, and a modernized kitchen that you could serve an army from. The floors and ceilings are handcrafted. I was wrong about the asking price. It's only three million seven. The view across China Lake itself is sumptuous. And the number of the Belker home is one thirty-three."

I tracked us as she talked. All the roads were named China Gate. There were little signposts indicating which number-clusters were up which cute little streets.

"I appreciate this, Josephine."

"Just don't steal anything when you get inside, hey?"

"Scout's honor."

We swung into a curved driveway that led up to the

Belker house. It wasn't strictly Tudor, but a bastardized combination of Elizabethan and Jacobean the architects called "Jacobethan." Guys I'd worked with in construction called the same style "black-and-white," because of the half-timbering look—exposed exterior wood with brick and stucco chinked in between. The industry term for this chinking is "nogged."

A discrete sign from J. August Realtors said the house would be shown by appointment only. Josephine led me down a curved walkway into a courtyard guarded by the nasty metallic snout of a closed-circuit camera. The courtyard, which was a compressed imitation of an English geometric garden, needed some tailoring.

"Isn't this grand?" said Josephine, raising the door knocker.

"Isn't this where the English gentry ran down the squealing scullery maids for their aristocratic pleasure?"

"Your mind, Matt Murdock, is a—"

A Latino maid let us in. She wore a gray uniform and a white pinafore. From behind her pumped heavy rock music, tribal dance of today's teens. Josephine knew the maid, whose name was Amelia. Alas, the lady of the house was not at home. The entry way was parquet. I wanted to poke around upstairs.

The Belker place was sumptuous and over-decorated in an attempt to fake good taste. The parquet didn't work with the chintz. The chintz didn't work with the oriental rugs and the heavy gothic furniture. Someone was trying hard to impress. And not succeeding.

In the vast downstairs the only trace of Claude Belker was in the library. On the antique desk in a gold frame was a duplicate of the family photo from the Heartland file folder.

Through the French doors of the library, I saw two teens bronzing in the sun at pool's edge. The pool over-

32

looked China Lake. The teen on her stomach, buns facing the sun, was buck-ass naked. The other wore only a bikini bottom. As Josephine and I watched, she sat up and stretched, arching thin arms over her head.

"Naughty thoughts."

"The daughter?" I asked.

"Yes. Belinda Belker is the one lying down. And a friend. They're too young for you, dear."

"Let's see the upstairs."

Josephine guided me out of the library and up to the second floor. The bedrooms splayed out along a carpeted corridor that reached the entire length of the Belker house. The master bedroom was at one end, a bonus room at the other. The door to one bedroom was closed, and behind it I could hear the click of computer keys.

In the master bedroom I opened the closets. A hundred pairs of women's shoes, racked carefully and kept tidily in dirt-proof plastic bags. Rows and rows of dresses and skirts and blouses. Accessories, enough to start a department store. And no sign of Claude Belker. Behind some of the clothes I spotted a bank of drawers. No way to dig around in there without alerting Josephine.

"I heard the owner died."

Josephine stood at the door, tapping her foot. "Yes. Only a couple of months ago. I hear there's some problem with the insurance. I have a date, dear. Could we get on with whatever it is?"

"How about the bonus room?"

"All right, but let's make it fast, shall we?"

Just then a voice called from downstairs, and Josephine stepped to the corridor to answer. It was the lady of the house, back home, I assumed, from a tough day sweating out a case of mall-fever. I heard the throaty flutter of female voices as Josephine began territorial negotiations.

Josephine went downstairs while I ducked back into the closet and pulled open the drawers.

And there was what was left of the life of Claude Belker.

A few pairs of white socks, three new packages of sweatbands, a much-laundered T-shirt that said Golden Bear, and one of those little elastic harnesses to hold your eyeglasses on during sports.

I closed the drawers and walked across the ankle-deep carpeting to the corridor. Voices floated up from down below. It sounded as if they were bosom buddies. I hustled down the hall to the bonus room. The door was closed, and they had turned off the air-conditioning. The temperature was in the nineties, the air close and stifling. The room faced west and took the glaring heat from the afternoon sun.

The room was dominated by an expensive pool table. Along the end of the room was a full bar, with room for eight leather bar stools. There was no liquor, only Pepsi, Coke, Perrier, and six varieties of orange crush and lime-ade. Two walls were lined with doors that probably led to storage units. I began with the closet near me, which held camping gear. Two backpacks, some stuff with a Coleman label, a gold-plated trail cup from Early Winters. In the next closet, I found a tent. Going on down the line led me to fishing gear and two rifles, both in canvas cases. I did not take the time to open the cases.

In the fourth closet I found a new pair of hiking boots, still in the box. There were also books on wildlife and conservation. Several came from the Sierra Club.

I was checking out one of the books when the hairs stood up on the back of my neck. I turned to see the teen from the pool, the naked one. Now she wore a shorty robe, pale blue, cinched at the waist. Her legs were smooth and toasty tan. The robe ended at the tops of her thighs. She leaned against the doorframe and ran a comb through her short hair. The action raised the hem of the robe, and she watched my eyes. A real teaser.

"Are you a lookeeloo?"

I stood up, holding the book. "Someone likes camping, I guess. I'm a camping nut, myself."

"Daddy loved it in the woods. He used to take me."

"Where did you go?"

"Oh, everywhere. Mammoth. Big Bear. There was a place in Arrowhead he wanted to buy." She paused in her hair combing and crossed her legs at the ankles. She wasn't a pretty girl, but she had a body that was trim and smooth, and she knew how to jazz the guys. "Who are you, anyway?"

I grinned and put the book back and faced her. "Just a guy looking for a place to land," I said.

"I'll bet." Her mouth pouted. Her voice was fake sexy. Her hips gave a little twitch and the bottom of the robe parted, flashing her wares. She treated me to a throaty chuckle, one she'd learned watching bad television.

I was about to close the door to the storage closet when the girl spotted something and came over to kneel down on the carpet. As she passed me, I caught a whiff of suntan lotion and marijuana. She pulled out the box containing the new boots. She made a small strangled sound and stuck her head inside the storage cabinet. I heard her scrabbling around, searching for something. Before she found it, a voice called from down the corridor: "Belinda? Are you here, dear? Yoo hoo? Belinda?"

Voices came down the hallway and the girl, Belinda, kept up her search. The mother burst into the room, and you could see what the daughter would look like in twenty-five years, when the tan had faded and the body had gone the way of all flesh. The sexy pout had changed to an angry slit. The eyes were too close together. They narrowed as they landed on me, the man, in the room with the daughter. "What? Who are—?"

Josephine August came hustling in to stand behind her. "Gladys, this is—"

Before Josephine could finish, the girl backed out of the storage cabinet to stare at her mother, hands on hips. "Mother! What did you do with daddy's boots?"

"What?"

"Daddy's boots. What did you do with them?"

"Aren't they in the closet?" Belker's widow poked her head inside and came out with the box of new boots. "Right here."

"Not those. The old ones. The ones he always wore."

"I'm sorry, Belinda. Would you mind if we discussed this some other—"

"Mother!"

"Matthew," Josephine said, motioning me out.

I nodded and started out. The mother faced the daughter, and I had the feeling this scene had been placed on permanent videotape, so they could play it again and again, the same stances, the same tones of voice, with the single touch of a button.

It wasn't the boots they were arguing about.

It was everything else.

3

Josephine dropped me at the curb on the wide street outside China Gate, where the Ford sat. A pale yellow parking ticket was tucked neatly under the windshield wiper on the driver's side.

"Crap," I said.

Josephine blew a puff of smoke at me. "Matthew, I think I deserve to know what's going on here."

I was thinking of Claude Belker's hiking boots as I opened the door and climbed out. I squatted down and looked through the window. "As soon as I know, okay. You'll be the first."

She held out a hand sideways and I reached in and we shook. "And remember what I said about your little beach property. With what I'd get you for that, you could buy half of the Anaheim Hills."

"I like the beach, Josephine."

She let go of my hand and puffed a cloud of smoke toward her windshield and drove off. The big silver

Caddy parted the heavy afternoon traffic like a Sherman tank through an Oklahoma chicken ranch. I tossed the traffic ticket onto the seat and headed toward Coast Highway and Kristi's barber shop.

Kristi Flamingo had wanted to be a movie star. That hadn't worked out, so she'd decided to be a cop. That hadn't worked out, so she'd married herself a cop. That hadn't worked out, so she'd left Los Angeles the Fair and moved south to Newport Beach. She had a flair with clothes and makeup and hair, so she went to barber school to learn a trade. After she graduated, she worked the clubs and hotels until she made enough money to open her own place on South Coast Highway, across the street from Le Club of Newport Beach. Her going rate for a cut is twenty dollars. She works by appointment only, four days a week, which leaves her the weekends for play. Her favorite sport is two-man volleyball, and last year she won the local tournament and went to the quarter-finals in the nationals, held on Labor Day in Huntington Beach.

Kristi's clients are locals. They run the economic gamut from bankers to construction workers to lawyers to teachers to sports figures to mobsters. Kristi loves to talk, which makes you think she doesn't listen. Wrong. She has a great memory for detail and I was hoping she knew something about Claude Belker.

When I walked into her shop, Kristi was just finishing a customer. Her shop always smells clean, like soap. She saw me and squealed: "Sherlock!" She ran over, barber shears in one hand, clippers in the other, and a comb between her teeth. She gave me a hug, then stepped back for a critical appraisal of my hair. "You need a trim, Sir Sherlock. You need a trim in a very bad way."

"Thanks."

"Let me finish up, okay. Just a couple minutes." Kristi

went back to her customer, a jowly man with a frown and a large stomach. Kristi Flamingo possesses vibrant red hair, vibrant green eyes, and a smile to be envied by any game show hostess alive. Kristi is thirty-three. She was thirty-one when we met, six years ago, and she does not believe in birthday parties. Thirty-three is a good year, she says. It has symmetry. It has balance.

I opened up an old *Playboy*. Kristi's customers are mostly men. They donate copies of *Playboy* for the shop. Kristi's collection fills her back room, where she has a Macintosh computer and a harp and lots of poetry books. Her dream is to retire from the barber business and write poetry and study music in a conservatory back East.

Kristi's five-six and curvy. Today she wore lime green slacks, a white cotton shirt, and a barber smock that said Beatlemania. She was not talking to the customer, so I knew something was wrong. Kristi talks to everyone.

The lead story in *Playboy* was about how the DEA was spending a lot of the taxpayer's money and still not catching the dope smugglers. It was called "D-Men: Money Down a Rat-Hole." Last year, the total income from the traffic in illegal drugs was an estimated $70 billion. A colorful bar graph showed a heavy increase in coke traffic, from Colombia through the Mexican pipeline. A sidebar identified a thirty-mile corridor in southern Arizona as Cocaine Alley. The main smuggling outfit was La Familia. A second outfit called Los Primos was trying to grab a piece of the action away from La Familia. A DEA agent had been killed in Guadalajara. The feds suspected that the money was being laundered in the United States. A second sidebar, titled "Greenwashing," talked about the different ways that money can be washed clean of the underworld taint.

I was halfway through the sidebar when Kristi's customer paid her off and left, carrying his suit coat. She stared at his backside, looked down at the twenty in her hand, then walked angrily to her appointment book, where she made a notation.

"Goodbye, Mr. Friedland. Forever."

"No tip?"

She jerked open the cash drawer, dropped in the money, and slammed the drawer closed. "Not only no tip. The creep had the nerve to proposition me. Just before you came. What a slob!" Kristi shook the hair off the striped blue barber sheet and motioned me into the chair. "His old lady is out of town tomorrow, until Saturday, so he offered me two hundred lousy bucks to have what he refers to as a working lunch. Would you believe that? My boyfriend will kill him!" She tucked the sheet around me and latched the neck closed.

"New boyfriend?"

"Oh, yeah. Terry Rehder. A lawyer who works for the city of Long Beach. Not so handsome, but very dependable."

"Whatever happened to Deke Marin?"

"Out of my life, Sherlock. I mean like *way* out. He couldn't hold a job, so he was always sponging. Goodbye, Deke." Kristi tipped my chair back so that my head was over her sink for the ritual shampoo. The warm water felt soothing. After rinsing me twice, she sat me up for the treatment with the handheld dryer. "Hey!" she said. "You're dressed spiffy. Getting married, or what?"

I grinned, but kept my eyes closed. "I need some help, Kristi. On a local guy named Claude Belker. Maybe you remember, his car hit a gasoline truck down the road and he burned to death. He was the president of Golden Bear Savings and Loan."

The dryer turned off. "What do you want to know?"

"Anything. You know anything about him?"

Snick, snick, went the shears. I had the sense Kristi was

40

deciding how much she should tell me. "Sure, I know him. He was a customer for awhile, before he switched over to Harry at Le Club. What's your rap on this?"

"An insurance company has hired me to look into his death. He was insured for a bundle. There was some funny stuff with the way he filled out his applications."

"How much was he insured for?"

"Millions."

"The bum." The hair fell onto the barber sheet. "What's your angle?"

"They don't want to pay."

"They're bums too."

"They pay the bills."

"Sometimes I want to kick loose, Sherlock. Just close the door and go up to Big Sur and play my harp. You know?"

"I know."

The shears went faster, and closer to my ear. Sweat popped out on my forehead. "Hey!" Kristi said. "Sorry, Sir Sherlock. Didn't mean to get so close with the blades."

"It's okay. I didn't mean to hit a nerve."

She didn't say anything for awhile. She finished up my trim and used the brush to whisk off stray hairs. She lathered the back of my neck and scraped my neck clean. It wasn't until I handed her twenty bucks and a five-dollar tip that she nodded.

"Okay." She rang up the money on her antique cash register. "This guy Claude dated a friend of mine. Not a friend, really. More like an acquaintance. We were in a women's group together, one of those matriarchal support things, and she used to come in with stories about how Claude was going to divorce his wife so he could marry her. There were eight women in that group, and only one believed her story about divorce and marriage. I mean, you meet jokers like Claude all the time. They were losers in high school. They were geeks or nerds. They get out and try to un-geek themselves. They make money on some wacko invention. They marry and have some kids. Their wives gain a little in the buns, so the Claudes of the world start looking around for some fresh action. My customers talk about it all the time. Young stuff, they call it. Girls in their early twenties who still have the stars in the eyes. It happened to me a couple of times. These guys get un-geeked, and they dazzle you with money and gifts and flowers sent around to the workplace. They sneak out of town and meet you at a hotel up the coast. They goose you in the hot tub and in the shower, and they climb all over you before you're awake in the morning, and when Sunday noon rolls around, they go back to the wife and kids and you have another week of blue Mondays."

Kristi crawled into her barber chair.

"Look," I said. "I didn't mean to—"

She held up a hand, palm facing forward. "So the reason I'm telling you this is not because of the crummy insurance company, but because Claude was a bum. And all the guys like Claude are bums. And because the gal was nice. A real artist. Okay?"

"Okay. Thanks." I waited for the rest.

Kristi sighed and crossed her legs. Her face at that moment looked older than thirty-three. "She had two names. Mary Sue something, that was her real name. And Sheena Mandarin, her showbiz name."

"What kind of show business?"

"Exotic dancer."

"Where?"

"Private parties."

"Local?"

"Mostly. I know she had a couple of gigs in L.A. But

mostly around the county—Orange, Fullerton, Irvine—where the college kids hang out."

"Would you have a phone number?"

"Nah. You know how disorganized I am. But I might find out from a friend of a friend."

"Would you?"

"I'll try. The friend I'm thinking of doesn't get off work until later. How about if I call?"

"Great." I handed her the photo. "Is this Sheena?"

Kristi checked out the picture. "Where'd you get this?"

"Belker's office. Taped underneath his desk."

"It's her, all right. Little Mary Sue. And that's Claude, only in very different clothes. He'd come in for a trim, and his collars would be airtight, you know?" She handed me back the photo. "She won't get into any trouble, will she?"

"I don't think so."

I heard a heavy tread on the steps outside and more steps approaching and then a man appeared in the doorway. He was a construction guy, checked shirt, faded jeans, work boots.

"Hi, doll," he said. "Am I early?"

Kristi bustled around, getting him in the chair, shaking the hair off the barber sheet, tucking it around his neck. As she worked, she talked, asking questions, catching up on his life. It was a mother and son scene. She made the customers feel wanted. And safe.

I was almost to the Ford when she called my name and ran after me.

"Sir Sherlock?" She came running up. "I remembered something. About that guy Claude."

"Shoot."

"He played poker with a couple of my regulars. Wendell Barrymore and Bobby Maclean. Wendell was a big tipper. Bobby used to be the mayor of Newport."

"Have you seen them lately?"

"Wendell died in January."

"How?"

"A fire, I think it was. He was a car collector. Something caught fire in his garage while he was doing some work."

"What about the other guy, the ex-mayor?"

"I haven't seen him in awhile. A month, maybe. He could have changed barbers."

"Thanks, Kristi."

She put a hand on my arm. "There's something else."

"What?"

"Claude introduced me to a guy, a business friend. He never was a customer; but he sure gave me the rush."

"In what way?"

"He wanted to pay for my time."

"No kidding."

She looked back over her shoulder, toward her little one-chair barber shop. "He offered me a thousand at first. When I said no, he went up to two, then three. He wanted me to play motel tennis. I kept saying no. He sent flowers. He invited me to dinner. I had just kicked Deke out and I was lonely, so I went. That was a mistake. This guy was all over me. Drove a big Mercedes, threw money around. He scared me, he was so darn hot."

"When was this?"

"February. Claude introduced us one day and this guy was on me the next."

"What was his name?"

"Mendez," Kristi said. "First name of Emiliano. The reason I remember is because that was Zapata's name. *Viva Zapata* was one of my dad's favorite movies, and he watched it all the time on an old VCR player."

"You mean Mendez-Madrid?"

"Yeah. That's it." She peered at me in the twilight. "You know him, too?"

"Just heard the name."

"He said he played poker with Claude."

"Thanks, Kristi. I owe you."

She hugged me again. "Let's have dinner. You bring your lady. I'll bring Terry."

"Great idea."

And then she turned and ran back to her shop.

There was no lady in my life at this time.

I drove home, wondering where Belker and his pals had played poker.

4

Back home at my place, I jotted down the names on the back of a power company billing envelope. Barrymore. Maclean. Mendez-Madrid.

I picked up the phone book and thumbed to the M's. There was no listing for Maclean, Robert, or Maclean, Bobby. There was no listing for Mendez-Madrid. There were several Barrymores, but I didn't have the first name. Information had no record of their numbers on the phone company computer.

I put the envelope into the Belker file and drank a Bud. Kristi called at 5:40, with the name Robert L. Vitrione, who owned a party-house in Lemon Heights. Sheena Mandarin, a.k.a. Mary Sue Something, was dancing there tonight. Kristi didn't know Mr. Vitrione, so she couldn't help me wangle an invitation.

I phoned Wally St. Moritz at the John Wayne Club. He plays doubles every afternoon from 3:00 to 5:00, and Wednesday was his day at John Wayne. They said Wally had left, so I phoned him at home. He was just getting into the shower. I told him what I wanted and he said he'd call me back. I finished the beer and read the sports pages. The season had barely started and my Braves were in trouble. A half hour passed before Wally called back with good news. The party started at nine or so. Vitrione's house was in Lemon Heights, snuggled up in the hills east of here. The man on the door was a surfcat named Tiger, and he owed Wally money for two Japanese boards and three surf-leashes.

Best of all, Wally wanted to come along.

We made a date for 9:30 and I phoned Bruce Halliburton, to alert him about the party. His answering service took the message. I hung up and phoned Webby Smith, at the Laguna Beach PD, to ask what he knew about the death of Claude Belker. He was working late. His voice sounded summer-weary. I asked him about Belker.

"I read the reports, is all."

"So what happened?"

"This a case you're working on?"

"Yes."

"Who's the client?"

"An insurance company."

"Hey, hey. Okay. Let me get the file."

He was back on the line in a couple of minutes. I heard the sound of papers crackling. "There isn't much, Sherlock. Just after midnight on a Thursday, this guy Belker slams into a gas truck. He's coming out of one of those high-rise condo projects in Laguna Niguel. The gas truck's heading south on Coast Highway. They estimated Belker's speed at fifteen miles an hour. He must have been on something, but there wasn't enough left of him to tell. The gas truck, they figure, was doing sixty."

"Did the driver live?"

"Yes."

"What happened to him?"

"He was in the hospital for awhile. He was treated and released."

"Did his statement look okay?"

"Yeah. He says Belker just drove in front of his truck. No time to swerve. Which insurance company you working for?"

"One of the biggies. Where had Belker been?"

"No one knew. It was around midnight. There was talk he might have been visiting a lady friend, but none turned up. The death was ruled accidental." Webby paused to speak to someone with his hand over the phone. He came back on. "Wasn't Belker the savings and loan guy?"

"Yeah. Golden Bear Savings and Loan."

"A cousin of mine's got some money in there. He keeps asking me should he take it out. What do you think?"

"Good idea," I said.

"Tell him to take it out?"

"Tomorrow."

"Why?"

"Intuition."

"That crap again?"

"Instinct, Webby. It's what links us with the animals."

"Let me do some real work, okay?"

"Okay."

"And you owe me a lunch."

"You got it."

The phone was ringing when I stepped out of the shower. It was Bruce Halliburton, returning my call. He did not say where he was calling from, but it sounded close enough to be next door. He seemed real pleased to hear about Belker's girl friend and the party in Lemon Heights. Good work, he said, his voice bristling with praise. He took down the address, a street called Argyle, and said he might join us there, if he could break free.

At 9:30 I picked Professor Wally St. Moritz up at his house on the Balboa Peninsula and we drove northeast on the Newport Freeway, heading toward Lemon Heights. At Seventeenth, we headed east, winding up into the high-rent district where houses perched on the hills like medieval castles. The Vitrione party would be extensive, Wally said, two hundred people, maybe three hundred. It was intended to make money, so our door fee was welcome. Wally handed me a plastic envelope containing something that looked like grass and smelled like illicit plant-life product from our neighbor to the south, Colombia.

"What's this?"

"A magic potion that loosens tongues and paves the way to perdition."

"Where'd you get it?"

"From Dolly, a recent runaway turned shopgirl."

"It's illegal, Wally. A controlled substance, they call it."

"Which is why I liberated it from innocent Dolly."

"Nice work."

"Thank you."

Wally St. Moritz loves California. His full name is Wallace Arthur St. Moritz, M.A., Ph.D. The master's degree is from CCNY, in literature. The doctorate is from Colombia, in cultural anthropology. He'd done the academic trip as a learned professor, climbing the ladder into a soft berth called tenure, getting his fill of committees and trustee politics, then dropping out. Back there in his professorial past he had two ex-wives and four kids. At Christmas he sends them all the same card—a man on a beach, wearing ragged Robinson Crusoe shorts, his face shaded by a straw planter's hat—postmarked Honolulu, or Tahiti, or Rio. He has ninety Robinson Crusoe cards, which he keeps in a drawer in his surf shop. On New Year's Eve he gets drunk and talks through drippy tears and a box of Kleenex about his previous life, which he refers to as his Academic Incarceration. Wally is stocky, five-ten, brown from the sun, and near-sighted as an owl. He speaks five languages, reads a dozen, knows acupuncture, homeopathy, Rolfing, and hypnosis. His pad on Balboa Peninsula is cozy and tastefully decorated. He calls it his California Cocoon. Sometimes a woman friend drops by for a weekend. Wally's women are bright, moody, managerial, and on the way up. They all sport advanced degrees in economics or political science and address him as Wallace. He lets them come, he says, because they remind him of the life he left behind, the gray grimness of academe. He's a liberal and a scholar. In any library, no matter how small, he hums to himself and turns into a sleuth.

The beach kids call Wally "The Saint," punning on his last name. They got him to change the name of his shop to the Saintly Silver Surfer, who is a comic book superhero. I call him Prof. He has four passions: food, tennis, ecology, and saving runaways who land on the beach. He finds them a place to stay and a "cultural cushion," a support group of runaways who have stopped running. He needles the city fathers for money. He finds them meaningful work. When distraught parents arrive, Wally speaks learnedly about the troughs of society and counsels them with mounds of wisdom.

For the party, Wally wore white trousers and a blue blazer, double-breasted, with brass buttons. As we wound onto Argyle Road, he blinked at me through thick glasses and rubbed his palms together. I twisted up Argyle until

I found the party-house, a brick and glass whopper up a steep driveway. It was a two-story job, California Laid Back Modern, a patio, a swimming pool, a wall of glass for the view of the ritzy homes blinking away from the surrounding hills. Music pumped from the house and behind the glass you could see swingers gyrating to the beat.

"Welcome to Paradise," Wally said.

I parked the Ford around the corner and checked the Walther PPK and we walked back through the soft California air to the party-house. We came up the stairs into the light from the porch. Tiger, the baboon on the door, was big-shouldered and husky, with a suntanned face and hair bleached white by the sun.

"Tiger, this is Icarus. He's with me."

"Hiya, Icarus. You pay. The Saint gets a freebie."

I handed over a ten and two twenties. Tiger stamped Wally's wrist, then mine. "Okay, boys." Tiger grinned at us as he flexed and waved us inside. "This is Funland. Don't get it caught in a tight spot and remember the age in which we live."

The purple ink from the rubber stamp took me back to high school dances, when the worst sin was sneaking a gulp of rotgut rye whisky as you looked over your shoulder for the heavy-footed approach of the assistant principal. Times had changed. These days, kids started pot on their tenth birthday. By the tender age of thirteen, they'd tasted coke and smoked weed and had started sex and psychiatry.

The Vitrione living room was long, running the front of the house and then bending left into an L that reached back into the south side, where there was a raised stage in front of two leaded glass windows. Five musicians were thumping out the music. Two had pigtails, two had crew cuts, and one had rag-mop hair that needed a shampoo.

All five wore leather pants and matching leather vests that showed off their hairless chests.

In front of us, a hundred people danced to the music, which was loud enough to drown out any idle talk. The music was a mixture of punk, hard rock, acid rock, Jesus rock, and something indefinably ugly and profane. I grew up dancing with pretty, sweet-smelling girls to oldies like "Volare" and "Tom Dooley." It was a simpler time. A redhead came up and said hello to Wally, who introduced me. Her name was Rhonda. She had a sardonic smile and laughing eyes. We had a dance, and she told me Sheena would be on around ten, and then I offered her the plastic envelope.

"Oh, wow," she said. "To accompany this, I need a drink."

Rhonda led me by the arm around the ragged edge of the dancers to the kitchen, where a muscular black man sold us a beer and a white wine for ten dollars. The black man had a shaved head and Oriental eyes. He resembled a younger Woody Strode. She watched as he rolled two joints on a cute little cigarette machine.

"Thanks, mama," he said, holding one out.

Rhonda and I stood against the wall, sipping our drinks, while I scanned the crowd. A lean, raw-boned kid was dancing with a fluffy sun-bunny, using the center of the floor, where a strobe light pounded his face. The kid wore faded jeans and cowboy boots and a western shirt with pearl buttons. He looked as if he had just arrived from Sticksville in the boonies.

"Have you seen Sheena dance?"

"Oh, sure. She's wonderful. They say she could go to Hollywood any day."

"This is my first time."

"She oozes sex appeal," Rhonda said, inhaling the smoke. She turned her long face up to give me a long wistful smile. In this light her eyes were pale green and a little nervous. She had the kind of skin that would burn, and you could tell she stayed out of the sun. She wore her hair long, down to the middle of her back. I figured her age at early thirties, young enough to be lonely, too old for the young beach turks. I wondered what she did for a living. Something brainy, I thought. Marketeer. Copy writer for an ad agency. Teacher. "Sheena's beautiful. She turns the whole room on."

"Swell," I said.

Rhonda stepped close, and I got a whiff of her perfume as she reached under my bush jacket to put the ziplock bag away. Her hand brushed the butt of the PPK. "What is that?"

"A gun."

"It feels huge."

"Nah. It's normal."

She caressed the gun. "You're a cop, aren't you?" Her knee pressed into mine.

"Private cop."

"A manhunter."

"Sometimes. Tonight, I'm a woman hunter."

"Who?"

"Sheena."

"That's right."

Rhonda's face clouded. "Damn!"

"Maybe you could help me."

Her hand left the gun and she moved her knee away. "Why should I?"

Before I could answer, the music stopped abruptly, the musician's comment on how the world will end, and there was a drum-roll and an expectant titter from the audience. Smoke drifted across the spots as the announcer, a short tanned guy with Popeye forearms, called for attention. He wore tight white pants and a purple shirt. Light bounced off his monk's bald spot.

"Do you know Roberto?" Rhonda whispered.

"Roberto who?"

"Roberto Vitrione. This is his house."

"So that's Roberto."

"He's Sheena's manager, sort of."

"I heard she had a boyfriend, an older guy, some daddy from Newport Center."

Sheena opened her mouth and I saw a thin tendril of smoke. "You really are a cop, all these questions."

Onstage, Roberto Vitrione lowered his arms and smiled at the crowd. A door opened to my left, back in the short arm of the L, and a blonde made her dramatic entrance. Her hair was platinum and it hung down her back to her buttocks. She wore a long black cloak that covered her from neck to toes. Her lipstick was silver. Her eyes were hidden by a silver cat-eye mask. A coordinated costume.

"Sheena, Sheena!" the crowd chanted. "We want Sheena!"

"Ladies and gentlemen and anyone else!" Roberto cried. "Presenting Miss Sheena Mandarin!" He held out his hands toward Sheena, at the same time backing off the stage.

A photographer with a rat's tail haircut settled in against the wall near the window, with his camera pressed against his cheek.

The camera flash lit up a widening triangle of the room as Sheena strutted onstage. The cloak opened, revealing high buccaneer boots and a gleam of stockinged leg, with plenty of tanned thigh above. Applause rattled through the room as Sheena gave the signal for the music to start, a tilt of her chin and one arm out straight, hand held out indolently, beating time. The leader of the band, his vest

54

flying open, jerked his head at his players. A guitar twanged, then began a steady beat.

"Wow," Rhonda said.

"A hundred people here, that makes five thousand bucks."

"Shh," Rhonda said. "This could get really New Age."

The music was sharper now, thump, pappa wump, thump, pappa wump. "What's the tune?"

"Bolero," Rhonda whispered, digging sharp fingernails into my arm. "This is wonderful stuff. Why aren't you hitting?"

"I'm still on duty."

"Oh, poo. Don't be a party-pooper."

The cloak swirled out as Sheena, keeping time to the music, entered the first phase of her dance. It was a heavy cloak, velvety on the outside, with an inner lining of shining silver stripes to match the mask and the lipstick. The music pulsed. Sheena gyred and pirouetted, the cloak roping out over the heads of the nearest onlookers like a flat black stingray with a wicked striped belly, then swirling back to wrap tightly around her body. In the flickering instant while she was unwrapped, you could see the buccaneer boots, a wispy sash, a black leather bra, and a bikini girdle with a golden padlock.

"Some dance," I said.

"Shh." Getting friendly again, Rhonda pressed into me. All around us people swayed hypnotically to the music. The room was dark except for two floodlights flooding the stage with white light. Marijuana smoke filled the room. I was sweating now.

As the music built to a climax, Sheena's dance step resembled more and more the measured cadence of a Sioux warrior heating up the tribal blood for the warpath. Without missing a beat, she began stripping, taking off items of clothing, tossing them out to the crowd. Out came the filmy gossamer sash, floating through the cone of whispery light to vanish in the crowd. Out came the leather bra.

"Oh, Lordy," Rhonda said, gripping my arm again. Her hips gyrated in time to the music. I wondered how many women wanted to trade places with Sheena.

Gasps came from the audience as the pump of the music built to a frenzied peak. I wondered if the composer, whose name I could not remember, had envisioned a scene like this one to accompany his tune. Onstage, beneath the white lights, Sheena pirouetted like an ice skater and the cloak soared like the wings of a great vampire. Some guy in the audience sighed, "Oh, baby, take me, take me." I guessed we had a minute left, maybe ninety seconds, before the blood-thumping climax.

There was a scuffling over near the front door, where Tiger was inking people's hands with his stamp. You couldn't hear anything because of the music, but I saw Tiger backed up against the screen door, and then he was shoved aside as someone bigger and meaner opened the door and entered the room. Rhonda glanced that way and her face got pale.

"Uh-oh," Rhonda said. "Trouble."

5

Rhonda's pink fingernails dug into my arm as the trouble came inside, shoving the Tiger ahead of him. The man had the narrow face and snake eyes of a circus geek.

Tiger's back was straining in an unnatural arch because his arm was rammed up behind him in a wrestler's hammerlock. The laid-back surfer smirk had been replaced with pain. Tiger was my height, six-two, and the man who had his arm in a hammerlock was three inches taller.

He maneuvered Tiger toward the stage, and then the door opened and an accomplice came in. He was short and thick, with a head shaved clean and a leather vest thrown open to show off a thatch of wiry chest hair. Silver chains winked from the vest. "Bikers!" Rhonda whispered. "They broke up a party in Orange a couple of weeks ago!"

The geek muscled his way through the crowd, heading for Sheena's stage. I searched for Wally in the strobe-whipped darkness, but could not find him.

The music thumped away, the musicians sweating toward climax, but over near the front door people sensed trouble and shuffled aside, the nervous herd making room for the barbarians. On the lighted stage, Sheena kept right on dancing, earning her money, a pro to the end. Her blonde hair flew in bright sparks. The cloak was off now and the bare shoulders gleamed whitely. The gold padlock winked in the light as she ground her hips and pelvis for the customers. Smiling, she held up a gold key.

The geek liberated a beer bottle from the raw-boned kid with the boots, took a swallow, and then muscled Tiger through the audience, heading for Sheena's stage. The kid said "Hey!" and grabbed for his beer. There was a muffled thump, not part of the climactic finish for *Bolero*, and then a quick scuffling motion as the geek shoved Tiger at the kid and stepped onto Sheena's stage. The kid lost his balance and fell down with the Tiger on top of him. Wide-eyed, Sheena came out of her trance to see a big hand reaching for the silver mask.

The man onstage was tall, six-four, with an Army Ranger crewcut and a shaggy rat's tail down the back of his neck. His head knifed out at a funny angle from corded shoulders. Sheena backed away from him, one hand out for protection, but he snatched her mask, jerking it away, just as the music died.

"Get away from me!" Sheena cried.

"Hot buns," said the intruder, reaching for her golden girdle.

Without the cloaking ritual of the dance, she seemed naked and terribly vulnerable. A light flickered on across the room. Some guy near us, high on weed, said, "Outstanding! Go for it!" For him, the looming geek was part of the act. Roberto Vitrione, landlord and manager, pushed his way through the crowd.

"Who are you?" Roberto demanded. "What do you want here? What—"

The geek shoved our host sprawling into the crowd. Shaved Head, his eyes like gun-sights, angled toward me like I owed him money. He knew me. I didn't know him. We were about to be introduced. The raw-boned kid, shaking his head, was on his feet, clawing his way toward the stage. One more guy wanting to play hero. Onstage, a big surfer in a white sportcoat took a wild punch at the geek, who sidestepped and raised a knee into the man's crotch, doubling him over. Shaved Head elbowed his way closer. More screams now, as I picked up a chair. "Look out!" Rhonda said.

And someone grabbed me from behind in a choke-hold.

I smelled men's cologne, something heavy, and Juicy Fruit gum. People see-sawed toward the door and I saw Rhonda edge toward the kitchen.

The voice behind me said, "Outside, mate." It was a British accent, or maybe Australian. "How'd you like to lose an ear." Hot breath on my neck. Chummy Britisher.

I felt something sharp touch my skin, a knife, maybe an icepick, and I stomped down hard, planting my heel on his foot. He loosened his choke-hold and grunted. Light flashed off metal, and I jerked my head to the side, pivoting, ramming a shoulder under his chin, knocking him away.

"Knife!" someone yelled. "He's got a knife!"

I touched my neck, at the jawline under the ear, where the blade had been. My fingers came away spotted with blood.

"You're bleeding!" a woman cried.

My own biker was heavy, weight about 235, with burly shoulders and meaty white arms. He was down on one knee, his eyes wide from having my shoulder bump his

59

chin. He wore black jeans, heavy boots, and a T-shirt that said "Twisted Sisters, Yeah!" As he stumbled to his feet, preparing for a second rush, a whirling strobe lashed his face, and I saw that he had pale eyes, almost pink, and stark white hair. His face was expressionless, like a robot's. Shaved Head was coming up on my left. There was no room to use the PPK.

I picked up a chair and leveled it at White Hair.

Wally St. Moritz appeared from the shadows, holding a wine bottle. Wally is in his mid-fifties, but his days on the court keep him in shape. He bent his knees to get his body into the swing. He weighs about 210, a lot of beef if you get it going out of inertia. White Hair shouted a hoarse warning, but the bottle was already in motion, making an arc. At the end of the arc was Shaved Head. The bottle made contact, driving the biker to his knees, but did not shatter. Good glass. Shaved Head sagged to the floor.

I saw the odds tally up in White Hair's pale red eyes, like those clickety-clicks from a Vegas slot machine, whirling while you wait for the tumbling cherries to label you a winner. Then he shrugged, turned on his heel, and got his ass out of there.

Blood stained my shirt as I moved toward the stage. The chair felt antique, flimsier than what I needed.

The geek was having some fun with Sheena. He held her by the arm, leering down at her like a bad dream. Then he saw White Hair go. He saw me coming up on him. In one smooth rotation, he let Sheena go and whipped off the chain from around his waist and made a lethal looping motion, his teeth bared. The chain clunked against my chair, the business end whipping around, slapping my shoulder and ribs. He aimed a kick at my crotch. I dodged, taking his heel on my thigh. Pain shot through me as I feinted with the chair, edging him back a couple of steps. He grunted and swung the chain again in a wicked arc, metal clashing with wood. I waited until the arc was finished and then rushed him, the chair legs jamming his chest and Adam's apple, and shoved him through the picture window.

There was a cheer from the crowd.

Glass shattered as he crashed through. He let out a yell, cursing, flailing his long arms. I stepped back to avoid falling glass. Branches cracked as the geek kept on rolling, out of the wedge of light into the darkness. He called me names. I heard footsteps, stumbling off.

The chair was in two parts. People stared at me from the darkness beyond the stage. A woman said, "What is happening?" A man said, "Beam me up, Scotty." My legs were shaky from the continuing rush of adrenaline. From the street, I heard the cranking motion of a starter pedal and then the roar of a big bike.

Woody Strode appeared from the kitchen, wielding a butcher knife.

"Nice timing," I said.

Woody shrugged. "Not my fight, daddy. I'm just tending bar."

"Find something so we can tie this one up."

Woody nodded. "Hey, daddy. You can sure handle a chair."

The kid sat against a wall, holding his stomach. His face was white. He gave me a weak grin and tried to speak but could only wheeze. The wind had been knocked out of him.

Shaved Head lay face down on the floor, his hands roped behind him with a necktie. Wally was sitting on him, looking smug because of his quick action with the champagne bottle. Our host was across the room, slumped in a chair while someone handed him a joint and a restorative drink.

Sheena swept out of the bedroom, dressed in baggy slacks and a soft shirt, carrying a valise which probably contained her togs for the erotic dance. Some buttons were still undone and the tails of the shirt were not tucked in. Lady in a rush. She stooped down to pick up the black halter, then grabbed the filmy sash from an onlooker. I was disappointed. I had assumed those were relics for the hope chests of her vast army of admirers.

The door opened and guests who had escaped the action filtered back in, to view the scene. Sheena bent down to peer at the kid. "Hey, Country!" she said. "Are you all right?"

"Got the wind knocked out of him," I said.

She turned to me with a practiced hardness. Tears had clogged her eye makeup. In closeup, she looked younger than she had onstage, and more vulnerable, more like the hiker in Belker's photo. I figured her age at twenty-five, about right for a middle-aged guy like Claude Belker. "Thank you for—" She shook her head and walked over to Roberto Vitrione, who stared at her. She said something to him and he reached into his pocket and brought out a roll of bills. Sheena tucked the bills inside her blouse and came back to look down at the kid.

"You know him?"

"No."

"You called him Country. He came to your rescue."

She shrugged. "He's been following me around."

Outside, in the night, a police siren moaned.

I motioned to Wally, who helped me prop the kid up so I could wedge a shoulder under him for the fireman's carry. The kid was dead weight, heavy as three sacks of potatoes.

"What are you doing?" Sheena asked.

"Can't leave him here."

"Why not?"

Too roustable," I said, heading out.

Our transportation was a block away and the kid made me sweat. That gave me an idea. "Where's your car?"

"The Toyota. Across the street."

I headed out of the house. "Can you drive?"

She shivered. "Sure. Who were those guys?"

I stopped at the Toyota. "Crazies. Open up."

She fumbled for her keys and unlocked the door. The sirens were louder now. Wally helped me load the kid into the rear of the Toyota. He gave me some pellets from a glass vial. "Arnica," he said. "For shock and shakes." He put a couple of pellets between the kid's teeth and then offered some to Sheena, who shook her head.

"I don't do drugs."

"Better roll. The cops could get pushy."

Her keys clattered on the tarmac. I picked them up. "Want me to drive?"

She hesitated, then nodded. "Okay. Thanks."

Wally jogged off toward the Ford. I got behind the wheel and started up. Sheena sat rigidly in the passenger seat, staring into night beyond the windshield. The Ford's lights swung in behind me as I drove back down Argyle to Foothill. The streets of Tustin were quiet. We had just turned onto Newport Boulevard when a police vehicle appeared at the end of the street, its blue light bar cranking. We kept moving well below the speed limit. The cruiser passed us and turned up Foothill, toward the party.

"Where do you live?" I asked Sheena.

"Huntington Beach. Where did you come from, anyway?"

"They say around town you knew a man named Claude Belker. They say you two were sweet—"

She didn't let me finish. "Damn you!" She kicked me

on the shin and the Toyota weaved over into the other lane. She knew him, all right. "Stop the car and get out!"

I stopped the Toyota, turned off the engine, set the brake, and said, "They think Claude might have died under mysterious circumstances."

"Get out! Get out of my car!"

I opened the door and climbed out, but held the door open. "Look, I'm just a guy doing a job. I work for a living, just like you. Did you know he tripled his insurance?"

"Up yours, fuzz!" She climbed over the gear shift with no trouble. She slammed the door closed and started cranking the engine. It caught, throwing a blue exhaust plume into the night. A light summer fog was rolling in from the west and the night air had grown cool. She roared off, laying rubber.

Wally pulled up behind me and I opened the door and got in beside him. "Did you ever consider, Matthew, how barbaric is the stick shift?"

"Keeps you young, Professor."

"Any luck with Mademoiselle Danseuse?"

"I hit her with the concept."

"How's our young gladiator?"

"I think he's faking, doing the wounded hero bit."

Wally grinned. "Before you met me, Matthew, did you know any of this terminology?"

Up in the next block, the Toyota made a U-turn. "What terminology is that?"

"Wounded hero, cycles of nature, grail quest—that sort of terminology."

"Prof, everything I know I learned from you."

The Toyota wheeled to a stop in front of us. The driver's door opened and Sheena charged over to rap on the window of the pickup. "Hey!"

I rolled the window down. "What's up?"

"Him," she said, jerking her thumb at the car. "That country boy. He won't wake up. He's too heavy to move."

"Try the ER. Tustin has a wonderful hospital."

Her voice was a squeak. "Damn you for this!"

"Drop him on the side of the road. He's just another heartsick admirer. One more out of thousands."

She sighed in defeat. "Help me out, okay?"

"As a favor?"

She sighed. "I knew Claude, okay? It's not a crime, knowing him. We were . . . friends."

"How about a drink?"

"I don't drink."

"Coffee? Tea? Cocoa? Pepsi?"

"You'll help me?"

Wally poked me in the ribcage and I felt a jolt of pain. There would be bruises from my tussle with the geek. Where was he now? I climbed out of the pickup.

"Can't say no to a lady in distress."

Sheena stamped her foot angrily and walked with me back to the red Toyota.

6

The kid didn't die.

When we got to my place, I wedged a shoulder under him and helped him up the steps. I smelled beer on his breath but no weed. On the way up he burped with each step. At the top I braced him against the railing to let him puke. He coughed and hunched his insides, the vomit dribbling onto the sidewalk below.

Wally brought out a wet towel, and I mopped the kid's face.

"I'm okay," he whispered. "Thanks."

Inside the house I laid him out on my bed, and he grinned at me. "How's Miss Sheena?" His accent sounded like Texas, or maybe Oklahoma.

"She's okay."

"Like to see her home, if it's all right with you."

"I need twenty minutes, kid, then you make your pitch."

He stuck out his hand. "Name's McCloud. J. W. McCloud, from Mexia, Texas."

He pronounced it Muh-HAY-uh.

"Matt Murdock," I said. "Pleased to meet you."

"What you hit that sucker with, anyway?"

"The landlord's chair."

The kid grinned in appreciation. He had a big long face and lots of farm-boy teeth and eyes set wide under a broad forehead. His boots were scuffed, and there was a hole in the right elbow of his cowboy shirt. I figured his age at twenty-five, like Sheena's. I knew the story already. He'd played high school ball but had been too short for college ball. Money was scarce. He'd tried several jobs, watching the economy of his town sag with the rest of the oil patch. So he'd loaded his jalopy and headed west, to California, where he'd fallen in love with an exotic dancer who wore a chastity belt with a golden padlock. And here he was, fighting bikers in Lemon Heights. Tonight, he'd had his chance to play hero.

"Dang," he said. "Wish I'd thought of that."

"You helped with your diversion."

"I blew it, Mr. Murdock. I surely did." He rubbed his solar plexus thoughtfully. "Gosh dang."

When I came into the living room, Wally was sitting in my easy chair, and Sheena sat on a straight chair, her ankles crossed. The blouse was buttoned up now, the tails tucked in. Wally had poured us brandy. Sheena was drinking a Pepsi. "Nice place," she said.

"Thanks." I pulled up a director's chair and sat down carefully.

"What do you want to know?"

"Where you met Claude Belker. How well you knew him."

"We met in the mall, South Coast Plaza. I didn't know him all that well."

"Did he see you dance?"

"A couple of times."

"Did he take you to lunch? Dinner? Out for a drink?"

"No. Nothing like that. We were casual acquaintances."

I pulled out the hiking photo and showed it to Sheena. She stared at it and then glared at me, her neck tight, her spine rigid with anger.

"Where did you get this?"

"It was taped to the underside of Claude Belker's desk in his office at Golden Bear Savings and Loan."

"So?"

"So where was it taken?"

Sheena sagged in her chair. "In the mountains. I think it was Lake Arrowhead. Or maybe Tahoe."

"Did someone else take the picture?"

"No. He had a time-exposure thing on his camera. He'd tie the camera to a tree trunk and set this little switch and hurry on over."

"Where did you stay overnight?"

She set the photo down on the table. The fingers of her left hand dug into her leg. "Look. It was a day hike. We drove up. We drove back. We walked in the mountains. Nothing happened." She stood up. "I have to go now. It's been a hassle, and this lady is tired."

"The people I work for think Claude's still alive."

Her face went into contortions and her eyes got wet. "You're mean, mister." She grabbed for the doorknob but missed and had to try again. She snatched open the door and hurried out into the night, shoes clicking on the wooden steps.

The kid came to lean against the doorframe of the bedroom. The color was not yet back in his face. "Where's Miss Sheena?"

Wally raised an eyebrow at me as I went out the door, following Sheena Mandarin.

A bank of summer fog was rolling in off the beach as I trailed Sheena's red Toyota north on Coast Highway. She started out driving over the speed limit, zipping away from me and her trouble, but then at the Santa Ana River I saw the brake lights glow bright against the gloom as she slowed down to 45 miles per hour, then 35. By the time we reached Huntington Beach, she was down to 25 miles per hour, and all I could see through the shadowless gray was her lights. She turned right and drove inland for three blocks and parked in the driveway of a frame duplex. I cut the headlights on the Ford and waited. The dashboard clock read 11:40. I wished I had brought the brandy bottle.

She was back outside by 11:55, and this time she was dressed for a hike. She wore baggy green pants and a shirt with big pockets and hiking boots. Over one shoulder was a red rucksack.

She climbed into the Toyota and started up the engine and backed out. The fog was heavier now, and I was not looking forward to tracking her in the murk. Wherever she wanted to go, the trip seemed urgent.

Crawling along at 20 miles per hour, we headed east, away from the beach, and toward the San Diego Freeway. I made a right turn and barreled down to the corner, where I hung a left on the next street, driving parallel to her for two blocks before making another left. I was at the corner as the Toyota crept by, still edging for the freeway.

It took us ten minutes to reach the freeway. She stopped at an Exxon station to make a phone call. She was in the booth about a minute. It looked to me like she was listening to the phone ring. She stared at the phone before hanging up. Then she hurried back to the Toyota and took the south on ramp.

The fog was no better here. Big semis eased along at 15 miles per hour, so you knew it was a bad night for driving. We covered about six miles before Sheena made her exit and headed for home on the surface streets. I sat outside her place in Huntington Beach until the lights went out, and then I drove slowly back to the pier.

Something I had said about Claude Belker had set her in motion.

I drove Wally home to Balboa. Then I taxied the kid back to his car, a 1978 Camaro with Texas plates. It was after 1:00 A.M. when I got home, too late to call Bruce Halliburton and report. I set the alarm and dove clumsily into a weird sleep.

The alarm punched me awake at 5:00. My ribs ached from the geek's chain, and my left shoulder was stiff. I stumbled out onto my deck for a reconnoiter. There was no wind, and you could not see through the fog across the quad. Muttering to myself, I made coffee and warmed up a week-old danish. I dressed and strapped on the PPK. The Ford started with a cough and an unfriendly gurgle. By 5:40 I was stationed down the block from Sheena's house in Huntington Beach. The red Toyota, windows streaked with beach-mist, sat in the driveway. I yawned, kept drifting off to sleep.

The fog hung around until almost eight o'clock, and I remembered one more reason why I'd stopped being a cop—wearing out the seat of your pants on stakeouts.

Sheena made her appearance at 8:05, wearing the hiking clothes from the night before. Through the binoculars, she seemed fresh, rested, eager for the day, moving with energy and verve. In the pale gray light the rucksack was a spot of red.

We drove east to the San Diego Freeway and then south to the Newport Freeway, where we encountered one of Southern California's main events—a traffic jam. While I maneuvered the Ford, changing lanes, keeping the Toyota in sight, I went through what I knew about the case:

Item: In December Claude Belker starts building up his life insurance, using six different companies to spread the money. Heartland's share is over $5 million.

Item: Claude meets Sheena. On a hiking trip he takes a photo.

Question: Did they meet before he started building up his insurance or after?

Item: Claude is playing poker with cronies at Bobby Maclean's place. Other players included Wendell Barrymore and a horny guy named Mendez-Madrid.

Item: In April, midnight on a Thursday, Claude drives in front of a gasoline truck and burns to death.

Item: The boots are missing. The house is for sale. The people at Golden Bear are hungry for deposits.

By 9:30 the sun was trying to burn away the fog, and we were heading northeast, toward the San Bernardino mountains. We drifted through sleepy San Bernardino and cruised up along a twisting four-lane through Waterman Canyon. The elevation at Lake Arrowhead is just over five thousand feet, but seems higher because you come right up off the desert floor. One minute you're in flat San Bernardino, feeling sea-level. The next you can smell the tang of the pines. We drove through Crestline and Lake Arrowhead, with Strawberry Peak on the right. Along the highway were colored snow poles that marked the edge of the road. Summertime heat makes snow poles look strange.

The sun had peeled away the overcast as we came into the town of Big Bear. It was a weekday, and the town looked buttoned up. There were signs for motels and fishing and boating. An Italian restaurant advertised Guido's pizza for four dollars, one giant coke included. We eased through town, still heading east into the sun. I hung back, keeping two or three vehicles between us. When I got too close, I waited until the little Toyota had rounded a curve before speeding up to keep her in sight.

About five miles out of town the Toyota made a right turn onto a gravel road that led into a forested area. I waited until she was into the trees before following. The road was steep and muddy. The trees were scrub pine. I counted three cabins on the right and four more on the left. None of them showed any signs of life. Through the trees I caught flashes of sunlight on her car windows and occasional glimpses of red. The wheels of the Ford slipped in the mud, and I wondered how much farther she could go in her car.

I got my answer as I came around the corner and spotted the Toyota. It was angled off the road, tilted to the right, its right rear fender mashed into a clump of small pines, its right rear wheel stuck in the mud. Sheena was not in sight. I parked the pickup in a stand of berry bushes and hiked up the narrow road until I came to a clearing. Tire cleats marked patches in the muddy road. There was no way to tell how old they were.

In the center of the clearing was an A-frame cabin. There was a wood pile off to the left and a big stump someone had used for splitting firewood. The roof was red metal, steep on the south side and punched out to form a dormer room. The windows were streaked with dirt from a recent rain, and the front door stood open. I checked the PPK and walked to the front door. I could hear her crying inside the house, snuffling, blowing her nose. The sound came from the direction of the dormer room. It was gloomy inside and gray with cold.

I rapped on the door with my knuckles and stepped inside. She called out: "Claude? Claude, honey?" Her voice was plaintive, full of terrible hope. She came around the corner at a quick trot, blonde hair flying, face streaked with tears. When she saw it wasn't Claude Belker, she stopped, digging in her heels. "What are you doing here?"

"The same as you. Waiting for Claude Belker."

"Damn you!"

She clenched her fists and ran at me, lashing out at the world through me. I grabbed her wrists and dodged her kick. She was strong, with dancer's muscles. She spat in my face, and her eyes were crazy and red-rimmed from crying. When she got close enough, she tried to sink her teeth into my hand, and when I jerked away, the back of my hand bumped her nose. Not hard. Just a little. Blood dripped out, spattering the floor.

The sight of her own blood, bright against the chill gray morning, settled her down. With a muffled curse she let me go and flung herself away. She was in the bathroom a long time, running the water, bumping around and snuffling. I found the circuit box and flipped the master switch. Lights came on. I poked around in the kitchen. The dishes were clean. The knives were sharp. There was half a can of Folger's coffee near the stove. The fridge contained a loaf of French bread, sourdough, hard as a rock. Next to the bread was a half pound of butter, an unopened package of Jimmy Dean's bacon, and a carton of eggs. The eggs were extra large. I picked up the wall phone and listened to a dial tone.

I left the kitchen and went into the bedroom. The bed

was a king, with a red Hudson Bay blanket on top, set on a Hollywood frame. The closet contained two pairs of khaki trousers and a half dozen shirts. Three of the shirts were women's size twelve. Above the bed was a home-made shelf loaded with books. Half the titles were westerns—Luke Short and Louis L'Amour. The other half were metaphysical—crystals and channeling and the wonders you could do with the Tarot.

I found the hiking boots underneath the bed.

The soles were caked with dried mud. I carried them into the other room where Sheena sat, her chin in her hands, her elbows braced on her knees. She had dried her eyes and combed her hair. Seeing the boots brought tears to her eyes, and she started wailing again. I thought I knew why.

I set the boots down in front of her and then I waited for her to calm down. "He was here, wasn't he?"

"No. How should I know?"

"The power is on. He was here, only you didn't know it."

She shook her head, making the ponytail swirl. "That's not true."

"You were waiting for him to make contact. You've been waiting for a couple of months. You called him last night from a pay phone."

"No. That's not true." She stood up and walked to the door and stared out at the morning. In the forest a bird chirped, ter-whit, ter-whoo, ter-whit, ter-whoo.

"He wouldn't have left the boots," she said, tight-lipped.

"Where is he, then?"

She turned to look at me and the movement brought gaunt shadows to her face. Her expression was pale and without hope. "Where did you find them?"

"Underneath the bed."

She shook her head sadly. "Claude didn't put them there."

"Who did?"

"He wouldn't put anything under the bed. It was a rule."

After one last, sad look around Sheena locked up the A-frame, and we walked down the road to her Toyota. It started up all right, but the right rear wheel was buried axle-deep in the mud. I hooked a line from the Ford to her Toyota. There wasn't much room to maneuver, so it took the better part of an hour to haul the car out. By the time the Toyota was free, we were both sweating. When you stepped out of the shade, you could feel the heat of the sun. I suggested food.

She led me to a health food place called Middle Earth in the center of the village of Big Bear. We ordered salads. Her face was still pale with sadness, but when the food came she ate with appetite. I stayed away from questions about her and Belker. She had lost him twice. That was enough trouble for one day. As she ate the last bit of lettuce topped with sprouts, she told me how she and Belker had met.

"Claude and I ran into each other—I guess you could say we collided—at South Coast Plaza. He was coming out of Eddie Bauer and I was looking the other way and in a rush and ker-boom, we just collided. I liked his face. It was soft and pleading, sort of. It was just before Thanksgiving, and he was doing a little early shopping. We got down on our knees to pick up his packages, and he offered to buy me a cup of coffee. I had tea. Claude was a wonderful listener. In no time he got me talking about myself, my childhood, my family, that sort of stuff. I knew he was married, but he seemed so much nicer than the creeps I meet working, if you know what I mean."

"Sounds like a good guy."

"He was a wonderful man." She stared at me, then took a drink of her carrot juice. "On the outside he was gruff. You know, all business and bottom-line and numbers on financial reports. He was very organized, and he understood people really well. On the inside he was like a kid, a kid about seven years old. He loved to play. He had a nice singing voice, and we used to do duets. He was a wonderful lover. He told me his wife didn't care about that part any more. She was busy having lunch with her friends and being Mrs. Rich Bitch."

The tears started up again, and Sheena excused herself for a trip to the ladies' room. When she came back, her hair had been combed. I paid the check and walked Sheena to her Toyota.

"Well, it's been wonderful meeting you, Mr. Detective. Just swell."

"You were going away together, weren't you? You and Claude?"

She sighed, her chest rising nicely inside the shirt. "We were in love. That's all."

"Did you see him the night before he died?"

She nodded. "Yes. For an hour or so. He usually came by before he played poker."

"Was this at the Maclean place?"

"Yes."

"Do you know where Maclean lives?"

"South of Laguna somewhere. That was Claude's other life, the one he wanted out of. I didn't care about it."

"Did he mention the name Barrymore to you? Or Mendez-Madrid?"

"No."

"What did you guys talk about?"

She blushed, remembering now. Her voice was thick with emotion. "We talked about us. He told me about growing up in Omaha. I talked about growing up in Detroit. Look, mister." She grabbed my arm. "I loved Claude. When he died, it killed me. Later on, when the shock had worn off, I started remembering the things he'd said. Like if he went away suddenly or if something happened to him, that I should just sit tight. Hold the thought, Claude said. Hold the thought. He talked like he might be coming back, like he had a plan or something. So when you said what you did last night, about him being alive, I hoped maybe—" She stopped to brush a tear from her cheek. "So I came up here with my heart pinned to my sleeve, and the only thing left was the boots."

"He was here, wasn't he?"

She brought out a Kleenex and blew her nose. "I don't know. It's all so—" And then she said: "Darn!"

She dug into her rucksack and came out with a business card. It said Sheena Mandarin, Exotic Dancing. There was a phone number with a 714 area code. With a slim gold ballpoint, she wrote something on the back of the card. "My name's not Sheena," she said. "It's Mary Sue." She handed it to me. The back of the card read Mary Sue Janowitz. She looked around at the health food place. The sun beamed down. It would be a beautiful day in Big Bear.

"Would you let me know if you find him?"

"Sure."

"Claude's gone. I can feel it. I don't think you'll find him." She stared at my eyes and face with a sudden new interest. "I like a beard on a man. I like yours."

The wonderful and disarming directness of youth. "Thanks."

"Even with gray in it."

I grinned, increasing the generation gap that already yawned between us, and she turned on her heel and climbed into the Toyota. Mountain mud was still caked underneath her right rear fender. She started up and made a smart little U-turn on the gravel lot. She pulled up beside me. "That kid," she said. "The one I call Country. You know his name?"

"McCloud," I said. "J. W. McCloud."

"Hmm," she said and drove off.

7

Bruce Halliburton made contact that night while I was busy watching the eleven o'clock news on Channel Three. My favorite anchorperson, beautiful Linda Calderon, had been promoted to network—that elusive East Coast heaven-on-earth for the chosen among happy-talk newscasters—and her Channel Three replacement was a dazzling redhead named Megan McGuire. I'd heard rumors that anchorpersons in L.A. made a quarter of a million a year. Network paid even more. The test for success as a news anchor was simple: You had to keep smiling and talking happily as you summarized the day's horrors. Tonight Megan McGuire was earning her dough as she chatted merrily about the death toll in Asia, Europe, the Mideast, and Central America.

A bomb had killed four civilians in Paris to kick off the summer tourist season. The friendly Palestinians had allowed one hostage to send a message to the White House on videotape. Very convenient for the terrorist community, videotape. The hostage, a newsman with a scraggy brown beard and dark circles under his eyes, looked beaten down and starved out. Violence was flaming in Korea and the Phillipines. Down in Nicaragua two factions were battling, killing innocent people, but from Megan's bright-eyed delivery you couldn't tell who was winning, or whose side you should be rooting for.

Bruce called in during a Heartland commercial. I told him about Sheena/Mary Sue and the boots of Claude Belker. Bruce kept his cool. No surprise in his voice.

"Is that Sheena as in Jungle Girl?"

"Right." In the background I heard classical music and a woman's voice. I wondered who Bruce was bunking with.

"Good work, Captain. Excellent. How old is she?"

"Mid-twenties."

"Pretty?"

"If you like jocks with tight muscles."

"You have her address and phone handy? I think I'd like to interrogate her."

"I'll trade you, Bruce."

"Hmm? Trade for what?"

"Those bikers came for me. Made a bee-line. I'd never seen them before. I'm wondering how they knew."

"Leak in the organization, Captain."

"Only two people besides me had the address. Wally and you. Wally was with me."

"What are you saying, Captain?"

"Did you finger me, Bruce?"

He laughed. A short, curt sound. "What for?"

"You tell me." I was tired of all the dancing around. "While you're at it, tell me about Mendez-Madrid."

Bruce's voice dropped to a guarded whisper. "What about him?"

"He was poker pals with Belker and a guy named Mac-lean. I saw a file on him in your briefcase."

"That's Need to Know, Captain. I assumed you factored that in."

"Where are you, Bruce? Where are you calling from?"

Bruce sighed. "All right. There are some bits and pieces I haven't told you. Look. Let's schedule a meet tomorrow morning. I'll ring you when I'm free. I'll buy your breakfast and fill you in. Deal?"

"Why not tonight?"

"Sorry. I'm otherwise . . . ah . . . occupied. Hope you understand."

A woman. How nice for Bruce. "Okay. What time tomorrow?"

"Ten or so. I'll just dial 'M' for Murdock." He chuckled. "Now, how about those numbers on the little dancer?"

"Tomorrow, Bruce." I hung up. Bruce was jerking me around and I knew what that meant. His need for Murdock was finished.

After hanging up, I stared at the television as the zany weatherman reported on the force of a small tidal wave in Alaska. I like weathermen. They're crazy. They get glee out of nature. Honest rip-roaring glee. Maybe I should have been a weatherman. There was one swallow of Bud left. I finished that on my way to the fridge for another can. Bruce's gin bottle sat on the top shelf, keeping cool, waiting for the next dry martini. I popped open the Bud and stood leaning against the island, staring at the television, thinking about Bruce.

Superagent Bruce Halliburton was the original Golden Boy—East Coast upbringing, Harvard degree, Navy career, a decade hanging out in the marble halls of government in Washington, D.C., coat and tie required—and now he was working the marble halls at Heartland Mutual and still wearing his coat and tie. He'd hired me to poke around in the life of Claude Belker. Move fast, he'd said, and save the company millions. I'd uncovered a girl friend, bikers, boots, some poker cronies, a mountain hideaway with the power still on. I smelled a conspiracy. Leads were piling up, begging to be tracked down, but Bruce wasn't eager for me to do the follow-ups on Mendez-Madrid and the poker crowd.

Why not?

The phone dragged me out of a dream about a muddy brown river crowded with crocodiles. On the bank of the river people were waiting in line to board a barge. A gong sounded each time someone boarded. Bong. The mallet was swung by a bald-headed monk wearing a white cassock. When I moved in for a close-up of the next man waiting to board, I saw he wore a white death mask.

Bong.

I fumbled with the receiver, one foot still locked in the dream. My bedside clock said 6:48. The light outside my window was dark gray. I was up on one elbow, and my ribcage was sore from being on the receiving end of the geek's chain.

"Yo."

"Mr. Murdock?" It was a woman's voice, soft, liquid, and low.

"Yes."

"I'm a . . . friend of . . . Bruce Halliburton'."

I rolled over to lie on my back. "Wonderful."

"He said to phone you if he didn't get back by six-thirty."

I checked the clock again. 6:49. "Why don't we give him another ten?"

There was a pause. "I woke you up, didn't I?"

"Yes." I still didn't know her name or her connection to Bruce. Was she the voice in the background?

"I got . . . nervous. When he didn't get back, I mean."

"Where did he go?"

"To meet someone."

"What time?"

"Just before five."

In the back of my head a tiny alarm sounded. "Do you have any idea where the meeting was?"

"Somewhere on the beach. When he left, he told me he would be back by six-thirty. If he didn't get back, I was to call you."

I was coming awake now. "Okay. Mind telling me your name, ma'am?"

"Oh. Of course. My name is Mrs. Mendez-Madrid."

Bingo. "Where are you calling from?"

"I'm at . . . Coco's. Near Fashion Island."

"Was that where you were supposed to meet Bruce?"

"No." She paused, and I thought I heard her sigh. "I came here because someone was coming to the house."

"Who?"

Her voice broke, faltered. "A man."

"Where were you supposed to meet Bruce?"

"At my house."

"Where's that?"

"Near here. On Spyglass Hill."

Spyglass Hill was the high-rent district in Newport Beach, a town that was mostly high-rent districts. "And now you can't go back."

"Right."

"Because of the man."

"Right."

"So you called me."

"Bruce said you were very . . . resourceful."

Good old Bruce, always full of compliments. "This man. You think he'll still be waiting?"

"I hope not. Can you help me?"

"Sure. I'll be there in about twenty minutes. How will I know you?"

"I have dark hair," she said. "I'll be wearing white slacks and a white shirt and sweater. I'm at a window table."

"Order me some coffee," I said and hung up.

I came into Coco's just after seven and looked around for Mrs. Mendez-Madrid. She saw me first, from a booth against the windows. Behind her in the window was Fashion Island, the big shopping mall, white construction limestone looming grayish white in the California morning. Her eyes swept me quickly, and she tilted her head back and waved me over. She had dark hair, like an Apache, and high American Indian cheekbones to deepen the impression. The cheekbones and the hair had caught the attention of the corporate types who stopped in for breakfast before leaving to slug it out in the wonderful world of mergers and takeovers. At least a dozen guys in snappy three piece suits were drooling over her.

She was too far away for me to see her eyes. I guessed they'd be dark, black as night, with pale yellow flecks that danced when she got riled. Or when she got turned on. I walked over, feeling the corporate scrutiny on my jeans and work shirt and yellow windbreaker. I wondered what turned her on.

"Mr. Murdock." She held out a brown hand. "Thank you for coming."

"Right." I liked the feel of her hand.

I sat down across from her in the booth. She signalled the waitress, who came over with a cup for me and a fresh pot of coffee. I added cream and sugar and took the first survival sip.

A floppy purse of dark leather sat on the bench next to Mrs. Mendez-Madrid. The purse was roomy, like an overnight bag. She had wonderful wrists, lean and sculpted. Her brown hands were the hands of an artist. On someone else, the white outfit might have looked like a uniform. On Mrs. Mendez-Madrid, it could have been the centerpiece for a fashion layout in a fancy women's magazine. The collar tabs on the blouse protruded perfectly from the neck of the white sweater. She seemed lean and fit, groomed and educated. I guessed her age at early thirties. How tight was she with Bruce? Tight enough to know Bruce was carrying a file on her husband?

I had been wrong about the eyes. They were not dark, but ice-blue, the same shade as Aqua Velva shave lotion, the brand touted by my old man, the Sergeant, during his thirty years of Army.

"Sorry to ruin your morning, Mr. Murdock. I hate being startled awake."

The coffee was reviving me. "Tell me about this meeting Bruce had. And about the guy at your house."

"All right. Last night, Bruce was on the phone for almost an hour. He called you, of course, to set up a meeting. He was very thoughtful when he got off the phone with you. Earlier, he'd spoken two or three times to someone from his office, Ken Trager, I think his name was. In between, he spoke to someone else, I don't know who. There was some talk about numbers, money I think. Bruce seemed . . . argumentative. Finally he said, 'all right'. This morning he was up before five. I'm an early riser, myself. I thought we were going running. Then Bruce told me he was going out, to meet someone. He didn't say who. If he wasn't back by six-thirty, I was to contact you."

"What was the meeting about?"

"One of his cases. He didn't say which one."

"On the beach, you said."

"Yes. I think it was Huntington Beach, but I'm not certain."

"What was his mood after the calls to this Trager?"

"Excited. Although Bruce was good at hiding his emotion."

"How does this connect to the other guy?"

She stroked her coffee spoon. "I was waiting for Bruce to come back when I received a phone call. The caller was . . . a client of my husband's. He said he was coming over. I said it was too early for visitors. He said he had to speak to me about something concerning my husband. The way he spoke made me feel threatened. So I dressed and drove here and phoned you."

"You could have called the police."

"Yes. I could have. I phoned you."

"Who is the client?"

"His name is Cantu. Rudolfo Cantu."

"Foreigner?"

"Rudolfo is a Mexican national. He lives in Guadalajara."

"And he's bothering you?"

She blushed and her lip trembled. It was a very pretty lip, and the trembling made her seem vulnerable. "Yes."

"Where is your husband, Mrs. Mendez?"

"Mendez-Madrid," she said, correcting me. "He's dead."

She said it with a flat tone and a nervous shake of her head. To cover that, she picked up her coffee cup. Around us Coco's was filling up, people standing at the receptionist's desk, waiting for a table. Her fingers were dark brown against the pale crockery cup. My wrist watch said 7:30. "Maybe we should get back to your place and wait for Bruce."

"All right. What if . . . Rudolfo is there?"

"How big is he?"

"About your weight, only shorter."

"Age?"

"Late forties, I think."

"Does he carry a gun?"

"I don't know."

I patted the PPK in its shoulder rig. "I do."

"Oh."

I left the pickup in the lot at Coco's, and we drove to Spyglass Hill in Mrs. Mendez-Madrid's Chrysler. She was a good driver who took the corners with just the right amount of acceleration. As we climbed, the real estate prices climbed with us. Her house was in a cul-de-sac on an upscale street called Spyglass Rim. The structure was Moderne, flat roofs and ramps instead of steps, with glass brick and a white Mediterranean exterior. The front of the house sported an angry little balcony, with steel tube railings, a style dating back to the thirties. The view of the coast and the ocean beyond was spectacular. Spyglass Rim was one street-level below Spyglass Circle Drive, the top of the heap in Newport Beach. There was a "For Sale" sign in Mrs. Mendez-Madrid's front yard. Up the street in the cul-de-sac a big black Lincoln was parked. I scooted down in the seat, to decrease my visibility.

"What kind of car was he driving?"

"A white one. But that was three weeks ago."

"He's been here before?"

She nodded and pressed a button to open the garage door. Going in, she came close to clipping off the side-view mirror on the passenger door. When she stopped, she braked with a jerk. The lady looked smooth as sculpture on the outside. On the inside she was jittery.

The door closed, and we got out and went inside, entering through her kitchen. One wall was lined with packing boxes, stacked four deep and sealed with brown tape. The furniture in the living room was right out of *Architectural Digest*. We stepped from expensive tile onto a deep, plush, green carpet. A balcony ran the length of the house. It had a political feel. If you ran for office, you could stand on the balcony and make showy speeches to your voters.

A big cat with blue-gray fur slipped into the room and walked up to Mrs. Mendez-Madrid. She picked it up.

"Manxman," she said. "This is Mr. Murdock."

The cat gave me a stony stare, then shrugged and meowed. She put it down.

"Do you like animals?"

"Sometimes."

"I named him for a sailor in *Moby-Dick,* a minor character really. Have you read it?"

"No."

Mrs. Mendez-Madrid smiled and indicated the boxes in the room. "Manxman and I have to move. It's too expensive. The bank's selling it out from under us. I feel like an orphan."

She walked away from me and disappeared through a door leading to a downstairs study. I heard the whir of tape and then the static crackle of her answering machine.

The blue cat had vanished.

On the wall across the room was a wall-size television. To the right sliding doors opened onto a terrace where a black metal sculpture of a bird spread its wings and tried to soar vainly off its marble pedestal into the wild blue yonder. The patio was dotted with green plants. A fountain gurgled happily, softening the harsh stone. Mrs.

Mendez-Madrid appeared at the door to her library, smiling wistfully. "No new messages."

The PPk felt heavy against my ribs. The house felt empty and forlorn. There was no sign of Bruce.

A car door slammed outside. I walked to the curtains and peeked through. A man was coming through the gate. He wore a white suit and white shoes and a white hat with a fancy red hatband. His face was dark and his heavy body moved with deliberation. Mrs. Mendez-Madrid came to stand beside me. She seemed perfectly still, but I could feel her trembling with fear.

"Is that Rudolfo?"

"Yes. What will you do?"

"Let's see what he's after."

"Let him in, you mean?"

"Sure. Talk to him. Maybe we can surprise him, figure out what he wants."

She shook her head. "I don't like it."

I touched her arm. "I could just shoot him first. But the law frowns on that."

She forced a smile. "I know. I know."

She told me to wait in the study downstairs. It was a warm-feeling room in a big empty-feeling house. The shelves contained a lot of books in Spanish and were labeled with names like Cortazar, Borges, Fuentes, Ocampo, Lispector, that I did not recognize. The desk was tidy. An IBM computer sat on one arm of the desk, with a printer down below. There was only the one chair, blue, with chrome arms and a chrome swivel.

The doorbell rang and I watched her open the door. She was a tall lady. The man in the white suit was about her height, but thicker, with that mean asshole look you get from having money in a country of beggars and poor folks.

He said something in rapid Spanish and she answered, equally rapidly. It surprised me, but then I remembered she'd been married to a Mexican. She stepped aside so that Rudolfo Cantu could come in. They had a conversation standing up. My Spanish is limited to *"huevos rancheros"* and *"cerveza, por favor,"* so I had no way of following what they said. Rudolfo wanted something. I heard the word *dinero*. The lady of the house kept saying no and shaking her head. They went at it for a couple of minutes, arguing in rapid Spanish, and then he grabbed her. Before I could get to her, he had ripped the white sweater and the blouse under it. Her throat was exposed, and one ripe brown shoulder.

Rudolfo's eyes got wide when he saw me coming. He let go of the lady and reached inside his coat, but I was on him by then. I slammed him up against the wall, making that side of the house shake. I shoved the PPK up under his nose and spun him around for a body search. I figured him for a knife artist, but he was carrying a five shot .32 in a belt holster. He kept speaking to me in Spanish, cutting his eyes at Mrs. Mendez-Madrid, who was holding her torn sweater and breathing hard. Her eyes, which should have been wide with alarm, were narrowed with anger. Rudolfo's breath smelled of corn tortillas, strong cigarettes, and a heavy spice.

She left the room and came back pulling on a fresh sweater, off-white and classy. We sat Rudolfo down for some Q&A. I asked the questions in English. Mrs. Mendez-Madrid translated. Rudolfo growled his answers and kept staring at the door. Maybe he expected help from the *rurales*.

Q: What did he want here?
A: Emiliano—that's my husband—owes him some money.

Q: How much?

A: Over a million, depending on the value of the peso.

Q: Money that he borrowed?

A: Yes. It's none of our business, he says.

Q: Is there a note, something to verify the loan?

A: No. Only the word of an old friend from boyhood days.

Q: Why did he come here for it?

A: He says my husband had lots of secret hiding places. Some of them were in the house.

Q: This house?

A: Yes. This house.

Q: Why did he tear your dress?

A: He says women are cattle. They eat and drink and talk too much. Their only function is to produce offspring for the marketplace.

Q: Tell him he's a wonderful person.

She told him and he smiled, showing us a gold tooth that I had not seen before. The questions had made Rudolfo sweat. He needed a bath, bad.

I wrapped Rudolfo's wrists together with some strapping tape. He grunted when I gave an extra twist to the tape.

"Did you know about the money?" I asked her in English.

"No. But I'm not surprised. Emmy was a stockbroker. He borrowed everything he could to invest in the market. He loved to flash hundred-dollar bills at waitresses and valet parking attendants. He owed money to a lot of people."

"When did he die?"

"Oh. Didn't Bruce tell you? Emmy died in March."

Rudolfo broke into our conversation by growling a question.

"He wants to know what we're going to do with him," Mrs. Mendez-Madrid said.

I knew another word in Spanish. I used it to charm Rudolfo.

"Policia," I said.

He spat at me, but his aim was lousy. He missed. Old Rudolfo was not having a good day.

8

We drove Rudolfo down the hill to the Newport Beach Police Station. The time on the dashboard clock of the Chrysler said 8:32. The parking lot contained only three vehicles, but there was lots of activity out by the side door, where five blue and white prowl cars were lined up.

We entered the lobby with Rudolfo between us. Mrs. Mendez-Madrid walked like an Indian queen, her dark face and hands set off by the white clothes. I wondered if she ever wore red, or black, or silver. I kept stealing looks at her. From every angle, she looked good.

It's always better at a police station if you get specific, so I asked the desk sergeant to page Sergeant Leon Book. Rudolfo said something in Spanish that sounded nasty, but the desk sergeant just stared at him with a face full of disdain.

Leon Book came out wearing his gunbelt. He's a gourmet who has trouble keeping his weight down. He's not as concerned about his weight as he is about forking over lots of money for new uniforms. He has a square face and blue eyes that twinkle. Leon is the only cop I know who's been married to the same woman for fifteen years. As far as I know, that's a world's record.

We shook hands and I introduced him to Mrs. Mendez-Madrid and explained that Rudolfo had attempted to assault her and that she would press charges. Leon handed Rudolfo over to the desk sergeant, who paged for an interpreter.

"Does Rudolfo do much business in the States?"

"I wouldn't know. Why?"

"You'd think he'd learn English."

She nodded. "Rudolfo likes working with interpreters. Young women, mostly. And my husband was bilingual, of course."

It took half an hour to fill out a complaint. I sat with her so she could ask me questions about police procedure. I enjoyed answering, Murdock the Expert. She printed her letters using a gold fountain pen she carried in her purse. In the age of the ballpoint, you seldom see a real fountain pen. The ink coming out of this one was bright blue.

I wondered again how she and Bruce were connected. Were they pals? Tennis partners? Lovers? Her husband had died a couple of months ago, in March, she'd said. Bruce was employed by Heartland. Had her husband been insured by Heartland, the same as Belker? Bruce was apparently sleeping at her place, but was he in the lady's bed as well? An inner voice told me to cool it. There was a good chance she was Bruce's lady, and therefore out of bounds. But she was magnetic, dammit. And beautiful. Well, it was not against the law to look.

I walked over to poke my head into Leon's office. "Got a minute?"

"Just one. This is a bitch of a Friday. The kids are

massing for a fun party weekend on Balboa. There's a murder up the road and two robberies at Fashion Island. The coke trade is up by twenty percent over last year. I've got six officers out with the summer flu. And my wife's mother is visiting from Scranton."

"Where was the murder?"

He glanced at a computer print-out. "On PCH, near Bolsa Chica."

"Huntington Beach?"

"It's county jurisdiction, actually. The body was found by a jogger. He called the CHP. They called the sheriff."

"Any I.D.?"

"Not yet." Leon eyed me. "How come you're interested?"

"A client of mine went out this morning, early, and didn't come back. He was going to meet someone on the beach. Maybe your guys picked up something."

"There's a lot of beach, Sherlock." Leon reached for a phone. I gave him Bruce's name and a brief description. I wasn't really counting on anything turning up. There we were in the police station, where they have all this fancy electronic gear, plus a direct computer wire to F.B.I. headquarters in Washington, D.C., and I just wanted to see what would happen. Leon hung up the phone. There was a long silence. Then he said: "What was he doing out there, this client of yours?"

"Early morning meeting."

"On what topic?"

"He wasn't dealing drugs. What have you got, Leon?"

Leon scratched his ear. "White male, mid-forties. Wearing green slacks, a golf jacket, rugby shirt. The tennis sneakers looked new."

"What killed him?"

"Three gunshot wounds, small bore. I don't know where he took them."

My stomach jumped with queasy fear. "When can we get a positive I.D.?"

Leon looked past me, where Mrs. Mendez-Madrid was finishing up with her complaint form. "Is the lady connected?"

"I'm not sure. We just met."

"Well, she's a looker." Leon stood. "I've got to head up that way. Where can I reach you?"

"How about if I go along?"

"This is police business."

"Come on, Leon."

He shrugged, settled his gunbelt around his gourmet's waist, and led the way out.

Mrs. Mendez-Madrid wanted to come along. I advised her to stay at home. Rudolfo was on ice. For awhile, anyway, he'd be no trouble. But the lady dug her heels in. She didn't want to go home. Stormy lights flashed in her blue eyes. She insisted on coming along. Okay, I said. Okay. We climbed in her Chrysler and followed Leon Book north along Coast Highway. She drove.

When the wind is right, the industrial oil reek carries down the coast from the refineries up in Long Beach, disregarding the real estate values, to poison serene and beautiful Orange County. The wind was right today. The smell along the beach was deadly, rank, ugly green, and medicinal.

The brownish summer smog had settled in for the day as we drove through Huntington Beach. A half mile beyond I saw the first roof lights of the police and emergency vehicles. Beyond that were the yellow ribbons of a police barrier. Four cruisers—two from the sheriff, one from the CHP, one from Huntington Beach—were angled in, their light bars slowly turning. An ambulance was backed up to the scene. Next to it was a station wagon that said "Medical Examiner, County of Orange."

Leon Book parked his car and came over to the Chrysler. "You people stay here. I'll find out what's going on." He walked heavily toward the barrier, where he showed his shield to the officer on duty, who passed him through to the crime scene.

The police had erected sawhorses to divert the traffic away from the right lane, and now the gawkers slowed to see what was happening. Just outside the barrier, a clot of pedestrians had gathered to watch the police at work. There were two bikers and an old party in a leisure suit and two beach girls with tanned legs and a Chicano who wore dusty work boots.

"This is awful," Mrs. Mendez-Madrid said.

"Yeah."

"You think it might be Bruce. Isn't that it?"

"The man who died was the same age, an Anglo."

"God." Her face hardened, and she looked older.

I watched the dashboard clock turn over. It was a digital that gave you a readout in seconds. "What was Bruce wearing when he left the house?"

"A windbreaker and some slacks."

"Remember the color?"

"He had them on last night. They were green."

"Shoes?"

"They were new Adidas. He'd just bought them last weekend but hadn't had a chance to test them on the courts."

The fear waffled me again. I rolled my shoulders, trying to shake it off, and said: "I remember in Saigon Bruce would wait up all night for a chance to play tennis."

"His backhand is marvelous. Do you play?"

"No."

With an electronic click the dashboard clock turned over another minute. It was hot in the car, so I opened the door and stepped out. I heard Mrs. Mendez-Madrid rustling in her purse. I heard her blow her nose. Then her door opened, and she got out of the car. There were tears on her cheeks. I looked at her across the roof of the car. It was not a good time for questions, but there were things I needed to know.

"Has Rudolfo bothered you before?"

"Yes."

"When was that?"

"Once, before my husband died. And then twice after."

"Was he always after money?"

She took her time putting on a pair of designer dark glasses. "What do you mean?"

"You're a good-looking woman. Rudolfo is an animal. You were alone. He could have thought you were prey."

She walked away from the car, head down, staring at her feet, her arms folded tightly over her chest. A Nissan four-by-four with three grinning teens in it honked at her. A teen with his nose plastered with zinc oxide cried: "Hey, baby! Wanta toot my horn?" Mrs. Mendez-Madrid did not notice. She crossed the lanes of traffic and headed toward the beach.

Through the massed vehicles at the crime scene I saw two paramedics in dark blue loading a body bag into the yawning doors of a police ambulance. The body bag was dark green, almost black, made of a slick rubbery material.

A photographer at the edge of the barrier began firing his camera. A police car started up. A walkie-talkie crackled. Sounds irritated me. A line of sweat trickled down my neck, wetting the shirt collar. I took the keys out of the ignition and followed the lady. She was sitting in the sand with her shoes off, staring out to sea. I sat down beside her.

"Yes," she said.

"Yes what?"

"Yes, Rudolfo was after me. The money first, then Roxanne. That's my name, Roxanne." She held out her hand and we shook. "I wish you'd stop calling me Mrs. Mendez-Madrid. It makes me feel like my mother-in-law, and she's dead."

"I'm Matt," I said.

"What am I going to do, Matt?"

"About what?"

"Everything." She put a hand on my arm and leaned close. "Will you help me?"

"I'm working for Bruce."

"Bruce is trying to help me."

"In what way?"

"It's . . . complicated."

I was about to probe some more when I heard my name called. I turned to see Leon Book standing at the edge of the beach, between two beach bungalows that had cost $12,500 to build and would now retail for $450,000 apiece. I helped Roxanne to her feet. There was sand trapped between her toes. Her hand was smooth, glossy. Touching her brought on the tingles. Nice.

Leon's face told us everything. "Okay," he sighed, bringing out his notebook. "It's him, all right. An officer found some I.D. up the road, where they must have dropped it."

"It's who?" Roxanne asked.

"Halliburton," Leon said. "Bruce J."

"Oh, dear God!" Roxanne grabbed my arm and squeezed, digging her nails in, then turned and walked away to lean against a building for support. I started to follow, but she waved me off. She gulped air and her body heaved with strong sobbing.

"She knew him, all right." Leon said, staring after her.

Cops love to probe. "What have you got, Leon?" I pointed to the notebook.

"The ME's about finished." Leon stared at what he had written down. "Like I said, the wallet turned up. Eelskin. Inside were a dozen credit cards, no cash, some receipts for meals. The driver's license was a half-mile away from the wallet. Joe Floyd, my counterpart in Huntington Beach, has robbery as a motive. The perps went through the wallet, tossing stuff out they couldn't use. We got a ring, Harvard, class of sixty-five. There were business cards saying he was a vice-president for an insurance company, Heartland Mutual. No photos of family. Was he married?"

"He used to be."

"Yeah. What kind of vehicle was he driving?"

"Volvo. Gunmetal gray. Late model."

Leon wrote that down. "No trace of the car. Where'd you know him?"

"We were in Vietnam together. He was with the Navy over there, mostly intelligence and recon. He'd hired me to work on a case." I brought out an envelope. "What's the address on the driver's license."

Leon read me the address, a street in Malibu, and I wrote it down. "Any idea about the weapon, Leon?"

He sighed. "Automatic."

"Jesus."

"They stitched a line of lead right across his chest." Leon traced his finger along my rib cage, all the way to the neck. He rapped my solar plexus with his knuckles. "A real mess, he was." Then he looked over at Roxanne, his eyes crinkled against the morning sun. "What are you working on, Sherlock?"

"Doing some security analysis."

"Ha ha. You make everything sound so big-time. Say it in English."

"Claude Belker, one of your upstanding citizens. He ran into a gas truck down on Coast Highway."

"Ok, yeah. The savings and loan guy. Lived over in China Gate. The big house. The good life."

"Right."

"What you looking for?"

"Evidence of malfeasance."

"Translate."

"Belker had some big-money life insurance policies with Bruce Halliburton's company. They thought he might have falsified his applications."

"They don't want to pay, right?"

"That's it."

"What's the link-up with the pretty lady?"

"Her husband knew Belker. Bruce was checking on him."

"Enter Sherlock Murdock, the human garbage grinder. How's the hunt coming?"

I shrugged. "I found a girl friend with long blond hair and a pair of hiking boots. Very suspicious."

"Jesus. You call that detecting? I see why you left the profession." He wrote something in his notebook. "How much insurance are we talking here?"

"The total comes to fourteen and a half million."

Leon whistled. "Nice piece of change. How's our friend Cantu involved?"

"He was annoying the lady."

"Were Halliburton and the lady—?" Leon wrapped his index finger around his middle finger in a King's X and raised one questioning eyebrow.

"You have a dirty mind, Leon."

Leon grinned, his cop's cynicism never far from the surface, and clapped me on the shoulder. "Watch your heart, Sherlock. She's the marrying kind. And keep me in your information loop, okay? When you go to work, all of

Orange County takes on this eerie glow. If you turn up something on this Halliburton business, anything at all, pass it along. I owe Joe Floyd a couple of favors."

"Right. Any chance I can retrieve those guns you confiscated back in January? A forty-four and a three-five-seven."

"How about the year 2001?" Leon trudged between the houses to the highway.

After awhile I walked with Roxanne back to the Chrysler. My mouth was dry. I needed a beer.

"I could use a drink," she said, right on cue.

I handed her the keys.

"No," she said. "You'd better drive."

I started up and eased past the crime scene. We passed the wildlife preserve, which was between the road and the Naval Weapons Station, and drove along until I spotted a place that was open. "Delphi's Marina," the sign said. The exterior decor was green and gold. I parked the Chrysler, and we went inside. The interior decor matched the exterior, green and gold, but was stark in the sallow fluorescent lighting. Roxanne did not seem to notice. We found a booth in the back and ordered. Roxanne got a rum on the rocks with extra limes. I got a draft beer. There were three drinkers at the bar, staring into their glasses and blowing smoke into the air. It was Friday. The clock over the bar said 10:02.

The drinks came, and Roxanne took her time squeezing the limes into the rum. By the time she finished, I had downed half the beer and was thinking seriously about another one. I always drink when someone dies. It takes the edge off the fear that coils like something cold and slimy on the back of my neck.

Roxanne took several sips of her drink before she was ready to talk.

"Are you okay?"

"Better. I feel all numb. Poor Bruce."

"Any idea how much cash he was carrying?"

"He carried quite a bit. One time I saw him with fifteen hundred-dollar bills and some fifties in his wallet. Why?"

"The wallet was empty."

"And that means?"

"Robbery, as a motive."

She shook her head to signal no. "The phone call. He was meeting someone. They killed him."

I thought of the bullets from the Uzi. "Yeah, but who?"

"Maybe Ken Trager knows."

"Maybe. Did you ever meet him?"

"No. I never even spoke to him. Bruce had everyone call his service. Then he'd call in for messages." She looked at me and lifted her drink. "He didn't want to involve me."

I decided to go ahead. "Was your husband insured by Heartland?"

"Yes." She reached a slim brown arm across the table and grabbed my wrist. "Will you help me?"

My client was dead. I liked being with her. "Maybe. Depends on the problem."

She held on for a moment before letting go. She sat back against the booth and her face took on a hooded look. She was a dark queen of the misty isles and her castle was under siege and her subjects were starving and the drinking water was running out and she was figuring out how to tell them cannibalism was okay.

"Someone else got my insurance," she said.

9

"Who got it?"

Her blue eyes flashed, and she leaned forward, the sweater pressing into the edge of the table. "That's what Bruce was working on. That's what got him killed!"

"You don't know that."

She nodded yes and swept her arm across the table as she reached blindly for her glass. The back of her hand hit the glass and knocked it over. Rum and limes and ice splashed across the table. She cursed quietly in Spanish and hurried off to the ladies' room. I got up and walked to the bar for a rag to mop up her rum.

"Another round?" the bartender asked.

"That would be great."

"On the house," he said. "T. G. I. F."

By the time she got back, I had cleaned up the spill and the new drinks had arrived. She wore fresh lipstick, a pale gloss that deepened her tan, and she had combed her dark hair. The skin of her face was pulled tight across those Indian cheekbones. She took the rag and mopped up one last sticky spot from the scarred brown table. Two sips of rum brought a tired smile and the insurance story.

"My husband died in March, Matt. He collapsed on the tennis court on a Sunday morning and was taken to the hospital. By the time he reached the emergency room, he was dead. I fainted. They woke me up with smelling salts and drove me home. I spent the day in bed. A friend made the necessary phone calls. Emmy's parents are dead; an only sister lives in Guadalajara."

"Guadalajara was his home town?"

"Yes."

"Did they fly him home to Mexico to be buried?"

"Only the ashes."

"He was cremated?"

"Yes. He had his will changed in January, when we returned from Europe."

"How did you feel about the cremation?"

She shrugged. "It was his body. He could do what he wanted to. His sister was outraged when I told her. But she was too ill to travel up here."

"Did you identify the body?"

She drank some rum. "Yes."

"What about your family?"

She shook her head. "My father died when I was young. My mother died before I married."

"So you were alone?"

"Yes." She went on with her story: "That afternoon I was weak and strung out. I drank some rum and threw up. It started raining. I put on my running gear and stumbled out into the rain. It was cold at first, and my skin felt icy, but then I took a few tentative steps and my body responded. It's really wonderful, isn't it?"

"What's that?"

"The way things work, so automatically. Your mind says the end of the world has come, and your body goes right on. It gets hungry. It gets tired. It sleeps. It chugs along, like the little engine that could."

"You mean, 'I think I can. I think I can'?"

She lifted her glass and gave me a forlorn smile. "Something like that, yes. The rain revived me, lifted me up. I discovered it was spring, the earth was bursting. I was reborn. The more I ran, the more I gained energy. The beach was deserted, except for a few stalwart gulls. One soared off, in search of lunch, and I stopped to watch it move in the air, the tilt of wing, the effortless soaring, and right then I knew."

She stopped to sip her rum drink. I wished I'd been a painter, so I could catch the angles of her face, the sweep of brown throat disappearing into the sweater, the look in those blue eyes.

"Knew what?"

"This will sound strange. But please try to understand. The shackles were gone from around me. The albatross was off my back. Emmy was gone and I was . . . free."

"I take it your marriage had not been all that happy."

She nodded. "I'd been wanting a divorce, asking for one. He'd made me wait almost a year, stalling, while he straightened things out."

"Financial things?"

"Yes. Emmy was Phi Beta at UCLA, in economics. He knew things about money that no one else knew. With money he was like a musician. He would wake up in the middle of the night and make phone calls all over the world, buying, selling, moving money around. He seemed to intuit when a country's currency was going to go up or down. He could play the stock market like a harpist."

"Sounds like a rare talent."

"Oh, it was. Last year someone very high up in the Mexican government asked him to take a job down there, to help straighten out the awful mess with the peso."

"He didn't go?"

"No."

"Why not?"

"Emmy hated instability. His grandfather, Alonzo Mendez-Madrid, was murdered in the thirties on the side of a dirt road in Oaxaca. He was a cabinet minister under President Obregon. The killing, the pictures in the newspapers, haunted Emmy. That's one reason he lived in this country." She looked out the window, toward the Pacific. "This rum has made me forget poor Bruce. Where was I?"

"Trying to get a divorce."

"Yes. The reason I wanted one was because he played around. Emmy was a ladies' man, only I was the last one to know. He fooled around on me. My wonderful tennis friends were whispering behind my back, smirking, and I went blithely on. Emmy was a flirt. He loved the spotlight. He had a thing for the young ones, the ones with the pretty hair and the smooth skin—Butter Brains, I call them. I found out what was going on one day when a man propositioned me. I was at the club, and someone I barely knew invited me to his bed. I laughed at him and that hurt his feelings so he decided to hit back. He called me a silly goose and then used that age-old line, only in reverse: 'What's sauce for the gander', he said, 'is even saucier for the goose'. His face was ugly and I was . . . shocked. I didn't believe him right away, but I did have the sense to ask one of the girls I played tennis with. She confirmed it—Emmy was having affairs, tons."

"Lots of husbands have affairs."

"Yes. I thought so, too. But when I tried to talk to Emmy about it, he got abusive and tried to slap me around. That scared me. I locked myself in the guest bedroom. He screamed at me, called me names, pleaded with me to forgive him. He left town for a week, to visit Mexico. He came back full of apologies, promising never to look at another woman. He gave me presents and took me to Europe. We recreated our honeymoon—Rome, Florence, Zurich, Gstaad, Nice, Menton, Paris. But when I went to London for a week to do research, he was right back to his old habits."

"And that's when you got serious about a divorce?"

"Yes. There was no more conjugal contact between us. I went straight to a doctor for a battery of tests—this AIDS thing had me worried—and thank God there was nothing wrong."

"How long ago did this happen?"

"What?"

"The proposition at the club."

"It was a year ago, in May, I think." Her look was stony and unforgiving. "I know what you're thinking because Bruce asked the same question, in about that same tone of voice. All right, staying was a mistake. Before I married Emmy, I was a poor scholar. After the marriage I was a rich scholar. I'm not the first woman to stay in a marriage after it goes sour. Have you been married, Mr. Murdock?"

"A long time ago."

"Was it perfect?"

I grunted. "For a couple of weeks."

"Well, mine worked for longer than that. But once I knew the truth, Emmy became a roommate, nothing more. He had his own bedroom. I had mine. I concentrated on my work—I translate South American writers, women mostly, from Spanish into English—and he went on chasing his Butter Brains. I went back to school, working on a Ph.D. at U.C. Irvine. Emmy paid the bills."

"Did you see a lawyer?"

"Of course. A man named Burton. He charged me a lot of money—his fees were outrageous—for checking Emmy's figures. The lawyer's assessment was that they were basically accurate. If I divorced Emmy before he was ready, he could tie me up in court for years. I couldn't have afforded the court costs."

"The house was half yours. Why not sell that?"

"The equity is very small. Emmy used the house for leverage so he could borrow more money to put into stocks. Two days after the funeral I discovered he'd missed four payments—they were thirty-three thousand a month—and the bank had started foreclosure proceedings. It will be sold to satisfy Emmy's credit line."

"The stocks are in his name?"

"Yes."

"So he had you locked in."

"He was clever with money. He knew how to hide it."

"From Rudolfo too."

"Yes."

"So you knew what Rudolfo was after?"

"Of course. He made it quite clear. But I don't have any money. Or I have very little. That's where this conversation started, remember?"

"Your insurance," I said.

"Yes. There was over seven million dollars, nine different policies with three different companies. Emmy had his beneficiary changed on all of the policies."

"Who was the new beneficiary?"

"For the Heartland policy, it was Amigo Land Development, of Houston, Texas."

"And the others?"

"A company called Ebco."

"Where was that?"

"Chicago."

"Any idea what kind of companies they were?"

"That's what Bruce was working on. Trying to find out."

"He told you?"

She shook her head. "Not everything. He asked me about Amigo when we first met. Emmy had made the switch back in January, after we'd come back from a Christmas trip to Europe. As the insured, he could choose the beneficiary. Bruce asked me a lot of questions, but he was a man who kept things to himself. He told me about Ebco, but he was more interested in Amigo."

"Did Bruce go to Houston?"

"Yes."

"When?"

"Last month."

"What did he find?"

"Whatever it was, he didn't tell me. Bruce was not given to discussing the secrets of his business."

I pulled the envelope out of my pocket and showed her the address I'd gotten from Leon. "Is this where he lives?"

She held the address up to the light. "No. He moved from Malibu to Westwood."

"You've been there?"

She nodded. "Yes. The street was Belshazzar Drive. I have a key."

"That makes things easy." I reached into my pocket for some money to pay for the drinks.

"You think he kept files at his home?"

"There's only one way to find out." I stood up and held out my hand. "You want to tag along?"

She gave me the ghost of a smile. "I have the key, remember." Then she put her hand in mine, and it seemed even smoother than before.

10

We started north with Roxanne at the wheel. Traffic on the San Diego Freeway was heavy, and the sun pounded down like it was August instead of June. At the La Cienega exit she said she felt woozy, so I took over. I had several questions, but she was keeping to herself, arms folded, eyes closed, chin on her chest.

Had Bruce hired me because there was a connection between Mendez-Madrid and Belker? Was he in a body bag, getting cold, because he'd kept me in the dark?

My stomach was edgy as I thought about Bruce.

I hadn't been that close to him. We were war buddies, united for a time by the stupidity of Vietnam, but always separated by that invisible wall of social class. Bruce had learned his stuff in school, a snappy boys' school back East, where he'd played squash and tennis. Then he'd learned some more good stuff at Annapolis, majoring in political science, then more at the Harvard Business School, where he'd earned his M.B.A. In the CIA he'd run some good operations in the jungle and was adept at recruiting top guns. In civilian life he drove a Volvo, probably leased, and wore suits. The Volvo was gone, stolen by his killers. Bruce was dead, stitched with an Uzi. His Airweight .32 hadn't helped much.

"You want to exit on Sunset," Roxanne said.

"Thanks."

I took the Sunset exit, and she directed me through the upscale labyrinth of Westwood, a red brick area where trees shaded the streets. It was cooler here. I turned off the air-conditioner and rolled down the windows. That heavy smog tang filled my nostrils. Welcome to the L.A. Basin. The neighborhood felt smug, nestled in its own protected urban pocket. Nothing bad could happen here. Belshazzar, Bruce's street, was a two-hundred-foot lane that ended in a cul-de-sac.

"It's the condo," Roxanne said. "The cute one, at the end of the street."

The cute condo was Spanish style, red tile roof, stucco exterior, surrounded by a wrought iron fence. Roxanne opened the gate with a plastic key card, and I parked in a slot marked number eleven. We were northwest of the UCLA campus.

"Bruce loved it here. He'd just moved before I met him."

"Where did he live before?"

"Malibu, at that address on his driver's license. But this was closer to his office. The daily commute from Malibu was driving him crazy."

Bruce was on the second level. We walked up the stairs together. Roxanne produced a shiny gold key to unlock the door of number eleven. It was one of three entries on a plant-infested balcony that looked west.

The living room was furnished in Scandinavian Hi-Tech—a sleek sofa, sling chairs with chrome frames, an eight-by-twelve area rug of deep blue, chrome lamps to carry the motif through. The kitchen was tidy. A Cuisinart food processor sat on the cabinet, next to an Osterizer. Copper cookware, burnished to a high sheen, hung on a brass ring suspended from the ceiling. Everything was sparkling clean.

"Bruce loved cole slaw," Roxanne said, with a catch in her voice.

"Yeah."

"He could eat it three times a day."

I didn't say anything.

Then she whispered: "I can't believe he's dead."

I left her in the kitchen while I checked the rest of the condo. The bed in the master bedroom was neatly made, the covers tight enough to pass military inspection. I pictured Bruce standing over his bed, dropping a quarter onto the covers.

The second bedroom was set up as a study. One wall was filled with books. There was no fiction, nothing for fun. There was history and geopolitics and a whole shelf on Japanese management techniques. The desk, a sober-looking antique that had the flavor of an oak-paneled office from a nineteenth-century mercantiler, was locked. The lock was tough. It took me ninety seconds to open the top drawer, thirty seconds for the file drawer. The tumblers moved with a smooth, well-oiled precision.

Roxanne came to stand in the door while I went through the files. I smelled coffee brewing.

"Was it locked?"

"Yes."

"How did you get in?"

I pointed to my leather case of lock picks. "A lock-wizard in Germany made them, especially for me."

"My, my, aren't you resourceful." Her voice sounded

peevish. When I didn't answer, she said, "I'm making coffee. Would you like some?"

"Yes. Thanks."

There was nothing filed under "Amigo" or "Ebco." Nothing under "Belker." Nothing under "Mendez-Madrid." I gave some files to Roxanne, and she took them into the living room. I didn't know what I was looking for as I paged through the manila folders. I scanned tables and computer print-outs of long columns of numbers. Reading over the material made me happy to be on my own, outside the cage of a big corporation.

Roxanne brought coffee and cream and sugar. She left me alone and went back to her pile of folders. Feeling I'd missed something, I started through my pile again.

I found it under "M," for "Medical," near the back of the folder. It was a single sheet of paper in a neat handwriting that was almost printing. There were two lists. The first list began in September. There was a month, a name, a city, and then one word in parentheses. I recognized two names—Belker and Mendez-Madrid. If the parentheses meant anything, everyone on the list was dead:

September—Strich, Laguna Beach (burning)

October—Bennett, Tustin (burning)

November—Logan, Huntington Beach (burning)

December—Marlow, Irvine (burning)

January—Barrymore, San Juan Capistrano (drowning)

February—Townsend, Corona Del Mar (drowning)

March—Mendez-Madrid, Newport Beach (cardiac arrest)

April—Belker, Newport Beach (burning); Samson, Costa Mesa (drowning)

May—Arquette, San Clemente (drowning); Spencer, Laguna Beach (burning)

At the bottom of the list in the lower right-hand corner were two numbers, printed in block letters. One looked like a phone number with the 714 area code. The second was $120 million, followed by a plus sign.

Was that the total amount of insurance they were carrying?

Six had died from getting burnt up; four from drowning. Emiliano Mendez-Madrid stood out because he had died of a heart attack.

The second list reached a little farther out geographically. The only names I recognized here were Amigo of Houston and Ebco of Chicago—both had been named beneficiaries of Emiliano's policies. The other names were from major metropolitan areas:

Amigo Land Development Corporation, Houston

EBCO Future Guaranty, Chicago

Everglades Forever, Ltd.—An Environ Group, Miami

Full-Scale Mortgage, Inc., San Francisco

The Future is Scottsdale, Phoenix

Greater Atlanta Futures, Atlanta

Long Island Warranty, New York City

Sunrise Projects, Ltd., Los Angeles

I read the list twice. I checked in the phone book for Sunrise Projects, the only name from Los Angeles. There was no listing. I called 411 for information and was informed that number was no longer in service. I tried the

602 area, but there was no listing for The Future is Scottsdale. I tried 415, for San Francisco. Nothing.

Sweating now, I worked my way across the country, phoning information for each name listed. Roxanne came in, dabbing her eyes with a tissue, and I showed her the list. By the time I reached Miami information and swung north to New York, my voice was hoarse and the sinking feeling in my stomach had turned to lead. I knew I wasn't going to get anything this way. I phoned 212 information anyway. There was no listing for Long Island Warranty.

I hung up and stared at Roxanne. My coffee was lukewarm. Her eyes were red from crying. Her hand shook as she pointed to Barrymore.

"There was a Barrymore who was a member at Le Club. And Emmy did business with Claude Belker."

"What kind of business?"

She shrugged. "The usual. Money. Borrowing. Lending. Numbers on a ledger. I never paid much attention. Claude was vice president of a savings and loan. Didn't Bruce hire you to look into his case?"

"Yeah. What did Bruce tell you about Belker?"

"Not much. The Belkers are members at the club. I didn't know them. There were rumors about hanky-panky between the daughter and the tennis pro."

"Did Bruce mention Belker?"

"Yes. When he hired you. And a couple of times on the phone to Ken Trager."

"Did you know about the Thursday poker game?"

"No. Where?"

"The name I heard was Maclean."

"Bobby Maclean?"

"I think so."

"Bob and Betsy Maclean were with me when Emmy—" She shook her head. "Emmy was out almost every night.

He'd come in late, sometimes not at all. I stopped asking because I got tired of hearing him lie about the other women. If he'd said he'd been playing poker, I wouldn't have believed it."

"How well do you know Maclean?"

"They're tennis friends. Emmy did some business with Betsy, some real estate things. Not well, I'm afraid."

I kept at her, Murdock the Grand Inquisitor. "Have you seen Maclean lately?"

"No. I had to drop my membership. With the packing and everything that's happened, I haven't played much. My game is shot."

I pointed at the list. "What about Barrymore?"

"His boat capsized or something. Off Catalina, I think. There was some talk at the club, but I tuned it out."

"You stay in your own cocoon, don't you?"

She glared at me through puffy red eyes. "You could call it that."

"What do you call it?"

"Minding my own business."

I laid the list on the desk. If I stared at it hard enough, maybe some magical writing would appear to point the way. "Tell me about Barrymore."

"I knew him to speak to. He was a tall man, rangy. He had a beautiful backhand."

"Remember what business he was in?"

"Coins, I think."

"Old coins? New coins?"

"I don't know."

"Did your husband do business with him?"

She shook her head. "I don't know."

"Jesus."

"You make it sound as if it's my fault."

"Sorry. Didn't mean to shatter your plastic bubble."

She stood up. "I'd like to get out of here."

She was right. I was pressing. There was nothing more we could do here. My coffee was stone cold. Bruce was dead, and what he'd known had died with him. I put the folder marked "Medical" back into the file, under "M," but I kept the single sheet with the two lists. When I folded the list and put it into my pocket, I touched the envelope with Bruce's old address. I walked into the other room to find Roxanne resting on the sofa, knees tight, one arm flung over her eyes, protecting her mind from the light.

"Have you been to Bruce's old place? The one in Malibu?"

"Once. He'd lost a book, something on the Persian Gulf. He thought it might be up there."

"We're close. Let's drive up."

"I don't have a key." Then she saw the leather case with the lock picks. "Oh, I forgot. You bypass little things. Like locks—" She paused. "And keys." With an angry motion she pushed herself out of the chair and stalked out to the car.

Bruce's old address was a block away from the beach in ritzy Malibu, one of those sunburnt, unpainted houses stained Mendocino gray by salt spray and salt air. The lot was narrow, thirty-five feet along the front, and the houses were packed in tight so that the builders could use every inch of beach real estate. There was no garage, which meant your car would soon become a gray twin to the sunbleached house. Maybe that's why he'd bought a gray Volvo. One of the treads on the front steps needed repairing. The front porch creaked. On damp, foggy nights, ghosts would glide here.

My lock picks weren't needed. The door stood open, the lock had been smashed. I hauled out the PPK and went in, with Roxanne behind me. When you charge, it's always a judgment call to take civilians along. If the intruders were still around, she wasn't safe outside. Inside, she might hamper my movements.

The place was a mess. There were ragged slashes in the sofa. Pillows had been ripped open and small piles of synthetic stuffing dotted the carpet, off-white on deep purple. Two easy chairs had been tumped on their sides, with jagged tears in the upholstery. The expensive coffee table lay on its back, legs sticking up in the air like a dung beetle with rigor mortis. Magazines lay everywhere. *Cosmopolitan. Vogue. Ms.* The new tenant was a woman. At the walnut entertainment center, the shelves had been swept clean.

"Sick," Roxanne said. "Sick."

Fluffy white feathers met us outside the bedroom door. Inside, the mattresses and pillows had been slashed. Our feet stirred feathers along the floor, where they ran in a rough track down from the queen bed. The lid was off the toilet and the tank was leaking onto the bathroom rug. A bikini hung on the towel rack. The rug was turquoise.

In the kitchen, the door of the refrigerator stood open. Someone had gone through the cabinets, spilling out dishes and glassware onto the floor. In the center of the tile floor was a fresh pile of human excrement.

"Oh, God," Roxanne said.

"Calling card," I said. "From the creeps."

Roxanne turned green beneath her tan, and her eyes widened. She clapped a hand over her mouth as she staggered to the kitchen sink, where she leaned over and vomited. I held her shoulders, bracing her while she heaved. When she was finished, I mopped her brow with a cold washcloth. She murmured a weak "thank you."

Her lips were pale and bloodless. Her smooth brown hand was cold as ice.

Back in the car, heading south, I asked if she was okay.

"Yes. It's just that . . . seeing those . . . animals. That pile in the floor. That rape of a house. My God, what kind of people are they?"

"Sleazeballs," I said.

We had reached Sunset Boulevard before Roxanne tried to piece it together. "All right. They, the murderers, find Bruce's address on his driver's license, only it's the wrong address. They come up here looking for something. But what?"

"How about the list." I tapped my shirt pocket.

"Very well. I'll accept that as an assumption. But how did they know Bruce had the list?"

"Maybe he told them."

Her mouth opened in surprise. "Told them? What for?"

"So he could sell it."

Her color went away again. "Sell it?"

"Yeah. You said he was talking about money on the phone."

"But I thought he was paying them. Buying information."

"Is that what he told you?"

"Not in so many words."

"You made an assumption." I sounded like a tweedy professor.

"An inference."

"Okay. Inference. What did he say?"

"That he was meeting someone on the beach. To discuss money."

"Was he buying? Or was he selling?"

120

She folded her arms and stared out at the beach. "I thought Bruce was your friend."

"So did I." I told her about Sheena Mandarin and Claude Belker and the bikers coming at me Wednesday night in Laguna.

"You think Bruce sent those people?"

"They came looking. They saw me and made a beeline. Maybe he said, 'Look for a man with a beard and a bush jacket. He's ready to deal.'"

"Bruce wouldn't do that. He wasn't like that."

I slowed down for a furniture truck. Time to shift the battle lines. "Did Bruce tell you he thought Claude Belker faked his death?"

She coughed before answering. "Ugh. No. What a ghastly idea."

She was lying. I can always tell. I locked my fingers onto her left wrist. She was stronger than she looked. "Okay, lady. It's confession time. Was that your husband in the hospital?"

She tried to pry my fingers away. "You're hurting me. Please?"

I let her go, and she sagged against her door. "Was it?"

"Yes."

"You saw him?"

"For a moment, just before I fainted. I told you."

"How was the lighting down there?"

"Dim and pale green."

"But you looked at him. You saw him?"

"Yes. And seeing him put me into considerable shock. I know you find that difficult to understand, but . . ."

"Who else was there?"

"In the room, you mean?"

"Yes."

"An attendant in a green hospital smock."

"Where were your pals from Le Club?"

"Upstairs." She rubbed her wrist. "Are you trying to say—?"

"You fainted. Then what?"

"They gave me smelling salts."

"The attendant, you mean?"

"Yes. And Dr. Ames."

"Who the hell is Dr. Ames?"

"Please don't raise your voice like that. It frightens me."

Her voice was tight. She was right on the edge. I wanted off the freeway, but the traffic had us boxed in. "Okay. Sorry. Who's Dr. Ames?"

"Emmy's doctor. He was there, in the hospital. He must have heard about it. He came down. He gave me the smelling salts." She made a face. "I hate that smell."

"Town meeting," I said. "Whee."

"What?"

"A fun crowd in the morgue. You. Your upscale tennis pals. Your husband's personal physician. Anyone else?"

"It wasn't like that." She put a hand on my arm. "It wasn't that way at all."

I braked at a stoplight. Up ahead I could see the dark mouth of the tunnel that would lead us back to the San Diego Freeway. Bruce was dead. He had left me a list of dead guys and a sexy scholar and a hornet's nest of unanswered questions. He had paid me for three days. It was past noon on Friday. I owed Bruce a day and a half.

"I'm afraid," she said.

"Afraid of what?"

"Afraid that something will happen."

"It already has."

Her mouth was primed for a reply, but now it snapped shut. We drove back to Newport Beach in silence.

11

It was 2:30 when we pulled into the steep driveway at Spyglass Hill. The sun burned down from the west. It felt nice to be in the shade.

"Would you like something? A beer? Iced tea?"

"A beer."

"Are you hungry?"

"No."

She brought a bottle of Michelob from the kitchen and a glass. As she handed them to me, her lip trembled, and she looked like she wanted to tell me something important. Then she gave a little shake to her head and her mouth snapped shut.

"Cheers," I said, drinking the beer.

She stepped closer. "Will you stay? I need to rest awhile. I could pay you?"

Bruce had already paid me. "I'll stay. Sure. Get some rest."

Roxanne checked her machine for messages and then

went upstairs to lie down, followed by the big blue cat. She looked down at me from the balcony before turning right into a room. The door closed.

I sat in a big soft chair amidst the packing boxes and drank the beer. Roxanne was jumpy, but so what? Her cheekbones were like smooth cold stone, but so what? Her body movements were stiff, but so what? She had good reasons to be acting edgy. Lots of good reasons. Let's count them up. One, her husband dies, leaving her in a tight place. Two, Rudolfo puts the squeeze on her. Three, Bruce dies, and she watches the paramedics carry him away in a body bag. Four, reading Bruce's list of supposedly dead guys, her lip trembles because she's making some kind of connection. Five, the sight of the filth at Bruce's old place in Malibu is—

So her jumpiness, the edginess brought on by stress, was logical. I could quantify it, write down the items, and then add them up like a shrink.

Her reaction made sense. But there was something else, a gear that wouldn't mesh, a hum out of phase with the rest of the machinery. It was as if we were in a room, Roxanne and Murdock, dancing a slow and terrible dance to some old and haunting tune from the fifties, only between us there is this thick sheet of plastic, pliable enough so that we can almost touch, but still keeping us apart. I can feel her, see her, watch her. She smiles at me through the plastic. But every time I try to put my face close to hers, every time I take in a deep breath, sucking in my gut, boosting my courage to make my move, the plastic sticks to my mouth and nose so that I can no longer breathe.

I knew she wasn't telling me everything. What was the truth? What was Roxanne holding back?

I finished the beer and walked into Roxanne's study to make some phone calls. The first one was to that number at the bottom of Bruce's list. A man's voice told me this was a recorded message from the Bob Robertson Insurance Agency. The agent was out, the machine said. Leave your name and number and the agent will get back to you. There was no address, no emergency number. It was not a message brimming with leads. I phoned information. The address they had for Bob Robertson was a P.O. box in Dana Point. This guy knew how to hide.

My next call was to Bongo Bodette, a computer techie who lived in the Newport Dunes mobile home park, across the highway from the Reuben E. Lee, a restaurant made up to look like a Mississippi paddle-wheeler.

I read him the information from the list. In the background, I could hear the click of his computer keys as he plugged in the names. Bongo hails from Arkansas. He avoided the military while he worked on computers that worked on military hardware that was supposed to work on the enemies of capitalism. He was with Kaypro when it went under and he has a standing offer to work for half a dozen competing firms, inventing software or hardware or both. He weighs 280 and half of it is brain. His memory is encyclopedic. He likes thin ladies from the Deep South, dog races, and Coors beer. His heroes are Doc Savage, Humphrey Bogart, and Robin Hood. He has a vast movie library, tucked away on videotape, and talks like a redneck:

"No first names on them dudes, Sherlock?"

"Sorry. Belker's first name was Claude. He was a banker who owned Golden Bear Savings and Loan. Barrymore's was Wendell. Mendez-Madrid's first name was Emiliano. He was a stockbroker with his own firm in Newport Beach."

"*Was* means they're deceased," Bongo said.

"That's my guess."

"How much dossier you want?"

"Anything you can get, Bongo. The big insurance company involved is Heartland. It would be great if you could find out how many of these guys on the list had policies with Heartland. And who else covered them."

"You'd want the face amount of each policy, I reckon. And the beneficiary?"

"Yes. Or beneficiaries."

"Them big spenders," Bongo mused. "They get to be specialists in backstopping their debt load. They borry to the goozle. Then they piggy-back them policies. Knew an old boy back in Eldorado who loaded up two million in policies, changed the beneficiary from his wife to his galfriend, and run his Cadillac off the road into a river. His name was Claude, too. Claude D. Brisko."

"What happened?"

"Never heard of him again. The girlfriend collected on two policies and high-tailed it out of town."

"When was this, Bongo?"

"Shit, it was just before I dropped out of junior high. Twenty years ago, at least." There was a pause. "Make that twenty-five. Time does fly, don't it?"

Before we hung up, I asked him to check medical records on the names from the list. And I gave him the name of Dr. Sylvan Ames, Emmy-baby's physician.

My third call was to Ken Trager at Heartland in Los Angeles. It took seven minutes to get through the corporate maze. The voice that finally answered was young, cocky, and full of confidence. In the background I heard people chatting and the regular staccato whir of a computer printer. I identified myself.

"Have you heard about Bruce Halliburton?"

"No. I'm waiting for his call. Who did you say this was?"

"My name's Murdock. I'm a private investigator retained on the Belker case, down in Orange County."

"Oh? Bruce didn't say anything to me."

"I was hired Wednesday."

"Well, there's nothing in the file, friend. Is this about payment? You'll need a memo, something from Bruce, before you get your remuneration."

"Listen, Trager. Bruce is dead."

"What's that?"

I told him the circumstances.

"Is this some kind of a joke?" he asked. "I've got a busy day, and—"

"Call Sergeant Book at the Newport Beach PD. It's no joke."

"Newport Beach? I thought you said Huntington."

"Sergeant Book can vouch for me."

"All right. What's your number there?"

I gave him the number, and he hung up. I sat in Roxanne's pretty blue chair and stared blankly at the titles of the books in the shelves. The computer was an IBM, gunmetal gray, the same color as Bruce's Volvo. How much more had Bruce not told me?

The phone rang, and I picked it up. It was Trager, and he sounded shook. "All right. So Bruce is dead. So they say he was murdered. What's that got to do with you?"

"Look, Trager. I'm on the trail of something that could lead to his killers. You worked with Bruce. I was hoping you could fill me in on some details."

I heard a voice in the background. Trager covered the mouthpiece while he responded to whoever it was. When he came back on, his voice was gruff with suppressed emotion: "What is it you want to know?"

"Did you set up the meeting he went to this morning?"

"No."

"But Bruce was on the phone with you last night."

"How did you know that?"

"He told me," I lied.

"It's that lady, the one he's seeing down there."

"What lady?"

"I don't know her name, but you can tell when some-one has someone."

"How?"

"He was gone on the weekends. His departure ruined our doubles foursome."

Tough life, losing your fourth. "But he did call you last night?"

"He calls in every night. With Bruce, that was S.O.P."

"But you set up the meeting."

"Not at all. I gave him some information. The informa-tion might have led to a meeting. I couldn't say."

"What information, Trager?"

He sighed, heavily. "An informant."

"What kind of informant?"

"One who said he had information."

"What was the information about?"

"Bruce didn't say."

"But he went out this morning and got himself killed. The cops are very interested in this one. I can lead them right to you, Trager. You're the last person to make con-tact with Bruce. Or I can lead them away. It's your choice."

"I've done nothing wrong." His voice was a squeak.

"Yeah, but they can bug you to death. I was a cop, and I know."

There was a long pause. "I don't have much."

"Whatever you've got is fine."

"All right. A man phoned me here at the office. It was yesterday, around closing time. He said he had informa-tion about a case we were working on. He wanted thirty thousand dollars for the information. He gave me a number where he would be at ten, and another number for eleven, and a third number for midnight. After midnight, the deal was off. I relayed the information to Bruce, and he took it from there."

"What case?"

"The one down in Newport. Bruce was working it solo. A man died on a tennis court. He was a stock-broker. He had a Spanish name, hyphenated. Mendez-Madrid, I believe."

"What did the voice on the phone sound like?"

"Muzzled, as if he were speaking into a handkerchief. I thought I heard the trace of a British accent."

"British?"

"Um, yes. You know, like in the movies. Jolly good chap and all that rot."

"Did the informant know it was Bruce's case?"

"What do you mean?"

"Did he know Bruce's name?"

"If he did, it didn't come from me."

"So he didn't know who was meeting him on the beach?"

"Not to my knowledge."

"Okay, Trager." The air whooshed out of me, and I realized I'd been holding my breath. I wondered how much he knew about Bruce and Roxanne. He had seen more files than I had. He had a computer to help him out. I wondered what his angle was now that Bruce was dead. A job had opened up at Heartland. Maybe Trager would get promoted and then pick up the trail where Bruce had left off.

"Is that it?" Trager asked.

"Yeah. You've got my number."

He hung up. I went into the living room and lay down on the sofa and closed my eyes. It was early afternoon, and I felt as if I'd been up for a week without sleep. I slept for awhile, dreaming of steamy jungle trails and a gray Volvo loaded with fat-faced men carrying shotguns.

Each man wore a name tag. I could see two tags. One said Barrymore. The other said Belker. Sweat slickened my hands, my face, ran down my chest. Belker opened up on me and harsh vines slapped at my eyes.

At a dead run I came out of the jungle and sped for the glassy river. I entered a clearing where people stood in line to board a shallow-draft barge. A boatman stood near the back of the barge, his arms crossed over his chest. A hood hid the boatman's face in brown shadow. The gray Volvo roared out of the jungle, guns blazing. No one standing in line seemed to notice as the shotgun blasts tore up the green leaves. The driver lost control of the wheel, and the Volvo tumbled over the mossy bank into the river. There was a ripple and then a soft gulping sound as the car sank. A poker chip floated to the surface.

The people in line for the barge shuffled forward. A hand reached out to take my hand. A familiar voice called me Captain. I turned to face Bruce Halliburton. He wore a pale green golf jacket and a green pullover shirt, and he was holding his head under his arm. I screamed. And the gong sounded, hauling me awake.

I woke up hearing a phone ringing. Roxanne answered from one of the rooms upstairs. I couldn't hear what she was saying, but it sounded like she was talking Spanish. Maybe Rudolfo was out on bail and getting ready to bug her again. This time, I'd rough him up a little, teach him some manners. The sun was slanting through the jalousies. My watch said 3:33. Upstairs, Roxanne's voice sounded agitated.

She stayed on the phone for another couple of minutes. The phone banged as she hung up. She came out onto the balcony and walked stiffly to the door at the far end. Her back was ramrod straight. She opened that door and walked in. In a moment she was back, hands gripping the railing, staring down at me. Her knuckles were white.

"Would you come up here, please?"

I rolled off the sofa and joined her upstairs. My mind was mired in the dream. There were four doors, two closed, two open. I looked into the room where Roxanne had been sleeping. It was neat and orderly. I walked into a master bedroom with expensive furnishings and a carpet of bright whorehouse red. The big corner window had a magnificent view of Newport Beach and the Pacific.

"In here," Roxanne said, from the bathroom.

I went in to find her tugging away at the lavatory. The fixtures were black. The lavatory was pink marble. It was an ugly combination. "Help me, will you? It's supposed to swing out from the wall."

Together, we tugged on the lavatory. It pulled away from the wall on hinges to reveal a specially constructed hidey hole about two feet square and maybe four inches deep. Stacked inside the hole were some rectangular packages, about fifty in number, bound with packing tape. You couldn't see through the plastic, but each package was the length and width of a dollar bill. Roxanne opened a package to find hundred-dollar bills.

"Ahhh!" she said.

We hauled the money out onto the balcony, where we counted it sitting on the carpet. Most of the packets contained a hundred hundreds. A couple contained a mixture of fifties and twenties. There were fifty-seven packets, which meant over two hundred thousand. In cash.

Roxanne's voice was harsh as she muttered numbers under her breath. "Hundred and seventy. Hundred and eighty. Hundred and . . ." For her, this June Friday was turning out to be quite a day.

She tossed a packet of hundreds into my lap. "Matt, I'd

like to hire you." Her voice shook. The smile was weak as water.

"What's the job?"

"Bodyguard."

"Whose body?"

"Mine."

"I get three hundred a day. Plus expenses."

She picked up another packet of money and handed it to me. The smile was better now, more secure. If the packet contained hundreds, I was holding ten grand in cash. She stood up and looked down at me. "Is it true what they say about private detectives?"

"What do they say?"

"Private detectives are like lawyers. What passes between the detective and the client is . . . confidential."

"It's semi-true."

She held out her hand, and I took it. She braced herself and hauled. Again, I was surprised at her strength. I got to my feet, and we stood there, surrounded by U.S. currency wrapped in plastic, and I could feel the connection between us change. Chemistry, they call it. She lowered her chin. The motion allowed her to study me from under the shelf of her dark forehead. Her eyes narrowed. Her lips skinned tightly back, showing her white white teeth. Through her fingers, I felt her vibrating.

"Would you hold me for a moment?"

Surprise, surprise. "Sure."

She came softly into my arms. Without her shoes, she was still tall, her eyes almost level with mine. Her mouth was close to my ear, her breath warm on my skin. I smelled her perfume. Now I was doing some vibrating of my own. She felt what was happening and eased away, to hold me at arm's length. I saw promise in her eyes.

"Matt, will you fly to Santa Fe with me?"

"What for?"

She indicated the money. "To deliver some money."

"Who to?"

She didn't answer for a moment. She let me go and turned away to lean on the balcony, arms straight, shoulders tense now, as she said: "I don't know how to say this, except to say it. That was my husband on the phone. He's . . . not dead. He's in trouble—running from someone, he said—and he wants me to bring some money to him in Santa Fe."

She turned to me. Her face was tight as a skull. In her eyes I saw a heap of old bones, sun-bleached, drying in the desert. And then she began to cry, the tears streaming down her tanned cheeks, and I knew why she had come into my arms, so subtly and so softly, sinuous as a snake.

"God forgive me," she said.

‖‖‖‖ **12** ‖‖‖‖

It took a stiff shot of brandy to calm her down so she could tell me about the phone call. She was in shock. She was out of shock. Then she was back in again.

Her voice seemed uncontrolled, low volume, high volume. I could tell she hated being out of control, even for a minute.

I asked the standard questions. When I probed too deeply, her eyes widened with fear, forcing me to back off.

There was no mistake that it was her husband, Roxanne said. It was his voice, and he had called her *"querida,"* a name used when he was trying to be nice. He wanted her to meet him in Santa Fe, at a motel called El Chulo, and bring twenty-five thousand dollars.

"Is that where he is now?"

"I don't know. That's where he wants to meet."

"Who's after him?"

"He wasn't specific. He said they had tricked him in

Europe. He had escaped. Now they were hunting him down in this country. He needs the money to survive on."

"Where's he been?"

"Europe, for awhile. Switzerland and Spain. And then Houston."

"Checking out Amigo Development?"

"Yes. His voice was very . . . subdued. He sounded hurt or maybe just tired. There was no one at the address in Houston, he said. Just an empty office."

"Did you ask him what happened from the time he did his act on the tennis court?"

"Yes. All he said was, there was a plan. But then the plan changed. They had stolen everything."

"He didn't say who They were?"

"No. He sounded beaten. He said he was in some pain, or he'd come here." She set the glass down and buried her face in her hands. "This is all so . . . unreal."

"What about that guy, the one on the slab in the hospital?"

"I didn't think to ask."

I wanted to touch her, hold her, shake her, but when I reached out she shrank away from me. "Please," she said.

I sat back against the cushions of the sofa. "Why Santa Fe?"

She shrugged. "I think I know that much. Emmy was very superstitious. A couple of times we skied in New Mexico, and he went through a sort of religious conversion in the snow on a mountain above Taos. He thinks the whole area around there is enchanted and full of good luck. He talked about moving there."

"When?"

"He wanted to sell his share of the business and move away from California. Mexico scared him. The next best place was New Mexico. Like going home, he said."

"And he can't come here because they're after him, right?"

"Yes." She looked up at me. "Are you going to help me?"

"You hired me. And I'd love to meet Emmy."

"Is that the only reason?"

"The only reason for what?"

"For helping me."

There was that vibration again.

"No," I said. "It's not the only reason."

"I have one favor to ask," she said.

"Shoot."

"Don't hurt him."

"Jesus," I said. "Why would I hurt him?"

"Because you're so angry with me."

Before we left town for New Mexico, we packaged the money and shipped it via registered mail to Wally's surf shop. Roxanne phoned a neighbor and asked her to look after the blue cat. There was a direct flight from John Wayne Airport to Albuquerque, but no connection to Santa Fe. It was late afternoon when we parked her Chrysler in the Main Street lot and climbed on a plane for New Mexico.

On the plane, droning east across the desert, I asked a couple of questions. Roxanne yawned, then handed me a photo of her husband. "Could this wait? I'm so tired."

I studied the photo. Lean handsome face, Indian cheekbones, good head of black hair, shrewd eyes. He wore a tennis shirt. Around his neck was a gold chain. The smile was a winner.

I ordered a beer and watched Roxanne sleep. Then I pulled an envelope out of my pocket and made a quick list of events that had begun back in September with the death of a man named Strich:

1. Strich burns up in September. Barrymore drowns in January. Emmy-baby collapses in March. Belker burns up in April.

2. Bruce contacts Roxanne in March, three weeks after Emmy collapses. Bruce sees the pattern and smells big money. The figure of $120 million could be the total of payouts to beneficiaries. Bruce is curious about Emmy, who didn't drown or burn up.

3. The beneficiaries are not family folks, but corporations set up to handle debts. So Emmy's insurance is not paid to Roxanne, but to Amigo and Ebco.

4. Bruce needs some help, a cat's paw to distract the enemy, so he hires Murdock. Murdock tells Bruce about the Lemon Heights party. Three bikers show up at the party and head straight for Murdock. That means Bruce talked to them and tagged Murdock: "Look for a tanned face, a beard, a safari coat."

5. Meanwhile, Bruce is planning his own little shakedown. He has information to sell in list form. He wants them to know he's an agent, so he makes contact through Heartland. They don't know Bruce's name.

6. While Bruce is working the other side of the street, the Heartland folks think he's buying information.

7. Who was Bruce trying to peddle the list to?

8. Bruce gets killed on the beach. Rudolfo comes after Roxanne. Murdock turns up the files. The phone at Bob Robertson's insurance agency is answered by a machine.

9. Emmy calls for help. Says he's in Santa Fe, running for his life.

10. What does Emmy know?

11. What does Roxanne know?

We were coming into Albuquerque when Roxanne opened her eyes. She smiled at me and touched my arm. "Thank you," she whispered.

"Yeah," I said.

You lose an hour flying east into Mountain Time, so it was 9:30 instead of 8:30 when we landed in Albuquerque. I studied the deplaning passengers, trying to pick out suspicious characters. There were Indians and cowboys and businessmen wearing boots and two college girls with slick faces and snake hips that went snick-snick under their acid wash miniskirts. A kid with spiked purple hair met the college girls and led them outside to his van, which was decorated on the door with a turquoise and silver logo that looked vaguely Navajo. While I kept up surveillance, Roxanne rented a blue-gray Ford Taurus at $49.70 per day, plus mileage. We got the keys and our luggage—the PPK was back in Orange County—and headed north on Highway 25 toward Santa Fe.

On the big mountain to our right you could see a solitary light, which Roxanne said was a restaurant that you reached by riding a cable car. The mountain was named Sandia Peak.

"Okay," I said. "Time for twenty questions."

"All right." She stretched her legs straight out and

laced her fingers together. She was still wearing the white slacks and white sweater she'd changed into after our morning scuffle with Rudolfo. The movement of her arms tightened the sweater against her ribcage, outlining full breasts. "Fire away."

"How long have you known?"

"Known what?"

"Known about your husband."

"Since that first day."

"In the hospital?"

"No. Not then. It was later that afternoon, when I went running in the rain."

"How did you figure it out?"

"I examined my own feelings. I wanted him dead. Wished him dead. But when I thought back to that moment in the little room, it was so cold, so empty of feeling, I realized it wasn't Emmy on that table."

"Did Bruce know?"

"Yes. He came to me full of suspicion."

"And he knew you knew?"

"Yes. He was . . . well . . . relentless. All that probing. He'd wait until I was relaxed and having fun to spring it on me. Bruce wasn't terribly pleasant when he wanted something."

"Nice little secret. When were you planning to let me in on it?"

She shifted on the seat, but did not answer. I watched the speedometer climb to seventy-five, eighty. The air was close in the car. We were back inside that room, dancing, our skins separated by the thick hot sheet of plastic. Then she reached out and laid a hand on my arm. Her fingers were cool. With her other hand, she unlocked the seat belt. When she was free, she scooted across the seat to sit beside me. Her left hand rested on my thigh. Her perfume filled my nostrils. The unspoken message was clear:

We were together on this. We were a team. The question was: What game were we playing? I lifted my foot and the speedometer dropped back to sixty-five. Roxanne tilted her head, touching my shoulder.

"This will probably sound strange, but when I saw you this morning, crossing the room, I had a really powerful reaction. It was as if we'd met before. It was as if we'd known each other in another lifetime. I'm not a mystic. I don't believe in that sort of thing. So it was quite a shock to realize I thought I already knew you. I scolded myself. I analyzed the feeling as a déjà vu. You probably noticed how quiet I get?"

"I noticed."

"It's because I've been worrying this feeling all day, trying to come to terms with it." The hand left my thigh. Roxanne sighed. "Can I ask a question, Matt?"

"Sure."

"Did you feel anything? Did you notice anything happening? Or was this thing all in my imagination?"

There was a lump in my throat as I put my arm around her. I did not have to pull because she came willingly, pressing herself into my side. She squeezed my leg again and grazed my jaw with her lips and I heard a tight snuffle and then she pulled away and dug into her purse for a Kleenex. Half her face was in shadow and I had a sudden vision of her undressing for me in the New Mexico moonlight. She blew her nose and sat back against the door again. Her shoes were off and she placed her left foot against my thigh. I didn't trust her, but I liked staying connected.

"I'm all breathless," she said. "This took me by surprise."

"Me too."

"I generally take a long time sorting things out."

"So do I."

"But it does seem right, doesn't it?"

"It seems right."

"To answer your question, Matt, I was planning to tell you, not only about Emmy, but about other things too. I'd like to tell it my way."

"Okay. Shoot."

I held the speedometer on sixty, feeling the scrappy little engine laboring on the hills. The headlights stabbed the night. Roxanne began her story.

"I was born in Stony Point, a little town in Virginia, but we moved to Washington when I was a little girl because daddy got a job with the government. My folks were both hardline Democrats. Daddy played the violin and Mother played the piano. They used to give concerts for the neighborhood. Daddy died when I was seven, so my mother had to go to work in a department store. She hated waiting on people, other women, so she went to night school and got her teaching credentials. It took her three years. During that time, my brother Tommy died."

"I'm sorry."

"He caught pneumonia and never came out of it. I remember seeing him in the hospital. His face was blue. Tommy's death set Mother back pretty badly, so she clung to me and made sure I did all the right things. I was a chunky little girl, but boys were attracted to me anyway. It was like they smelled something. Mother ran them off. 'Time enough for that,' she said. 'Plenty of time for men in your life.' I liked reading, and I was good at languages, and my dream was to be an interpreter for the United Nations. I started in Latin in the sixth grade and went on to Spanish and French, and that's how I spent my junior year in South America. I was an exchange student, and I lived with a family and fell in love with that crazy culture down there."

"Is that where you met Emmy?"

"No. I'm coming to that. I was seventeen that year in South America, and I fell in love with a perfect rake named Eduardo Rampal. He was part gypsy and part Indian and part Argentinian and part German-romantic poet. I knew I was being a fool, but Eduardo made me hot and confused. He kissed me, starting with the insides of my wrists and working his way up. Eventually, he kissed me all over. It took him three weeks to prime me for his use, and by the time he stole my virginity, I was ready."

"Where is Eduardo now?"

"I never saw him since. He's probably fat, like Rudolfo, and making millions in the white slave trade. But the reason I'm telling you about Eduardo is because that's who Emmy reminded me of when we first met. They were both five-eleven, which is tall for that part of the world. They were terrific dancers. Their talk was witty, but edged with the Latino sadness, so they didn't come off glib and superficial. Of course, I met Emmy a lot later. I'd done a master's degree and had some real jobs and been engaged twice, so I was aware of the Latin Lover Syndrome. I'd had one abortion, which had made me very sad, but still, when I saw Emmy across the room my heart skipped a beat, the way it sometimes does, and when he asked me to dance, I was floating."

"Where was this?"

"In Washington. I was working for Congressman Standish, from Virginia. Isn't that a wonderful name for a congressman? I was a research assistant, and the Congressman had a crush on me, and he kept promising me he'd find me a job in the government where I could use my languages. Meanwhile, he kept me on his staff and made back-handed approaches to try to get me in bed."

"Where is the Congressman now?"

"He lost his seat and went back into law practice in

lovely Leesburg. And I lost my job and started to feel poor again, and that always makes me panic. Then Mother died suddenly, and I was all alone and very blue. It was February. I'd tried working in New York, for three different publishers, while I left my name at the U.N. But the winter drove me south, back home to Washington, and that's where I ran into Emmy again."

"This was the second meeting?"

"The third. We'd met at that party, the year before, and then he'd taken me to lunch, and now he found me in this bookstore in Georgetown. I was depressed and twenty pounds overweight. I had two degrees, but no money to get on with my doctorate. Scholarships kept falling through. My lover—a sad, wistful boy named Allan—had taken a teaching job in Australia. I was making five dollars an hour and freezing my feet because my boots had worn out, and in walks handsome Emmy wearing an Alpaca topcoat that cost seven hundred dollars and a suit that cost a thousand and gold jewelry to enhance the flashy smile. Well, he seemed warmth incarnate. I knew he lived in California, in a house near the beach, and at that moment I would have killed to escape the cold."

"When did you get married?"

Roxanne adjusted herself on the seat. "It didn't take very long. Looking back, I realize I acted hastily. Emmy's mother knew. Esmerelda was her name. She looked at me as if I were a *bruja*—that means 'witch' in Spanish—and I'm sure she warned Emmy not to marry me. She could have tolerated me as a mistress, a *yanqui concubina*, but not as a daughter-in-law. But Emmy was making lots of money and becoming a big man in Newport Beach. He'd been engaged six times—I found this out later—but had broken off because the girls were beautiful but not *simpatica*. That means an American girl who speaks the language. My Spanish is classical. I know French and Portuguese. Emmy had a lot of clients from Mexico and South America. My job was to charm them in Spanish when he brought them to the house."

"How did you like that?"

"Oh," she said. "There's Santa Fe!"

In front of us now I could see the nest of lights that was Santa Fe. Roxanne broke off her story to direct me to the El Chulo Motel, one block off the highway to Taos, three blocks from downtown. It was a long stucco building with a small parking lot and eighteen units. The sign in the window said "Vacancy." The lamp in the window next to the sign had a pink shade.

"What does 'El Chulo' mean, anyway?"

"There are several meanings. One is bullring assistant. Another is the streetlife in Madrid."

The desk clerk was a sad-looking man with a New York accent. He had two rooms at forty-five dollars apiece. Roxanne was impressed when I argued him down to forty. Her key said 8. Mine said 7. I carried her bag inside. There was no baggage rack. I set it on the television unit that also served for a desk and a dressing table. The walls of the room needed paint. The air smelled of old sweat and of dreams gone sour.

"Matt." She put a hand on my arm. "I'm so tired I could sleep forever. Do you think we could—"

"Sure." I didn't really mean it. I had questions. She had answers. She turned me on. I wanted to watch her undress. "Sure. Get some rest. See you in the morning."

She touched my hand but did not come into my arms. I left her alone and was alone in northern New Mexico. The air was cool and clear, with a hint of pine scent. The moon was greenish yellow. From a cantina came the sound of mariachi music, a trumpet, a man singing.

My bones ached from wanting her.

144

I unlocked my door long enough to toss the red canvas bag on the bed. The decor in my room was motel plaid, no better than hers. I got into the rented Taurus and tooled off in search of beer. I paid $2.99 for a six pack of Coors and went back to the wonderful El Chulo. There was a light on in Roxanne's window. I saw her moving slowly behind the shade.

I lay on my bed with my boots off, drinking beer and staring at Bruce's list as I tried to remember what it was like growing up south of here, in shaggy El Paso del Norte. Grim gray winters, summers of boiling heat. If you had one good day out of ten you sent up prayers of thanks.

I ran down the names on the list, playing If and What If. If Emmy was alive, maybe Claude Belker was alive, too. If Claude was alive, maybe all those guys on Bruce's list were alive, Barrymore and Strich and the rest. What happened when the bodies were switched and one of them woke up in a foreign country with a new identity? Did everyone get away? Or did they wind up like Emmy, running? It was a neat trick, dying for dollars.

There were eleven names on the list. For September through March there was only one name per month. In April and May there were two names. It looked like a growth business.

But who was the boss? Who ran things? If there were eleven guys from Orange County, how many were there from San Francisco and Phoenix and Miami and New York?

The beer had made me sleepy. I was dozing when there was a tap on the door.

▌▌▌▌ 13 ▌▌▌▌

I opened the door to find Roxanne standing there, backlit by the New Mexico moonlight. She had changed clothes and now wore a white skirt and a loose white blouse. She was barefoot and her dark hair hung loosely down her back. The light was behind her, throwing her face in shadow. Seeing her under the pale green moon made my legs shake.

"Matt," she said, "were you asleep?"

"Watching television."

"Oh? What program?"

"Hell," I said, grinning. "I don't know."

"May I come in?"

I stepped aside and held the door wider. She glanced over her shoulder at the parking lot. She entered the room, bare feet on the battered carpet.

"Did Emmy call?"

"No. Nothing. I've been thinking, going over everything. I wanted to thank you for . . . coming with me."

It was a good opening line, just right. Her costume was just right, too, the white skirt full and long, almost to her ankles. The material looked soft, as if from many washings. The white blouse, of the same soft material, had long sleeves and shoulder pads. Two buttons were undone, revealing smooth, dark hollows. I had the impression she was not wearing a brassiere. The only decoration was a wide leather belt with a heavy silver buckle. Her bare feet gave her a peasant-girl air. She was a gypsy, about to dance around the blazing fire. Castanets, guitar music. Just the slightest movement of her body made the rich, dark hair sway like magic.

"Beer?"

"Oh. yes, please. I forget how dry it is here."

I popped the tab top on a Coors and handed it to her. She hefted it in a toast before drinking, then walked to the chair and sat down. She curled up in the chair, one leg tucked under her, the other one swinging idly. Her ankle was tapered, the foot slim and brown.

"I want to tell you about Bruce. And me."

"I want to ask you about Emmy."

"All right. I want to make you understand why I did what . . . I did." She sipped the beer. "But Bruce first, okay?"

"Sure." She had me hypnotized all right. In the yellow motel light her eyes were hooded with mystery. I could feel them on my face, like a caress, stroking my cheek with the soft touch of butterfly wings. "Let's hear about Bruce."

"Yes. He came along at a time when I needed someone. Emmy had been . . . gone for three weeks and there hadn't been any progress on the life insurance claim. The funeral was over. My lawyer—the one I'd hired to check up on Emmy's figures—was getting nowhere with Heartland. I had very little cash and the bills were piling up.

The bank phoned, threatening foreclosure. Emmy had always taken care of the bills. He was five payments behind on the house. The total I owed, including penalty, was almost one hundred and eighty thousand dollars. Add to that Emmy's credit line, secured by the bank, which had an interest payment due of nine thousand. Both cars were leased. That was another three thousand. When I added things up, I was shocked by what he owed. It numbed me. All I could do was read. Books were my only refuge, my only safe harbor. Rudolfo had paid me one nasty visit and was promising to come back. When the insurance money didn't arrive, I felt the universe was paying me back for that moment in the cold room. It was too late to change my story. There was no way back, no way to find out what really happened. I had to let the maid go, and the gardener. I felt terrible. They depended on the income and now there wasn't any. I got a part-time job in the library, but that cut into my study-time. My doctoral advisor at UCI said I could get a teaching job in the fall. But I had no idea what I would do until then."

Roxanne sighed and took a sip of beer. "And then Bruce arrived in his Volvo and his lovely suit, all earnest and helpful, to tell me that Emmy had changed beneficiaries. The Heartland policies had been paid to Amigo Development. At that time, he had no information about the other policies. I was in shock again. My life was over. And I was so angry at Emmy I could have killed him."

"When did you find out about the other policies?"

"A couple of weeks later."

"What were the companies?"

"One was South Coast Life. The other was East Bay Fidelity."

"Okay, so you knew you were broke. Then what happened?"

Roxanne took a long drink of her beer. "I was very lonely. I was afraid and feeling guilty. Bruce was a nice man, decent and honest. His behavior made it clear he was attracted to me. He was so awkward declaring himself that it made me sympathetic, and that threw me off-balance. I knew what was happening, knew it wasn't for keeps, but I was clutchy and didn't care. I needed someone, and Bruce was it. After we'd made love that first time, I knew it was temporary, a thing of the moment. He was too restrained, too withdrawn. As a lover he was . . . well, sweet, thoughtful, caring. He took care of me. He brought me flowers. I liked him and respected him, especially his mind, the way it worked, but I was not in love with Bruce Halliburton."

"But you didn't tell him?"

"No."

"But now you're telling me."

"Yes."

"Why?"

"Because I want you to know, Matt. And because I have this terrible load of guilt. About Bruce."

"How long had Bruce known about Emmy?"

"It's why he came to see me. The others—those names on his list—had died by burning up. Or drowning. Horrible, ugly ways to go. Emmy was the exception, collapsing in public, on the tennis court. Bruce was clever. He told me I would get no money. He saw how afraid I was. Then he said I could go to jail."

"How much did he know?"

"I never really knew. He must have had his little list. Emmy must have been on it. But while he was pressing me, he didn't tell me much."

"What did you tell him?"

She looked at me and took a deep breath. "The truth. They didn't want me to go down there. Bobby went down first. He came back all gray-faced and said it was Emmy. I insisted on going, so they took me down. The room was icy, badly lit. They pulled back the sheet. I thought it was Emmy. I really did. Later on, I suspected it was someone else."

"Bobby Maclean. Was he in on the scam?"

"It's possible. I think everyone was in on it, except me."

"Did Bruce buy your story?"

"Not at first. He made me go over it. And over it."

"Meanwhile, he fell for you?"

She nodded, bleakly. "Yes."

"And he had a plan."

"That's what he said."

"And now he's dead."

"I feel terrible. It makes me sick to think about it."

"He was trying to shake them down, wasn't he?"

She brushed a stray strand of hair away from her face. "He wanted money. He'd bought plane tickets. We were going away."

"When?"

"Today. This morning. A ten-thirty flight."

Good old Bruce. "How much money in the shake-down?"

"A lot. Over a million, I think."

My face felt hot as I asked the next question. "Where the hell were you lovebirds off to? Tahiti? Bora-Bora?"

"Europe. And we weren't lovebirds."

"Why Europe?"

"Switzerland. Zurich, to be precise. For Emmy's numbered bank account."

"Bruce had the number?"

She nodded. "I think so."

"Where would he have found it?"

"He spent a long time in the house, going through

Emmy's papers. He could have found it there. He was close-mouthed about what he found."

"You think that's what Rudolfo was after?"

"Yes."

"Looks like Bruce had the bad guys by the short hairs. He had his list. He had Emmy's secret number. What did he tell you about me?"

"What do you mean?"

"You knew he hired me. Why did he go to the trouble?"

Roxanne coughed, then cleared her throat. "Tactical distraction. No. That's not right. 'Tactical diversion,' was what he called it."

"Did you understand what he meant by that?"

"No."

"There was a party, up in the hills, a snazzy house in Lemon Heights. Claude Belker's girl friend was dancing and I wanted to talk to her. I told Bruce about it in my report. A couple of hours later three bikers showed up. When they hit the room, they headed straight for me, like hunters after prey."

"But he was your friend!"

"You didn't know?"

Her eyes flared up. "How dare you ask me that?"

I crossed the room to stand over her. I grabbed her arm, pulled her halfway out of the chair. "Did you know?"

"No. You're hurting me, Matt. Please let me go."

I tightened my grip. "He did the same thing in Vietnam."

Instead of pulling away, she leaned toward me. There was a silence before she answered. "What?"

"He'd sit in an air-conditioned office, behind a desk,

and send men into the jungle to test the enemy strength. Probes, he called them."

She shook her head. "How awful."

"Yeah."

"So when I reported on the bikers—one through a window, one in jail—he thought he could handle them. He set up the meeting on the beach. They must have agreed to his terms for the list, or whatever he was selling. They killed him, got his address off the driver's license, and hustled up to Malibu."

"The old address."

"Yeah."

"I feel sick, Matt."

I gave her arm a shake. "Tell me the rest, Roxanne."

"The rest of what?"

"The rest of the story."

"Let me go, first. You're hurting me."

I let her go and she sank back against the chair. I walked back to the bed, feeling lousy. I drank some beer. It tasted bitter on the tongue.

"You have a right to be angry, Matt."

I sat down on the bed. "Let's have it."

Her voice was low and throaty. "Have you ever participated in a *ménage à trois*? A sexual threesome?"

"No."

"That's what Emmy wanted for me. For us."

My stomach turned over heavily. "Who with? Rudolfo?"

"Yes."

"What did you do?"

"Kicked him. Emmy, I mean."

"Where?"

She gave me a stony smile. "Where do you think?"

Roxanne put down the beer can and changed her position, bare feet on the chair's edge, chin on her knees. She locked her arms around her legs so that she looked like a troubled teenager. Her brown toes curled into the worn upholstery of the chair seat.

"For a week after that, he walked around very gently."

"When did this come up?"

"Christmas. Emmy was a stupid drunk. I told you about the threesome because I wanted you to know how I felt, the morning it happened."

"Okay. I got it."

"When Emmy collapsed, I ran to him. I did the wifely things. Cradled his head. Called for help. But down deep, I wanted him to leave, get out of my life. At Christmas, I'd wished him dead. Now my wish was coming true, and I did not retract. I held him in my arms and wished him dead at the same time, and suddenly the ambulance was there, and I didn't notice it had arrived awfully fast."

"How fast?"

"Emmy collapsed. I ran to him. The tennis pro started CPR. And the ambulance was just there. Like that."

"That's how they switched the bodies. On the way to the hospital."

"I think so."

"What did the ambulance people look like?"

"There were two of them. A driver, tall and thin, with a very narrow face. And a white-haired man with pale pink eyes, like an albino, and thick white arms."

"British accent?"

"Yes. The white-haired man. How did you know?"

"So did one of the bikers in Lemon Heights. At the party."

She shook her head with impatience. "Good lord. Why didn't you say something?"

"Hasn't come up. Okay. Emmy's in the ambulance. Go on."

"The white-haired man would not allow me in the ambulance. Regulations, he said. They started an IV. Rudolfo arrived. Emmy saw Rudolfo and lay down again. The ambulance drove off. I followed, with Bob and Betsy."

"The Macleans," I said.

"Yes."

"The same guy who went downstairs at St. Boniface?"

"Yes."

"And then, later, you started thinking it wasn't Emmy."

"Yes."

"But you decided to button your lip."

"It was all very surreal, like a dream. There was someone under a pale green sheet. The attendant turned the sheet back and I saw Emmy and things started to whirl. I fainted. When I came to, they were holding smelling salts under my nose."

"Good old handy Doc Ames?"

"Yes."

"Didn't you think that was odd? His doctor, right there?"

"Don't you see? Too much was happening! I threw up. I was weak as water. Bob and Betsy took me home. They stayed with me awhile, and then I was alone. That was the day that I went running in the rain. I felt then that it wasn't Emmy, there in the hospital. But I didn't care. He was gone, and I was free! Do you understand, Matt? Free?"

"The ambulance was right there. The doc was right there. That took some planning."

"Yes. I've wondered how they did that."

"They tried to keep you out of the morgue."

"Yes. I see that now, though not at the time."

"How close was the resemblance to Emmy?"

She shifted in her chair. "That's what made it so eerie.

The man lying down was the same size. The hair was the same. He wore Emmy's clothes."

"What about the eyes?"

"They were closed. He wore a gold chain around his neck, one I'd given Emmy when we were first married. I stared at him. He was all gray. I wanted to scream. I'd wished him dead, and then he was dead. That's why I fainted."

"But you knew he wasn't."

"Not then. Later."

"If he wasn't dead, you knew he'd be back."

"Yes. But by then I'd be gone. I'd sell the house and tuck the insurance money away in a savings account and work on my doctorate. I'd wanted out for so long. Now was my chance."

"It's pretty risky, pulling a stunt like that. Did you ask yourself why Emmy did it?"

"Of course. I thought it was women. Then Rudolfo came skulking around."

"Was Rudolfo in the stock market?"

"It's possible. I don't know."

"What's his business?"

"He exports statues, *objets d'art*."

"From Mexico?"

"Also from South America."

"Old stuff?"

"With Rudolfo, it's probably fake pre-Columbian." She gave me a sad smile.

"So you make your big decision, and then one day Bruce shows up with the bad news."

"Yes."

We stopped talking for awhile and just let the silence hang in the still New Mexico night.

"I wonder where those other guys are," I said.

"What do you mean?"

"The ten other guys on Bruce's list. Strich and Barrymore and Belker and the rest."

"Oh," she said.

"Let's run it again. Emmy calls you, says he's in New Mexico. He begs forgiveness. His big dream has turned into a nightmare. He's gone to Europe, probably to tap his Swiss account. But now he's back, running and hiding. I was just wondering if the other ten dreams also became nightmares."

"Those poor men," Roxanne said. "Those poor, sick, desperate men."

My neck felt stiff so I stretched. "Did Bruce check the ambulance out?"

"Yes. The phone at that company, Esprit, was out of service. He couldn't find a business address."

"Did anything happen at Emmy's so-called cremation?"

"Nothing out of the ordinary. Emmy's partners were there and a few acquaintances. I realized then how few friends Emmy had had. Rudolfo was there, of course, and a couple of his toadies. Emmy's sister was sick. I think I told you that. She was against the cremation so she wouldn't have come anyway."

"Did Rudolfo look at the body?"

"It was a closed casket." She gripped the arms of the chair and lowered her feet to the floor. She stood up. "I've made a mess of things, Matt. A terrible mess. What do we do now?"

"Tomorrow, we locate Emmy. We ask him some tough questions. We locate the snake's nest. We set fire to it and watch the snakes burn."

"Poor Emmy. I feel so sorry for him now."

She started for the door, looking lost and forlorn, and I grabbed hold of her wrist. She shook her head and said, "Please?"

I held on. We were locked in the moment, both starting to tremble. Her lips raked back from her teeth in a terrible grin, half want, half animal terror, and a low moan escaped her. Her arm was rigid as I pulled her slowly toward me. "I can't," she muttered. "I just can't. Please. Not tonight."

A sob came from her throat as I put my arms around her. She was rigid at first, shoulders tight, spine unyielding. I stroked her back, and she shuddered and then turned her face up to me. Her cheeks were streaked with tears. Her breath smelled of beer. "Don't die on me," she whispered. "Don't you dare die on me!" Fear made her press herself into me, curve of pelvis and solid thigh and soft breasts. Her arms were strong as they went around me. Her nose was almost level with mine, and I wondered how she had been with Emmy. And with Bruce.

"Don't think!" she ordered, hotly. "Not now." And then she shifted her body against mine. "Hold me tighter, Matt! Just hold me!" Guttural sounds came from her, from way inside, a thrilling hum, a dark gasp from a night creature.

We trembled together standing up, testing, blind tongues seeking. She was here and I wanted her and I didn't care what she had done before this moment. Blot out the ugly past. Now was everything. Heat pulsed from her body.

"Lie down with me, Matt." Her voice was a soft purr. "Lie down with me." We lay down together, arms locked. Her breasts pressed into my chest and her mouth went slack and I felt the rise and fall of her breathing, and then her throat tightened and throbbed and her lips skinned back to bare even white teeth, and she was looking at me, eyes wide open, accepting me, accepting this moment, no matter what. She twined her leg around mine and drove at me with her mouth. The kiss was demanding, her tongue pushing inside, strongly. My heart fluttered because this was what I wanted, had been wanting since I'd seen her the first time, early this morning, at Coco's.

We tore at each other, grunting like animals, but there wasn't that same awkwardness you get with a stranger. There was certainty, a deep sense of the known, the familiar. She knew. I knew. She was all moistness and curved softness and ripe, pulsing heat. As we kissed, I felt gripped by a primitive energy, a dark force, raw, earthy, magnetic. I wanted her. Nothing would stop me from taking. She was aggressive, more challenge than invitation. Her lips burned into mine. Her tongue met my tongue, jabbed it, tried to coil around it, and then her hands roughly tore at the buttons on my shirt and at the same time her blouse fell away from one smooth shoulder. I pressed my teeth into her hot flesh and she arched against me with her pelvis, thighs, belly, and moaned.

She undressed me quickly, with an urgency that was not scholarly. When I was undressed, she presented her buttons to me. I undid the blouse. "I need you," she said. "So much. Do you believe me?"

"Yes."

Beneath the blouse her breasts swung free. She stood up to take off the skirt and the bikini panties and to make me wait. A slant of moonlight caught the curve of bare buttocks as she stooped over. I wet my lips with my tongue.

She swung a leg across me and straddled my belly. "El Toro," she breathed. She was on her knees, swaying over me, making her breasts swing together, like bells.

"You're beautiful," I said, licking her arm. "My God, but you're beautiful."

"Ahh!" she moaned. "Ahhh!"

We were ready for each other, ready to snatch this

steamy moment, ready to shut out the world. There was no need for words. No need to ask, 'What do you like?' No need to say, 'I like this, and this, and this.' Because as she raised herself to accept me, there was a gasping intake of breath and a clutching of muscles and a wonderful awakening and after that I closed my eyes and let myself go wherever she led.

We made love there on the motel bed in Santa Fe, New Mexico, as the clock ticked and Friday rolled into Saturday. She was the oyster. I was the grain of sand. She was earth. I was sky. In that New Mexico motel the civilized world went away, and for a long suspended moment, I forgot about Emmy and the Belker case and Bobby Maclean and what Roxanne had done in the world beyond the door.

And for a short moment I even forgot about Bruce. And about how he had used me.

Matt Murdock, Tactical Diversion.

14

The ringing of the phone pulled me out of a dream. I was back on the riverbank with the barge and the monks and the big booming gong. I stood in line between Bruce Halliburton and a blond man wearing tennis clothes who wanted to sell me some life insurance. A million, he said. Premiums only seven thousand dollars a year. He held out a ballpoint pen and said, "Sign here, you're going to need it, pal."

Then I woke up and saw Roxanne going out the door.

Her door opened in the room next door. Through the wall, I could hear Roxanne's voice as she answered the telephone. I could not make out the words, but it sounded like Roxanne was doing most of the listening. My watch said 7:14. I levered myself out of bed and pulled on my pants. The morning air was chilly, and I remembered Santa Fe was up there, six thousand feet above sea level, maybe higher. The motel had a battered electric coffee pot—really a water heater—and two bags of Teacher's Choice instant. I filled it in the bathroom and plugged it in. While the water boiled, I finished dressing.

Roxanne came back as I was taking my first sip. She wore the white skirt and loose blouse from the night before and was carrying her sandals and the big leather purse with the shoulder strap. Her face looked worried. She came to put her arms around me, and I felt her trembling.

"You want coffee?"

"Yes. Please."

"Was that Emmy?"

"Yes. He's nearby—he wouldn't say where—and he wants to meet me at La Casa Sena at nine."

"A restaurant?"

"Yes. We can get breakfast there."

I poured water over the instant coffee and handed her the cheap plastic cup. "Anything more about Amigo Development?"

"No." She took her first sip of coffee. "He asked if I had the money. I said 'yes.' He told me again he'd been cheated out of a lot more than that. When I asked how much, he said it would be better if I didn't know. He called me *querida*."

"Did you ask him about the Swiss bank account?"

"That's when he hung up."

"How many trips did he take to Europe?"

"Two or three a year."

"Did you go with him?"

"Sometimes." She sipped her coffee and made a face. "This is pretty bad, isn't it? Ugh."

"Yes. You want to go out for something?"

"I need to freshen up first." She carried her handbag into the bathroom and stood in front of the mirror, running the brush through her hair. She looked good in the morning, very good. She saw me smiling and answered with a mirror smile of her own. She finished brushing her hair, tucked the brush into her purse, and came into my arms. Her lips were soft on my face as she gave me some quick butterfly kisses. "I don't want to leave here, Matt. I don't want to leave this room. Ever."

"I'm with you. We could order in a pizza. Sit here. Watch television. Drink this coffee every morning."

"You know how to change a lady's mind."

She kissed me again, then pushed herself away. She went back to the mirror and leaned forward to scrutinize her face as she applied pale gloss to her lips. "I wonder how much he had tucked away."

I finished my coffee and set the cup down. "Did he sound any different today?"

"Not really. He sounded tired and afraid. He usually speaks with a marvelous bravado." She studied my reflection in the mirror. "I told him you were with me."

"What did he say to that?"

"When I told him you were a detective, he said he would hire you to help him get what was his."

"Your husband has good footwork."

"Poor Emmy," she said, turning away from the mirror. "I'm ready."

We had another cup of coffee at an early morning café overlooking the plaza, and then we walked through the awakening streets of Santa Fe to La Casa Sena. It was warm in the patches of sunlight but quite cool in the shade. Along one side of the plaza Navajo silversmiths were setting up for the tourist trade. Roxanne, who knew a lot of history trivia, reminded me that the town had been full of Eastern intellectuals back in the forties, when

Oppenheimer and his boys were at Los Alamos building the big bomb.

At La Casa Sena we found a table in the courtyard. Our waitress was a fresh-faced woman with red hair and freckles who had just gone through a nasty divorce and had come to Santa Fe to save herself.

"I love it here," she said. "It's a sanctuary. All this magic."

Roxanne ordered an omelette, and I ordered huevos rancheros. I resisted an early beer. Emmy was coming, and I might have to perform and do some serious detecting. Roxanne positioned herself so she could watch both entrances. One was to her left. It led to the street outside. The other was to her right. It led to a hallway with several shops that sold turquoise and paintings and genuine Navajo rugs woven in the mills of Indianapolis. I could see the street door but had to turn to see the hallway door.

Our meeting was scheduled for nine o'clock, and by 8:45 Roxanne had torn two paper napkins into precise strips. Her edginess was making me edgy and I pushed the plate aside. Nine o'clock came, but no Emmy. We sat there, not talking, as time slowed down to a crawl. 9:05. Still no Emmy. 9:08. No Emmy.

"Damn!" Roxanne said. "Damn him!"

"Where was he calling from? This morning."

"He said he was in the area. Why?"

I was about to answer when I saw old White Hair, the biker from Lemon Heights. He wore a green jacket and white trousers and he was standing in the shadows under the archway leading to the alley.

"What is it?"

"That white-haired guy. From that party."

"The ambulance driver?"

"Maybe. Come on."

I tossed a twenty on the table and we hurried past the shops. The narrow hallway made a right turn before it opened out into a narrow alleyway. I went through in time to see him walking quickly away. At the end of the alley, he turned and saw us and then hurried out of sight. Even in shadow, you could see the pale hair.

"That's him!" Roxanne said. "The ambulance driver!"

As we ran after the white-haired man, I could hear Roxanne's sandals flapping and I cursed myself for not wearing running shoes. Boots are wonderful for showing off for the client, but lousy for running down the bad guys.

We came out of the alley into a street that was crowded with tourists on their way to breakfast. The white-haired man was jogging through the crowd, elbows high, moving easily.

"Let's get him!" Roxanne said, taking off her sandals. And we started off.

For the first three blocks, she was ahead of me, running like the wind despite her large flopping shoulder bag. The white-haired man cut into an alley and Roxanne followed. I was ten steps behind her.

The white-haired man had a nice lead now. Roxanne was still running strong, but I was feeling the altitude with every step. I was also feeling my age as I pounded up the next slope. Up ahead, Roxanne stepped on something, let out a cry, and stopped to examine her foot. Blood oozed from a small cut. "Damn!" she said. A tear ran down her cheek. She shook her head and started off, keeping pace with me.

The white-haired man was out of sight as we turned the corner. Shit, the way he moved told me he was younger, late twenties, early thirties at the most, a hotdog in his prime. The streets tracked like a labyrinth. I knew how we had come, but I didn't know where to go next. "This way!" Roxanne said, pointing. The road forked into a Y. We heard a car engine and ran that way, alongside an adobe wall stained pale orange. There was a narrow doorway in the wall and I ducked through on instinct and came into a parking lot behind a white stucco building. A sign on the building said Historical Monument, 1689.

The driveway was choked with early summer grass pushing up through the caliche. Breathing harshly from the thin air, I jogged down the driveway. Roxanne lagged behind now. I was just in time to see the white-haired man climbing into a Range Rover, maroon, with New Mexico plates. The door closed and the Rover pulled away. I could not see who was driving. Two blocks away, the Rover turned left and disappeared.

"Oh, no!" Roxanne said.

"How bad is your foot?"

"I don't feel anything now."

We stopped in a patch of shade while I examined her cut. The wound was dirty now from the street. It needed cleaning and dressing. I looked around, trying to get my bearings in this strange town. A river runs through the center of town. It's really a concrete aqueduct. The La Casa Sena was north of the river. The white-haired man had led us south of the river. Our motel, the El Chulo, was south of the river, but west of here.

We struck out for the motel, heading west. But the streets ran in funny little quarter-moon curves and we hadn't gone two blocks before I realized we were even more south. Roxanne was limping now and there were no taxis in sight. Sweat poured out of me. I was bareheaded, a habit you get into in California. My last trip to the desert I'd bought a straw planter's hat, but it was back home hanging on a nail in my house on the beach.

She sagged against a wall. "Find a taxi, will you?"

"Okay."

Feeling a sense of urgency at having to leave Roxanne alone, I jogged toward the sound of traffic until I found a main road. I stuck out my thumb and watched the cars slide past. There were Volvos and Saabs and BMWs and lots of varieties of the genus Mercedes. A cowboy in a Ford pickup gave me a ride back up the street. Roxanne met us halfway. The cowboy drove us back to the motel. I handed him a ten and he saluted and drove away.

In the bathroom, I gave Roxanne some arnica pellets and washed the cut clean. I got tape and a gauze pack out of my red carry-on.

"You come prepared."

"I get hit a lot."

"Why was he here?"

"I think he followed us."

"Why?"

"Maybe he's after Emmy."

"The money?"

I shook my head. "Could be. Seems like an awful lot of trouble for a couple hundred thousand." I touched her foot. The bleeding had stopped and the skin was now dry enough for the tape to stick, so I bandaged the cut.

"The pain is gone," she said.

"Arnica has its own magic."

"I like it when you take care of me." Her voice caught and she gulped and flashed me a shy smile. I didn't need much invitation. I took her into my arms. Her face was wet with tears. We lay down on the bed and she murmured softly into my throat. "Thank God you're here. Thank God I found you."

I held her close and murmured that things would be all right. I didn't believe it, but I wanted to comfort her, wanted to shield her from the nastiness of the world. In this life you can go too long without someone. For me, Roxanne was that someone.

One murmur from her and Murdock felt good all over. She was beautiful, smart, warm, intense, educated, sensitive, and loving. She was wonderful in bed. Watching her took my breath away and made my knees weak. With her arms around my neck I knew I was falling in love. She had given herself to me freely, like a willing and glorious flower to a horny honey-bee. She was earthy and musky and moistly ripe and she had made me erupt with feeling, something I hadn't accomplished in awhile. She was an expert at love-making, and I kept being jealous of the guy who had taught her how. There was just one problem: She was up to her pretty blue eyeballs in trouble. But I could handle it, right. Because I was Matt Murdock, Private Eye. And trouble was my business.

After awhile I left her on the bed and went in to use the facilities. When I came out, she was lying there with her arm thrown over her eyes.

"In the café, this morning, you were about to say something."

"Just a thought."

"What was it?"

"Try this scenario. Emmy wants you out of town, so he calls long distance and asks you to bring money. He knows you're broke, so he offers a split."

The arm came away from her face. "He's that sneaky." The idea brought her to a sitting position. "But the money's not there."

"But he doesn't know that."

"So he's going back for it?" She swung her bare legs off the bed. I never got tired of watching her move.

"And so are we."

"I am so tired." Roxanne padded to the bathroom to wash her face. Emmy-baby was not going to answer my questions. He was not going to lead us to the snake's nest, to the dragon's heart, to the eye of the wicked octopus.

But White Hair might.

If we could find him.

While Roxanne phoned the airline, I paid the bill. It was almost noon as we climbed into the rented Taurus and headed south, for Albuquerque.

15

At 7:03 we flew out of Albuquerque, heading west to Los Angeles International. There were no direct flights to Orange County until noon on Sunday, and we were both eager to get back.

Roxanne didn't say much on the plane. She had a couple of glasses of wine and then she closed her eyes and went to sleep. I had a couple of glasses of wine myself, but my mind kept on chewing over the events so far, trying to put them in order:

—Roxanne wants a divorce. Emmy says wait awhile, like a year, while he zips to Europe, land of the secret Swiss bank account, to deposit money.

—In January he switches to a new doctor, Sylvan Ames. His life insurance is up to $7 million.

—In March Emmy collapses on a tennis court at Le Club of Newport Beach. The Esprit ambulance arrives to whip Emmy off to St. Boniface. Bobby Maclean identifies

Emmy, then tries to keep Roxanne from seeing the corpse. She identifies him anyway, faints. Doc Ames is at the hospital, probably to sign the death certificate.

—Later that afternoon, Roxanne realizes it wasn't Emmy. But she's so glad to be free, she decides to let things ride.

—Rudolfo paws around Emmy's papers. He says he wants money. What he really wants is the numbers for the Swiss accounts.

—The bills are piling up. Thirty-three thousand a month for the house, another nine thousand interest on the credit line, several grand for the cars.

—Three weeks after Emmy collapses, Bruce arrives. Emmy had changed beneficiaries. Bruce asks tough questions about the collapse. Roxanne confesses. The bank starts proceedings to sell her house out from under her, to satisfy Emmy's credit line. Feeling stressed out, Roxanne gets cozy with Bruce.

—Bruce makes the Emmy-Belker-Barrymore Connection. A lot of money has been paid, over $100 million. He decides to cut a slice for himself.

—Bruce discovers the Doc Ames connection. He matches the list of insured guys with the list of beneficiaries.

—In April Claude Belker dies, adding another name to Bruce's list.

—In late May or early June Bruce contacts someone for his shakedown.

—In June Bruce hires Murdock. His ostensible reason is the Belker case. His real reason is to use Murdock to test the enemy strength. Bruce has tickets for Europe. He has numbers for some of the Swiss accounts.

—At the Lemon Heights party, the bikers, led by White Hair, make a grab for Murdock.

—Murdock trails Sheena to the cabin at Big Bear,

where he finds Belker's old hiking boots. Sheena admits Belker had told her to sit tight. She thought he was coming back.

—On Friday Bruce is killed when he goes to the shake-down meeting on the beach. Murdock meets Roxanne.

—Murdock discovers Bruce's file.

—Someone rips up Bruce's old place, hunting for the list or the numbers or both.

—Emmy phones, saying he wants Roxanne to deliver money to him in Santa Fe. He says he's been cheated, but doesn't say who cheated him.

—In Emmy's rococo bathroom, behind a false partition, Roxanne and Murdock find over two hundred thousand in U.S. currency.

—Roxanne and Murdock fly to Santa Fe. No Emmy. But White Hair from Laguna appears.

I asked the flight attendant for a ballpoint and some paper, and then I made a diagram that was all about money. A man dies and his insurance goes to a dummy organization. I wrote "Dead Man" in the center of the paper and I drew an arrow over to the word "ORG," short for Organization. What's the split? I wrote "50/50" down, then "75/25." Where does the money go? I drew an X through "ORG" and put an arrow and a question mark after the arrow. Emmy had $7 million in insurance. Belker had $14.5. I wrote those numbers on the paper. Add seven to fourteen, you get twenty-one. Divide by two, you get ten-five. There were eleven names on the list. If you averaged ten million for each one, the total take would be $110 million.

Okay, so what if Orange County wasn't the only arena for this business? What if the same thing was happening to middle-aged fellows all over the country? Chicago and New York and Miami and Scottsdale? I added those to the list. What if a guy was tired of his life and wanted to start over? So he makes a phone call and contacts an organization—call it Death, Inc., or maybe Rebirth, Ltd.—and they set up a deal whereby he turns over a portion of his insurance to a dummy corporation in return for a new life.

And the only problem is when he tries to get paid.

What if you headed up Death, Inc., and worked a dozen cities at $110 million?

I did some quick figuring and came up with $1.32 billion.

If you were Death, Inc., how long could you stay in business before the insurance people caught on?

On the surface Death, Inc., was a service business. But that was too easy. What if you were a really bad dude, a really evil sonofabitch, and you preyed on these guys? You knew what it was to be middle-age crazy. You offered them a way out. And then when they *were* out, they were caught in your spider web, ready for the slicer, man, regular chopped liver, yeah, and—

"Are we almost there?" Roxanne reached over and took my hand.

"Soon," I said.

She moved close enough for a nuzzle, at the same time pressing her knee into my leg. "I want to get home," she said.

"Me, too. I'm beat."

"Could we stay at your place tonight?"

"Love it."

"I'd like to stop by my house and get a few things, running shoes, shorts, a top. Then we can drive to your place. Bruce said it's on the pier."

"Yeah."

"I'll bet it's homey. Cozy."

"Why?"

"Because you are." She squeezed my hand and smiled, and I felt better again.

We landed at LAX in a light fog, a remnant of the smog from the day. While I found us some ground transportation, Roxanne went off to the ladies' room. There was a van leaving for Orange County in ten minutes.

I stood outside the ladies' room, guarding the bags, watching for suspicious characters. If my analysis of the situation was anywhere close and if Death, Inc., was as big as I figured, it wouldn't be safe for Roxanne to be alone.

Los Angeles is the City of Crazies, so among the punkers and the riff-raff you look for a wobble in the environment. It took me thirty seconds to spot him, a guy in a business suit, round face, big gut, and a boxy rear-end to balance it. The three-piece suit looked expensive, with hardly a rumple. He wore round-lensed glasses that made his face look even fatter. He had a fifty-dollar haircut. He wore a white shirt and a severe blue tie. His shoes were Marine dress cordovans, and his luggage was a leather under-the-seat case with gold buckles. He was pretending to read the newspaper, but he gave that up when Roxanne joined me.

"My God, I am so tired."

"Yeah."

"How long until we're home?"

"An hour or so."

Roxanne yawned. "Sorry."

The round-faced man was approaching, grinning, eyeing Roxanne with lust in his squinchy eyes. "Mrs. Mendez?" he asked.

She turned, still sleepy. He handed over a business card. She read the card and passed it to me. It said: Alfred Dugger, South Coast Life, with a Miami address and a phone number with the 305 area code.

"I'm Al Dugger, ma'am. South Coast Life." He moved

closer. Any moment now, a drop of love-drool would appear at the edge of his mouth.

Roxanne backed up a step. "What is it, Mr. Dugger?"

He turned to me, the car salesman grin still in place, and held out his hand. "You're Murdock, right?"

I ignored his hand, which wavered, pumping the air, before it dropped away. "We've got a bus to catch." I took Roxanne's arm.

"Hey, wait up. Where you folks going?"

"John Wayne."

"Hey, no problem. I've got transport. Ride with me." His voice was oily and irritating. "We could go over old times."

I piloted Roxanne out of the terminal toward the curb and our waiting van, a blue Dodge that said "Super Shuttle" in large yellow letters. We quick-marched. Roxanne's arm was hot beneath my fingers. Dugger hurried along beside her, moving with that deceptive ease of the mythical fat man. Traffic slid by in front of us and along the concrete traffic belt overhead.

"Bruce told me about you, Murdock."

"Bruce who?"

We were through the doors. The van driver, a woman in a hunter's red vest, was writing something on a clipboard.

"Hey, come on, you guys. Bruce Halliburton. We worked together on some cases. He said you were hell on wheels in 'Nam, Murdock. A regular gook-blaster."

When we reached the van, I swung back to confront Dugger. "You want something. What is it?"

Sweat ran down his forehead as he opened up his fancy case. "Got something you and the lady might be interested in." He pulled out a thin file folder marked "Mendez-Madrid, Claims." With a grunt, he set the case down, so he could open the file folder. Behind me, I heard Roxanne paying for our tickets to John Wayne Airport, where her car was parked. Dugger handed me a Xerox copy of a cancelled check. The light was dim underneath the concrete overhang. I edged toward the light. The check was from Ebco, with an address on State Street in Chicago. It was made payable to Mrs. Roxanne Mendez-Madrid, to the tune of $1.5 million, the amount of Emmy's policies with South Coast Life. The bottom half of the Xeroxed sheet showed a copy of the backside of the check, stamped through by all the clearing houses. Roxanne came over.

"What is it, Matt?"

I handed her the Xerox, but not before I saw the signature on the back of the check.

Roxanne Mendez-Madrid.

"Where did you get this?"

"The usual way," Dugger said. "It came in the mail, in an envelope from the bank, along with our other monthly statements."

"What do you intend to do with it?"

"Use it as leverage," he said, "to get our money back."

She shoved the Xerox copy at him. "I don't have it. That's not my signature."

Dugger took a step closer to her, but I blocked him.

"Go away, Dugger. Find your rock. Climb back under."

Sweating heavily now, Dugger tucked the Xerox back into his file folder. "Sure you folks don't want a ride? We're going to be seeing a lot of each other. We can do this the friendly way. Or we can bring in the law."

Roxanne climbed into the van. I followed.

"You riding with me, mister?" called the driver.

With a pudgy hand, Dugger waved her off. He was still standing there, holding his luggage, when we drove away.

Roxanne sat huddled against me, clutching my arm.

"That wasn't my signature," she whispered. "I'll show you."

I patted her arm. "No need to."

"I should have kept that copy," she said. "I could have proved it to you."

"No need." I kissed her on the temple, touching my lips to her dark hair, and the Super Shuttle wheeled south, toward home.

16

There was a ticket on my windshield when we stopped at Coco's parking lot to pick up the Ford. Roxanne clung to me as I started to climb out of her car. "What if he's there, Matt? What if Emmy's there?"

"Then we ask him some questions."

"Are we going to win, Matt?"

"We're the good guys," I said. "We will."

She gave me a wistful smile as she slid behind the wheel. I unlocked the Ford and started up. With the engine idling, I reached under the seat for the PPK and put it next to me. I waved at Roxanne, who led the way to Spyglass Hill.

On the drive up, I made some mental notes about what to do next. One, phone Bongo Bodette. Maybe he'd turned up something on Bruce's list. Two, find Dr. Sylvan Ames and do an intensive interview. Three, ask Webby Smith to check up on Mr. Dugger, whose first name was Al. Did Dugger really work for South Coast Life?

I squinted my eyes and tried to forget the headache pounding away at my brain. Roxanne's headlights swung across the dark landscape of Newport Beach, lighting up the eyes of a tomcat out for some evening entertainment. The tomcat reminded me of Manxman, her blue furred cat. I shifted down for the climb. After a fun morning in Santa Fe, panting my lungs out at six thousand feet, it was good to be driving the Ford again.

As we turned onto Spyglass Rim Drive, Roxanne's street, I saw headlights beaming onto the garage door. The vehicle was in Roxanne's driveway. At the same time a second vehicle was swinging out of the driveway, heading toward us. I was tired. Being tired made me slow. The headlights swooped straight at Roxanne's Chrysler.

Roxanne gave the car a blast of her horn. I pulled out the PPK, but the headlights blinded me. Tires screamed on asphalt and I heard a crunching sound, metal on metal. The headlights swung away from my eyeballs, and I saw rubber smoking as tires raked the pavement. I swung the Ford into the curb, trying to block him, but he blew past me by riding up over the curb and across some expensive planters at the edge of Roxanne's neighbor's house.

I couldn't see the driver as the car swept past, but I did see the car.

It was a late model Volvo.

Roxanne had braked near the curb, where one wheel had gone over, tilting the front end of the Chrysler so that the headlights silhouetted the car coming down her driveway. It was an American car, dark green, maybe dark brown.

I leveled the PPK at the dark car, but suddenly Roxanne was in my line of fire. The Chrysler was backing up as she cranked the wheel, slinging her rear end around so that the brown car had to slam into the rock pedestal at the entrance to the driveway in order to miss her.

There was a solid whump. The brown car backed up and slid through with a squeal of rubber. I had the Ford pickup half turned around when the brown car zipped past.

Roxanne was out of her car, running toward me. She jerked open the door and climbed in. "That was Bruce's car!" she said.

I backed around in a half-circle and roared back down the hill. Through my open window, I could smell burning rubber. On the first two turns there was no sign of either vehicle. On the third turn I caught sight of taillights just as the driver turned them off. "There!" Roxanne pointed. "Up ahead!" We lost him again on the fourth turn, where the twisting drive began to level out. "We're losing him, Matt! Hurry!" Then, down below, I heard a horn honk, twice, followed by the squeal of brakes, and then a thunk as metal hit metal.

I slowed just enough to keep all four wheels on the ground, but the back of the Ford slammed into a decorative fence, throwing Roxanne against me. I straightened out and barreled on down the street.

The wreck had taken place under an oozing green streetlight. A taxicab sat with one wheel on the curb, one headlight burning fuzzily in the light fog. The other headlight was out.

Twenty feet away, the brown car—it was a Chevrolet—angled up into someone's yard. The hood had popped open like an oyster shell and smoke was swirling out. A stream of water hissed out merrily. I braked behind the Chevrolet. The driver's door was half open and I could see the lumpy outline of the driver. No one was moving. I climbed down and told Roxanne to stay there.

There was no sign of Bruce's Volvo.

With the PPK in one hand, I approached the car. One booted foot came out of the wreck, followed by a leg wearing torn Levis, and then a large hand. The driver's face came into the light. It was the geek, Sheena's pal, from the party.

Behind me, the cabbie called. "Hey! Over here! I think I busted something. Help."

Roxanne left the pickup and ran over to help the cabbie. The geek slid down, out of the Chevrolet, onto a smashed bush. He grunted, rolled over, saw me, and began to crawl away from the wreck. I waited until he had reached the street, and then I stuck the PPK in his ear.

"Take off the belt, clyde, and then lie face down with your hands locked behind your head."

He took off the belt. His forehead was bleeding from where he had slammed into the dashboard or the steering wheel. I made the belt tight around his wrists. Very tight. When he was snug, I decided to check the Chevrolet.

A man was in the passenger seat, hidden by shadows. The momentum had crowded him up close to the dashboard, and his face was bloody from whacking the windshield. I felt the big artery in his neck, but the blood wasn't pumping through. The man wore black, with a priest's collar. In his jacket pocket beneath the lapel was a Spanish passport, made out in the name of Father Alonzo Dominguez Alcazar. He had a full head of hair, a small mustache, and a face that some women would consider handsome. He was dead, probably from a broken neck. I turned his head so his face would be in the light. The streetlight colored his skin pale green.

I knew him. His face was on the photograph in my jacket pocket. It was Roxanne's husband, Emiliano Mendez-Madrid. And this time, he was really dead.

I wiped off my prints and put the passport back in Emmy's pocket and man-handled the geek across the street, where Roxanne was asking someone in a house above us to call for help.

The cabbie could move his head, but his back was hurting him, and he was obviously pleased to being tended by an attractive nurse. I looked in the window. His passenger was an old party in a tuxedo, slumped down in a comfortable heap on the back seat. The window was partly open, and I smelled the fumes of liquor breath.

"Drunk?" I asked.

"As a lord," the cabbie said. "Where'd you come from?"

"Up the hill. Think you can stand?"

"Nah. I need a goddamn vacation, anyway. My insurance says I gotta wait for the paramedics."

He seemed lucid enough, and I was no doctor.

"I'm the one needs a doctor," the geek said, snarling. "I need medical attention."

"We're taking this man to the hospital," I said to the cabbie. "He's a fugitive from justice. When the paramedics get here, tell them we're at St. Boniface."

"Gotcha," said the cabbie. Then to Roxanne. "Anytime you need a ride, pretty lady, call Mario Maggio. That's me. You ride free with Mario, anywhere in the county."

"Thank you."

We walked toward the pickup. Water still hissed from under the wrecked Chevrolet.

"Emmy's in there," I said.

"What?"

"Looks like he broke his neck."

"Listen," the geek chimed in. "I'm a federal agent on assignment and these people are kidnapping me and—"

I stuck the PPK in his ear, and he stopped talking. Roxanne walked over to look inside the Chevrolet. I heard her gasp. She stayed there a couple of moments. When she came back, she was dabbing her eyes with a handkerchief.

"Damn you," she said to the geek.

"Let's get to your place," I said.

"I'm in a lot of pain, pal."

"Shut your face," I said.

"I need a doctor, pal. I'll sue your ass."

I rapped him on the kneecap with the PPK. Let him bleed to death, but not in my pickup.

"Mama." He grinned at Roxanne. "Eat crackers in my bedroll, any time."

We parked in Roxanne's driveway and I muscled the geek out. At the top of the ramp, he tried to kick me in the balls, and that gave me the excuse to topple him off the porch into some rose bushes. While he was there, Roxanne threw a flower pot at him. It missed by inches. I wrestled him to his feet. Roxanne unlocked the front door, and we went inside. All three of us were panting.

The house was dark. Roxanne flipped on some lights and called for Manxman, but no cat appeared. The geek's cheek was scratched. Tough.

Some of the boxes had been ripped open. A chair was turned over. A lamp lay shattered on the floor. The geek stood with his feet apart, leering at Roxanne, then grinning at me. He probably thought of himself as a sexy guy, a real gift. The blood on his face was drying, clotting. The mean-ass look in his eye told me he wasn't hurt too badly.

"Shouldn't we call the police?" Roxanne asked.

"Let's see what's upstairs."

He didn't try anything on the way up the stairs. Too bad. It would have been a pleasure to drop him fourteen feet on his beaky nose. The door to Emmy's study was open. Roxanne let out a gasp.

Papers littered the floor. Books had been dumped out

of the bookshelves. A desklamp threw jagged shadows from its place on the floor. The heavy chair had been overturned.

"What were you looking for?"

"Guess."

We walked on down to the master bedroom, with its carpet of whorehouse red. From the doorway we could see into the bathroom.

The lavatory had been swung out from the wall.

A long-bladed knife lay on the floor, near the bathtub. The blade was caked with dried blood and what looked like tufts of dark hair. It was too short to be a bona fide machete, more like a brush hook used by campers, but without the hook. I shoved the geek into the pink bathtub, where he sat down with a thump.

"What happened here?"

"Up yours."

Roxanne walked out and stood still as a statue in the master bedroom. In her hand was the knife.

"You okay?"

She nodded, but did not speak. We had to call the cops, and soon. First, I wanted some time with the geek. I walked him back downstairs and into the garage, where I roped his wrists together with strapping tape. I made sure the tape dug into his wrists. I sat him on the floor of the garage and had him watch while I found an electric drill. I took my time inserting a wood bit. It has a sharp little screw on the end and the cutting edges are sharp and polished. This one was dull, but it was a half-inch bit and looked mean.

"Ever use one of these?"

"What's your game, jack? You keep stumbling onto my turf, you could end up dead."

I plugged in the drill and pressed the button to make it whir. Then I moved it quickly to the geek's ear, a half inch away, where he could hear it whirl. He was a tough guy, but the sound made him sweat. I wanted it to work on his imagination.

I took the drill away. "Right through the ear, buddy. Take out a molar or two, hey? Or a bicuspid?"

He squirmed on the floor. "Give me a chance, okay?"

"Like you gave Halliburton? And the guy upstairs?"

"Hey, it was a job. I'm only the wheel man."

"Who hired you?"

He shook his head. I laid the drill bit on his knee, angled it in, and looked at him. I knew I wouldn't use it, but he didn't. He gulped, the sound hollow in the silent garage. I touched the tip of the unmoving drill bit to the exposed skin of his shin. He jerked away, his face pale. I started the drill and held it a half inch away from his knee.

"Wait!"

I stopped, looked up at him.

"Okay. Okay. I'll spill what I know. It's not much. On the first hit, the suit with the Volvo, we got ten grand apiece. The info comes to me at a mail-drop in a motel in South Laguna. There was a timetable, where he'd be and all, that parking lot near Huntington, and a mug shot. We zeroed in on the beach, but it was Jerome did the deed."

"Jerome. He's the guy with the white hair?"

"Yeah. And those eyes. They are fucking spooky."

"Then you went up to Malibu."

"Yeah."

"What for?"

"Jerome wanted some files."

"What files?"

"Hell, I don't know. We tore that place up for an hour and didn't find squat. We found some stuff. Turned out it wasn't *the* stuff."

"What about the priest?"

"He was here when we got here. Rent car in the driveway there. Door wide open. We come up the stairs and find the good padre tearing up the bathroom. Jerome stiff-arms him, and he's out."

"What did you do then?"

"Okay. I'm getting to that. Jerome says, 'It's him.' 'Who?' I ask. 'The laundryman,' Jerome says. So we load him into the Hertz buggy out there, and we look around, and just when we're splitting, here's a car turning into the fucking driveway."

"Where were you taking him?"

"Some freezer facility."

"What for?"

"Beats me."

"Where's that?"

"Hell, I don't know."

"What's the name of it?"

He lifted his bony shoulders in a shrug. "He didn't tell me, man."

"How did you know it was a freezer facility?"

"Called it the deep freeze."

"Local?"

"I was just about to find out, man."

"What did you make on this job?"

"Two bills."

"Where does Jerome hang out?"

"Corona del Mar, somewhere. He never took me to his pad."

I asked him some more questions, but he didn't have more to tell. I jerked him to his feet and walked him back inside. Roxanne was on the front porch, calling for Manxman. I told the geek to lie down on his stomach, and then I ran a strand of tape around his ankles. A stink rose from him, like garbage.

"Hey, lady," he called. "Try upstairs."

"What did he say?"

"Manxman. Upstairs."

We left the geek on the floor while we climbed the stairs again. The shadows in the study were deep, with a heavier darkness in the corners.

"Manxman?" Roxanne said. "Come on out, dear." And then she made a clicking sound with her tongue, part of the special animal language she had created for Manxman.

No cat appeared.

I set the lamp upright again and saw a lump in one of the corners. Roxanne and I walked over together. From eight feet away you couldn't tell what it was. From four feet away we knew.

"Oh, no!" Roxanne dropped to her knees and reached for the cat.

Except it wasn't a cat anymore. It was a mass of dead flesh covered with blue fur.

Only the mass didn't have a head.

That big knife, in the bathroom.

And the tufts of hair clinging to the blade, stuck to the metal by dried blood.

Then Roxanne screamed.

17

Looking out the front window of Roxanne's house, you could see police cars and the red lights turning on the roof bars and farther off to the right the oyster bed of winking lights of Newport Beach, where rich people come from all over the world to embrace the sea, and beyond that a single light from a vessel sailing past the California coast.

My PPK was locked in the Ford. I put it there just before the police arrived. They see a weapon at a crime scene, and they confiscate it and lock it away in an evidence room for a couple of years. At the Newport Beach station Leon Book's boys have four of my guns tucked away for eternity. With the PPK was the photo of Emmy.

The time was 2:38 A.M., and there was a cop on the door. The forensics guy, Abe Farquhar, was coming in from the front porch, blinking in the light. Abe glanced at me and then walked into the kitchen. Leon Book was sitting with me. Roxanne was next door, at her neighbor's house, trying to keep from coming unglued. They had taken the hit man away, and there was an all-points bulletin out for his pal, Jerome of the white hair. The geek didn't know Jerome's last name. As he gave me his scenario, Leon kept looking at the Spanish passport from Emmy's coat pocket.

"So you and the lady drive up and discover three perps doing a simple B and E at this residence. One perp escapes in a late-model Volvo—no license tag recorded—and two others slam into the lady's vehicle, a 1988 Chrysler Le Baron. The perps are driving a Hertz Rent-a-Car." Leon looked at his police notebook. "One perp's name is John Robert Townsend. He's wanted in six states, including California. In the Navy he had some Seal training. Isn't that the outfit where they teach you to blow up enemy ships without letting the newspapers know who did it?"

"It's all classified, but I think so."

"The other perp is dead. He's carrying a Spanish passport in the name of Father Alonzo Alkazzeer, or something close. You and the lady give chase. The Hertz car rams into a cabbie at the bottom of the hill. You haul the driver out and tell the cabbie he'll be at St. Boniface. Then you take him up here."

"And phone the authorities."

"Right away," Leon said.

"The moment we were inside. We did not make coffee. Did not go to the bathroom."

Ha ha," Leon said.

"Can I go now? I'm bushed."

Leon pointed at me with his notebook. "On the person of our dead priest are airline tickets from Madrid to Dallas, Dallas to John Wayne. He had reservations at the Côte d'Azur, where there is a whole convention of priests. He hadn't checked in yet."

"You must enjoy your work, Leon."

"We're trying to run his prints now. No record in the U.S. No word yet from Europe."

I stood up and stretched. "Well, when you find out, let me know. Okay?"

Leon stood up too. "I smell something, Sherlock. This guy Halliburton gets wasted. He knows the lady. You know the lady. This guy Rudolfo Cantu knows the lady. Tonight the lady's house gets burgled. A cat gets killed with a knife. You better tell me what's cooking, pal. Or your ass will never see daylight again."

"What happened to Cantu?"

"What do you mean, what happened?"

"Did you book him?"

Leon stared at me, then looked away. "He was sprung."

"When?"

"Yesterday afternoon. A high-powered lawyer from L.A."

"What was bail?"

"Ten grand."

"The wheels of justice," I said.

"The judge sets bail, Sherlock. Remember?"

"Who was the lawyer?"

"Milo Proctor. He's with Strauss, Johnson, and Ledoux."

"Didn't Proctor represent Chuy Palafox?"

"The same."

"Then Rudolfo's hooked in with the mob."

"Assumptions, Sherlock, do not hold up in court."

Abe Farquhar, a big, square man with a bald forehead, came up. Abe's main love in life was tennis. His nose was always sunburned. His right wrist was pale where the sweatband blocked the sun. He set his black bag down with a thump.

"What have you got, Abe?"

"Like we thought, Leon. Our priest in the vehicle died of a broken neck."

"The car crash?"

"Looks like it."

"When can we get an autopsy?"

"Monday," Abe said.

"How about tomorrow? Cancel your tennis game and do some work for a change."

"Sorry, Leon. Monday's the best I can do."

I left them arguing about leverage from their various positions in the great bureaucratic pyramid and went outside and started up the Ford and parked it in front of the house next door. Roxanne was inside, standing in the kitchen, nursing a rum drink while she talked to her neighbor, Marge Duquesne. I got introduced to Marge's husband, Charles, a tanned and youngish Newport Beach type with a pasted-on smile and a vigorous corporate handshake, and then Roxanne hugged Marge and took my arm and we headed out into the dark.

The death-river dream came back that night. The line of dead folks had been moving along, snaking toward the barge where the monk stood ready with his gong. I was behind Emmy, who was wearing his black suit with the snug little priest's collar. I was about to ask him why priests wore those little collars when the gong sounded and someone stepped on board. We shuffled forward and I raised my head and noticed that there were only four people between Emmy and the barge.

Five bongs of the gong and Murdock would be on board.

I woke shuddering. Roxanne was there to calm my nerves. She was warm and curved and supple. We made love. And she helped me push away the bad dream.

I made a pot of Murdock Blend and served her coffee in bed. I heated up a frozen Sara Lee, and we sat propped up against pillows while we went over what had happened.

"You were right, Matt. He did come back after the money. He wanted me out of there."

"We still don't know what happened when he got wherever he was going."

"Where were they taking him?" she asked. "Those two men."

"Jerome called it the deep freeze."

"What does that mean?"

"Some kind of refrigeration place. He didn't say where it was."

"Jerome has the white hair?"

"Yes."

"Now that he has a name, he's not so spooky."

"I don't read him as smart enough to think this up. He's a hired gun."

"What do we do now?"

"Exercise." I rolled out of bed.

"Not me." Roxanne pulled the sheet up over her face. "I am so tired. My God. We only met Friday morning, and I feel a hundred and twenty years old."

"Exercise," I said, bumping her hip with my heel. "Pump the blood through those veins."

She slid further down into the sheets. "Today, I am not leaving this bed."

I found some shorts and a top left behind by a lady. The shorts were white and the top was pink. I dug into Roxanne's traveling case and found her New Balance runners. I hauled her out of bed, all warm and naked-brown and curved, and when she came into my arms and tried to persuade me to come back between the sheets, I showed my knightly restraint by insisting we run on the beach.

While Roxanne was in the bathroom, I phoned the number for Dr. Sylvan Ames. After four rings an answering machine came on, telling me the doctor was unable to come to the phone and would I please leave a number if this was an emergency.

Then I called Bongo Bodette. He said he would have something by midmorning. Stop by, he said, and bring beer. I phoned Webby Smith at home and got his answering machine. I left my number and asked him to call back.

It was one of those June mornings when all should have been right with the world. The sun glowed on our backs. The air was clear and sharp. The beach people had not yet taken up strategic positions on every square inch of sand. We jogged along slowly at first, stretching, easing into it, and then when we were halfway to the Wedge, on Balboa, Roxanne increased her pace and gave me a bright competitive smile, and we were off.

She beat me by twenty paces. I showed her the back of Wally's house. She thought she had seen him play during an interclub match.

"That life seems a thousand miles away. And a hundred years."

On the way to the ferry Roxanne ran with me, side by side, shoulders swinging, one-two, one-two. She had a smooth running motion and an easy stride that seemed effortless. I wondered how good a tennis player she was. We rode the Balboa ferry across to Balboa Island.

On the way across she pointed out Duke Island and Duke Castle, at the tip of Balboa Island, and said she and Emmy had been invited to the Christmas party last year. They couldn't go because of the trip to Europe.

The ferry docked, and we stood for a moment on the

landing. A forty-two-footer was heading out toward the jetty for a Sunday on the water. A man in a striped sailor shirt stood at the wheel. A woman in a bikini posed in the bow. They were doing their best to become immortalized by a photo in a glossy magazine. Standing there, on the edge of the Good Life, it was tough to believe Bruce was dead and Emmy was dead and that Mr. X and Death, Inc., were out there switching bodies and collecting insurance into the millions.

Roxanne plucked my sleeve. "Is that Bruce's car?"

I looked around. Three Volvos were waiting for the light to change. Two were gunmetal gray. The third was gray flannel, a shade darker. "Three choices," I said. "This is Volvo Country."

On the opposite side of Coast Highway a young couple on twin ten-speeds waited at the curb, necks strained in argument. They wore black French racing shorts and identical T-shirts, red stripes on a white field, and biking shoes with hard soles. The woman shook her head, and the man pointed north. Her nose was out of joint. Too bad they had to argue on a day like this.

The signal changed, and we started across. So did the male half of the biking couple. We were halfway across when I heard the squeal of rubber on asphalt. The gunmetal gray Volvo was coming at us in the far left lane. The biker was right in its path.

"Look out!" I cried.

Tires smoking, the Volvo drove at us in a curving arc.

The woman biker was still on the curb, near the signal pole, trying to get her foot into the metal stirrup on her pedal. The man with her turned and called: "Angie?"

I grabbed Roxanne and propelled her toward the safety of the concrete curb. The Volvo switched directions and angled toward us. The woman biker screamed. The man swore and started to climb off his bike, but his shoe got caught in the stirrup. "Angie!" His voice seemed high and scratchy. The Volvo had windows tinted dark so you couldn't see inside. The license plate was white for California, the Golden State, but four of the numbers had tape over them. The first digit was L. Then two spaces of tape. Then 56. Then more tape.

You could hear the whine of the high-performance RPMs as the engine came at us. Roxanne was three long strides from the curb when she tripped and fell. The Volvo was coming. I hauled Roxanne to her feet and gambled the invisible driver thought we would dive for the curb. Instead, at the last minute I pulled her the other way, back onto the highway.

The right front wheel of the Volvo whumped against the curb as the driver fought for control. Behind the tinted glass I saw a shadowy outline. There was a scraping sound as the undercarriage tore itself on the concrete, then the right front fender of the Volvo hit the woman biker with a sickening clunk. The side of the vehicle scraped the silver metal pole that held the traffic signal, a long raking sound, and then the Volvo barreled on past us, heading south on Pacific Coast Highway.

"You okay?"

Roxanne nodded and toed the asphalt with her foot. "I twisted my ankle, I think. My knee got scraped. Who was it?"

"Whoever it was, they're after us."

"Or maybe me."

The man in racing shorts had left his ten-speed and was running across to where the woman lay. Traffic piled up and horns started honking. A crowd gathered, shutting the woman from view.

"Angie?" the man cried. "Angie baby!"

We left her at the edge of the crowd, where her friend was ministering to the hit-and-run victim. I dialed 911 and reported the accident. When the police came, we gave our story, along with the pasted over license plate. I did not mention Leon Book or try to help the police make a connection between this Volvo and the one last night. When you're in doubt, keep it simple.

We were near Bongo's place in Newport Dunes. I bought two six-packs of Coors, and we headed down to see Bongo.

▌▌▌▌▌▌▌**18**▌▌▌▌▌▌▌

Bongo lived in a double mobile home about twelve feet from the water. His blue van was parked under an aluminum carport, a CB antenna towering up from the rear bumper to a point six feet above the roofline. A TV antenna rode like a boomerang on the roof of the cab. And a foxtail was knotted onto the roof rack. The van was streaked with red desert dust. We approached the door and rang the buzzer. We heard at least two televisions going inside.

The door was opened by a pixie-ish girl in a red bikini. She had long straight dark hair that went down to her waist. Her eyes lit up when she saw us. "Hi," she said. "I'm Rima. Rima Beaukirk. I'm a cousin of Lucy June's, who sends regards. You must be Sherlock Murdock. I heard about you."

"Hello, Rima."

We shook hands, and I introduced Roxanne. Rima was no more than five feet tall, but perfectly built and nicely proportioned. Her skin was smooth and dark, the same shade as Roxanne's. She took the two six-packs from me. "Bongo's working on your problem. He's been to Europe twice since midnight, on his modem, and to Tokyo and Singapore. He let me search the local stuff, from here to New Yawk City."

While Rima showed Roxanne around, I used the phone to call Leon Book at the Newport Beach station, to tell him about the hit-and-run. The sergeant on the phone said that Leon was not available. So I gave him the information and the three letters I'd gotten off the license plate of the gray Volvo.

Our problem was clear: The enemy was gearing up for a major offensive, and I was not going to be taken out without a fight.

I joined Roxanne and Rima in the computer room, where Bongo Bodette sat in an awning-striped swivel chair before a curved computer table and three television monitors. Bongo wore a combat photographer's vest, jungle camouflage, with flap pockets and zipper pockets. His beard looked bushier than I remembered it, with more shots of gray muting the glorious pirate's red. His arms were still the size of Arkansas hams, but Bongo himself looked as if he'd slimmed down from 295 to a trim 240.

Bongo might talk red-neck, but he had a brain like Leonardo da Vinci.

The chair was on rollers and Bongo was in the process of wheeling across the floor from screen one, on the left, to screen three, on the far right. On two of the screens numbers raced across a field of green. On the third screen words forming on an electronic bulletin board moved slowly upward.

Bongo stood up when he saw me and shook hands. "Hey," he said. "Sherlock Murdock. Have I got a treat for you." He winked and pulled me down close, so he could whisper. "That's a purty lady, Sherlock." He meant Roxanne. "Hang onto that one, for sure."

"Okay. I got the message."

He told Rima to get some beer, and then he rummaged around in a stack of file folders until he came up with one labeled "Excalibur." He pulled up a chair for Roxanne, and then we watched as he opened the folder.

The first sheet was a list of the names I'd gotten from Bruce. Bongo explained as he ran a thick finger down the list. "All these fellers are dead, except for three in June. Robertson and Jones and this feller Maclean are still walking around, at least on paper. The others, they up and died in the month it says here. The first number after the name is estimated personal wealth, not including life insurance at the time of death. The second number is a total of life insurance held at time of death. Got to warn you, these numbers could be low. I tapped into some data banks back East, Boston and New York City. This is what I got."

I was reading down the list of names when Rima came in with four cans of Coors. Bongo popped one open, held it up. "Here's mud in your enemy's eye." We drank to that.

Bongo had not changed the order of the list, so the first name was Strich, Albert J., of Laguna Beach. Strich, the president of Prime Lenders, had died in September, with a total personal wealth of $17 million and a debt-load of $9 million. His insurance had totaled $6 million.

I kept reading on down the list: Bennett, George G., of Tustin. Personal wealth $21 million; debt-load, $14 million; insurance $9 million.

I came to Belker, Claude A., Newport Beach. Personal wealth, $25 million; debt-load, $21 million; insurance, $14.5 million.

Mendez-Madrid, Emiliano F., Newport Beach. Personal wealth, $16 million; debt-load, $14 million; insurance, $7 million.

The bottom line was higher than what I'd come up with on the plane. If you totaled up the insurance from these names, you had $157 million.

Where did the money go?

"My God!" Roxanne breathed.

"There ain't no end to evil, ma'am. Snakes under ever' damn rock. You're lucky to have run onto old Sherlock here. Honest as my granddaddy Bodette, back in Tula, Arkansas." Bongo turned the page. "What we got here, it smelled like one a them offshore combines where rich folks hide profits and stuff from the guvmink. It's like that there shell game my cousin Jason Bodette Ardus used to run on the city suckers. You put the pea under one shell and then shuffle them around and ask the sucker—usually some slick-hair dude with a fancy car and a fancier woman—where it's at. By the time he chooses, that pea has moved around so much it's sprouted a vine. So what I did was, I tracked the money."

"How?" Roxanne asked.

Bongo grinned at her. "It's all wire transfers, ma'am. Used to be money was gold in them Wells Fargo saddlebags. Then it was paper, and the gold stayed at Fort Knox, where the guvmink could fool around with how much it was worth. Now it's electronic, and we got us some hell to pay for. Whoo-ee." He flipped to the second page of the file folder, and while we read the numbers, his fingers went tap, tappa, tap on the computer keys, and a spreadsheet appeared on the screen.

The list contained the names of Amigo and Ebco and the other firms gathered together by Bruce Halliburton. The name of the corporation came first, then the name of the bank where deposits were held, then the amount of the balance, and finally the date when the account was closed.

The banks were in Texas, Oklahoma, and Arkansas.

Emmy's main beneficiary had been Amigo Land Development of Houston. The bank for Amigo had been Corsicana Merchants, in Corsicana, Texas. On May 15 the balance in the Amigo account had been a tidy $210 million. The account had been closed on May 16.

The list looked like this:

ACCOUNT	BANK	ON DEPOSIT	CLOSED
Amigo	Corsicana Merchants (TX)	$300,000,000	May 16
Ebco	First National (TX)	$250,000,000	May 20
Everglades	Lawton State (OK)	$189,000,000	May 10
Full-Scale	Abilene Natnl (TX)	$340,000,000	April 2
Ftre, Sctsdl	Throckmorton S & L (TX)	$275,000,000	May 1
GAF-Atlanta	Ardmore Security (OK)	$290,000,000	May 21
LIW-NYC	Bastrop Savers (TX)	$180,000,000	May 14
Sunrise Proj	Bank of Magnolia (AK)	$275,000,000	(open)

"Only one account open," I said.

"My home state," Bongo said. "Last one on the timetable, like the board for a home football game."

"It's all oil patch," I said.

"Good for you, Sherlock. They're paying top dollar on CDs down there, trying to bump up their cash flow and stand off them federal regulators, so they got lots of money coming in."

"Where did the money go?" Roxanne asked.

"Thought you'd never ask, ma'am." Bongo turned over another sheet of paper in the file folder.

There was the name of a bank, Sécurité de Bruxelles,

and then the name of a company, Excalibur, Ltd. Below that was a figure of $2 billion, U.S., converted from Belgian francs.

"I been all night trying to run this one down, but they got shells on top of shells." He worked the keyboard until a list appeared on the screen. A printer started, zipping across the page. On the screen were names of companies, starting with Alpenstock, Ltd., headquarters in Stuttgart, U.S. branch office in Armonk, New York. The printer stopped, and Bongo tore off the sheet and handed it me. "We got forty-nine known subsidiaries of Excalibur—that was the name of a sword carried by a storybook King—probably all dummy outfits. It starts hereabouts with Alpenstock, which pretends to be in the wholesale sporting goods business, and ends with Viking Ice, which says it's in the frozen yogurt business."

"Frozen yogurt?" I said.

"Yup."

"Have you got an address? A phone number?"

"Haw. Rima's gathering that data now."

"Any idea what they're doing with that money?"

"Buyin' something for Christmas, I reckon. Something fancy."

I shook Bongo's hand and handed him the hundred dollar bill. "Beer money," I said.

"Thanks, Sherlock. Got a little favor to ask you when you get this one wrapped up."

"Anything," I said.

"Pal of mine named Dinny Breen's in the slammer. Thought maybe you could speak to some of your pals in Santy Anny and get him sprung."

"I'll try. What did he do?"

"Drunk and disorderly. Busted up a saloon in Messikin town. Hell, it was eight to one, the way he told it."

"Okay."

"If I haul anything else up, I'll give a holler."

"Thanks."

Before we left, I gave Rima the name of Rudolfo Cantu. She said she'd do what she could.

Rima waved as we left, then turned back to her computer screen. As we opened the door and walked out into the California sunshine, a printer started up, merrily ticking.

The sound of the future.

▌▌▌▌▌▌ 19 ▌▌▌▌▌

We made it back to my place from Bongo's without a single hit-and-run attempt. I phoned St. Boniface Hospital. The woman biker—her name was Angie Smith—had a broken leg. Her prognosis was good.

Roxanne fetched us a beer apiece while I hauled the battered chaise lounges into position for some noonday sun. Roxanne lay with her eyes closed while I cleaned and oiled the PPK. We both needed some R & R.

The Sunday version of *The Orange County Tribune,* fat with advertising, sat unopened and unread near the door. Wally St. Moritz, the guru of Punker's Strip, says advertising is one clear symptom of a corrupt and dying civilization, where the only innovation is style. The market is glutted with waste products, so the advertisers come on board to pump away the sludge. It can only go on so long, Wally says, and then we choke ourselves to death.

Stylishly.

Roxanne was lying with her eyes closed. Her voice was

thick with depression. She was having an attack of the galloping guilts.

"I should have told someone. About Emmy, I mean. If I had told them what I knew, none of this would have happened."

"You told Bruce."

"Yes, but not officially."

"Who else would you have told?"

"The police. The insurance people. Someone."

"Unload it onto Big Brother," I said.

"You don't understand."

"Ease up," I said. "All Big Brother would do is take your house and toss your butt in jail. The murder machine would chug right along."

She stared at me, her eyes angry and tired. "You're a real cynic, aren't you?"

"Have you ever been in jail?"

"No. Have you?"

"Damn right. It's not someplace you want to go."

"I was confused, in shock. I could have set things right."

"An assistant DA would hang your confusion out to dry."

Roxanne hugged her knees to her chest and rocked slowly back and forth. "I just keep seeing Emmy, dead in that car. And Bruce on that beach. And that woman on the bike. Maybe Emmy asked for it. Maybe Bruce took a chance. But she didn't."

"Look," I said. "This thing is bigger than you and Emmy. He got greedy and walked into a buzz saw. You sacrifice yourself now, this thing goes on, but without you."

"I know that in my mind, but it doesn't help me feel better."

We sat there awhile, not talking. Roxanne had her

shoes and socks off, and her legs were slick and tanned and beautiful. Tomorrow, the money—$180,000 from Emmy's secret stash—would arrive via registered mail, and she could add that to the package we had carted to New Mexico. I wondered what she would do then.

She could run.

Or she could stay.

Roxanne was hungry, so she went inside to raid the fridge. My mind felt numb and covered with gray fuzz-balls from a vacuum cleaner. I knew I should be out there detecting, but my waning energy level told me to sit still. I should hunt down Doc Ames. I should drive over to Huntington Beach and interview Sheena Mandarin. Maybe she'd thought of something else about Claude Belker. I should phone Bongo Bodette, to see if he'd turned up anything. I should trek down to Mexico and ask Rudolfo some questions. Bobby Maclean was on the list for June. I should phone him.

I went inside. Roxanne was opening a can of kippers. She had prepared a tray of cheese and crackers and ja-lapeno peppers, medium hot. I asked her if she knew Bobby Maclean's number.

"It's in my purse."

She pointed at the food tray. "Don't you have anything else to eat in this house? I'm so tired of crackers and canned peppers."

I left her talking on the phone to one of her tennis pals and went back outside to read the sport pages.

I picked up the paper. When I work, I lose touch with sports. Baseball is my favorite. My team is the Braves. I wondered how they were doing. I like the stability of sports. I'd come back from a case and open the sports page and feel that the world was cranking along as usual. Scores. Batting averages. Clowning for the crowd. I opened the Sunday paper and glanced over the front page.

The top story was all about the Arabs and the president. The topic was the price of oil. The president said the West was not going back to being held hostage by petrodollars. Those days were over, and America was drilling again. Sounded like a good idea to me. The story below the oil one detailed an airliner crash in the Mediterranean. Seventeen were known dead, sixty-eight missing.

Lower down, the mayor of Los Angeles had come to Orange County to ask for votes and money for his campaign for the governor's office. The mayor should call Excalibur, I thought. They've got two billion.

Down at the bottom of the page was a story about another air crash, a small plane in the desert out near San Bernardino. Two persons had died. The pilot was Bob Robertson, of Dana Point. The passenger was Dr. Sylvan Ames, of Newport Beach.

The box said "See Metro, 1."

My hands shook. It was still going on. Roxanne came out, holding a piece of note paper.

"I phoned his home. No one answered."

"Is Maclean married?"

"Yes. I told you. His wife's in real estate."

"Forgot. Any idea where they could be?"

"I tried the club. No luck there. Marge Duquesne said she thought they were out of town, on their boat. Mexico, perhaps."

I handed her the front page of the newspaper. "Dr. Ames died. Plane crash."

"Our Dr. Ames?"

"Looks like it."

"Are you sure?"

"And a guy named Robertson. Ever hear his name?"

"No."

"He was a Heartland agent."

She read the story on page one while I finished the follow-up in the Metro section. The plane, a single-engine job, had been en route from San Jose to San Bernardino when it had suddenly lost power. The pilot had radioed a distress call, which had been cut off in midsentence: "There's something wrong up here and I—" And that was it.

Both bodies had been badly burned. Identification had been made from personal effects found in the wreckage. The pilot was survived by a wife, Norma Robertson, and two children. Dr. Ames, a widower, was survived by two children, both of whom lived out of state. There was a mug shot of Dr. Ames, showing a guy in his mid-sixties, with thinning gray hair and a tight mouth. Information about funeral arrangements could be had by contacting Winslow Lawn, in Santa Ana.

I finished reading and handed the rest of the story to Roxanne. Her face was thoughtful and worried as she put the paper down.

"Ames," I said. "Robertson. Add them to Bruce's list."

She looked distracted. Her face was pale beneath the tan as she reached over and grabbed my arm, digging in sharp fingernails. "Let's leave town, Matt. We've got Emmy's money. Let's just pack up and—"

Roxanne went inside, hugging herself. I reread the story about Dr. Sylvan Ames. I dozed, woke up, drank another beer. Just after five, Bongo called with the phone numbers and the locations of Viking Ice. There were a dozen outlets, all in major metropolitan areas. We had one ourselves, right here in Orange County. I wrote down the address, 126 Waverley Circle, an industrial park off Placentia, in Costa Mesa. I showed it to Roxanne. "I'm going over there."

She shook her head. "No. Don't."

"You can stay with Leo."

"Leo?"

"Leo Castelli. He owns the café downstairs."

She gave me a long, sad look. "No. Damn you. I'm coming along."

I said okay. While we waited for twilight, Roxanne spent a long time looking at the pictures of my folks. There was one of the Sergeant as a young buck just before he married my mother in the late 1930s. There were two of my mother. One showed her with her cap and gown, graduating from high school in Minnesota. The other showed her walking down the street in El Paso, looking feisty and attractive. There was one of the two of them together, taken when I was four or five. The war was over by then and the Sergeant was coming home from the Pacific, and so my mother had taken me on the train from El Paso to meet him. The photo had been taken in San Francisco. In the background was the Golden Gate Bridge.

Roxanne did not mention the three photos of the ladies on the wall. But she did rummage in the fridge for more cheese and crackers. There was no more bitching about the food. I drank a Bud. I could have downed a six-pack for my nerves, but I needed a clear head.

I spent an hour with my guns, doing the pre-battle ritual. I checked the PPK. I unlocked the drawer of my gun cabinet and took out the Colt Diamondback and two speed-loaders. The disadvantage of a revolver is that you can't use a silencer because the explosion blows back at your eyeballs. I checked the barrel, which needed cleaning, and then I swabbed it out.

At twilight, we climbed into the Ranger and headed off toward Viking Ice. My plan was just to look around. It was Sunday. I didn't figure anyone would be working. In the lock box in back I had a kit of tools—a magnesium flashlight, wire cutters, picture wire with a seventy-five pound test, a cat's paw pry bar, a tape measure, my leather case of lock picks, a rechargeable portable electric drill, a hole saw, and a flat metal rod four feet long. When I was in the carpentry business, I used the rod as a saw guide.

"You think he'll be there?"

"Who?"

"The white-haired man. Jerome."

"Nah. It's Sunday."

"He looks so . . . spooky. Those eyes. That white hair."

I patted her on the leg. "We'll get him, kid."

The sun was fading behind a dark gray cloud bank as we drove up Newport Boulevard into the warehouse section of Costa Mesa. We passed three moving companies, an electrical manufacturer, two blocks of solid warehouses, and Fiorentino's Car Repair.

Three blocks past Fiorentino's, we entered a labyrinth of narrow streets. Waverly curved right into a cul-de-sac. A yellow sign said No Through Street. I stopped the Ford, got out, and opened up the lock box. I put the picture wire in my pocket, along with the wire cutters, and jogged around the corner. Number 126 was surrounded by a cyclone fence. Inside the fence were four buildings. One was an office, a prefab temporary with beige walls and a matching roof. The other three buildings were industrial-size refrigerators, with those big wide doors that swing open so the forklifts can drive right in. A small sign on one of the refrigerators said Viking Ice and below that, Nordic Frozen Yogurt.

A gray Volvo was parked near the office. It had a dent in the left front fender and a scrape along the driver's door.

Two vans without markings were inside the fence. A

dingy brown one idled in a parking slot against Building #3. A gray van was backed up to the loading dock of Building #2. As I watched through the fence, a forklift whined out of the doorway, carrying an oversize cardboard drum, the kind used to store bulk ice cream. From this distance the storage cylinder seemed to be three feet in diameter and six feet tall.

The tines of the forklift raised the cardboard drum up to the level of the bed on the gray van and ladelled it on. There was apparently someone inside the truck to manhandle the drums into position. The forklift tuned and headed back inside.

Roxanne came up beside me, breathing heavily. There was sweat on her forehead. "Those containers look heavy."

"Just what I was thinking."

"What do we do now?"

"They're pulling out, going somewhere."

"Matt. Let's call the police. Someone."

"Right."

On the post above the main gate, a closed-circuit television camera swiveled in an arc of 150 degrees. The gate was closed. On the end nearest us was a hydraulic motor. To activate the motor, you shoved a coded key card into the slit of a black box mounted on a concrete piling in front of the gate. If you had the right card, the gate opened.

The forklift made one more grinding run at the gray van. When the loading was completed, a man in grease-stained orange coveralls jumped down and swung the doors closed. There was no departure ceremony, no checking of lists on clipboards. The man secured the doors, climbed up behind the wheel, honked his horn, and wheeled his van over to the gate.

The gate slid open.

I made a decision.

"Take the pickup and get to a phone and call the Costa Mesa cops. Tell them a burglary's in progress at this address. If someone tries to stop you, blow them away."

"You mean shoot them?"

"Yeah. Use the pistol."

"You're going in, aren't you?"

"That's the plan."

I checked the magazine on the PPK, hoping the ritual would steady my nerves. It didn't. The gray van was coming through the gate, and the brown van was backing up to the loading dock. From all the signs, it looked like Viking Ice was relocating its inventory.

"Matt." Roxanne clutched my arm. "I don't like this."

"No time, kid." I pulled back into the shadows as the van slid past. The gate had started to close. This was my only chance. The keys were in the pickup. With the PPK held high, I ran through the shadows to the gate of Viking Ice.

I slid through with inches to spare and hid for a moment behind Building #2, where a compressor went thump-a-whump, thump-a-whump. It looked like a five-ton unit, about the size for a restaurant fridge. It was a York. I'd worked on Yorks in Vietnam, where they were used to cool the staff HQ and make shaved ice for the general's gin and tonic. In the jungle they used ammonia instead of freon. Ammonia was highly toxic. A leak could mean an explosion. An explosion might give me time.

I noted the position of the York and jogged through the gathering darkness to the Volvo. It was unlocked. I popped the hood, cracked the distributor cap, pulled out the rotor, and jerked loose some wires. One strip of masking tape clung to the license plate on the Volvo. It was Bruce's car, all right.

I jogged to the prefab office, opened the door and stepped inside. A man was working the keys of a computer. He had a lean face and a Max Headroom haircut. The nameplate on the desk said Roger. He saw me and then he saw the pistol. His eyes widened. He hit a key on the computer, raised his hands, and stood up. The computer screen went blank.

I shoved him against the wall for a body check while I asked him about the contingent.

"Three of them are accomplishing the loading," Roger said. His accent was European, educated, snotty. "That does not include the driver."

"Who's in charge?"

"He is called Jerome."

"Where are they taking the containers?"

"To a new location."

"What's inside?"

He smiled. "Inventory."

I wired Roger's wrists together. He did not resist. He moaned and sweated. He smiled and wet his lips and stuck out his tongue in what could only be a flirtatious manner. I got the feeling Roger liked pain.

"What were you doing with the computer?"

"Communicating. With Europe."

"What about?"

"The inventory."

"Frozen yogurt, right?"

Roger's grin pulled the skin tight across his skull. "That is correct."

I waited around for thirty seconds, hoping to hear the sound of sirens. The vans could hold six containers, maybe eight. How many more to go?

There was one guy on the forklift and one in the van. I saw someone moving inside the warehouse, but there was too much shadow to make anything out. I waited until the forklift had wheeled around, and then I ran for the van.

The driver was a big bruiser in a yellow jumpsuit. There was sweat under his arms. His eyes narrowed when he saw the gun. His hands went up. I waved him back into the van and climbed on.

The van held six containers, with room for two more. The cylinder nearest me said "Strawberry Ice" in heavy black letters. The next one said "French Vanilla." The one next to that said "Frappe." I wired the driver's wrists together. You could tell the driver had seen guns before. He didn't say a word.

I heard the whine of the forklift approaching the van. The twilight had reached that point of near-dark which makes it hard to see. As the forklift raised the twin cardboard cylinders, I dropped down to the asphalt and shoved the muzzle of the PPK into the operator's ribs.

It was the white-haired man.

Jerome.

He stared down at me through bleak eyes rimmed with garish pink. His accent was British, bitter, snotty. "You are a dead man, mister."

I hauled him down and used the last of the picture wire on his wrists. With his hands behind him, I marched Jerome into Building #3, where two Asians in blue pants and matching white shirts were rolling a container into position for the forklift. The letters on the container said "Chocolate Mousse." It was cold in here, like a meat locker. There were five containers left. Two more would fill the van.

One of the Asians spoke English. I gestured him to the floor, with his pal and Jerome. Their hands were locked over their heads. Jerome turned his head to the side and stared at me out of his pale, pink-rimmed eyes.

Watching the men on the floor, I moved to the cylinder marked "Chocolate Mousse." A number was printed near the top, the letters two inches high. "CM: Unit 703." I popped the lid open and looked inside.

It was a man, top of the head, shoulders. He had dark hair around a monk's bald spot. He was nameless, and he was frozen solid. I popped the top on the next cylinder, "Blueberry Fruit," knowing what I'd find.

It was another frozen corpse.

One Asian was crawling toward the door. He stopped when he saw me watching and locked his hands over his head. As I squatted down next to Jerome, I wondered where the cops were. Roxanne had had five minutes, maybe more. Enough time to make a phone call.

"Okay, Jerome. Who are these guys, and where are they going?"

"You're a dead man, mister."

I stuck the muzzle of the PPK in his ear so he could hear the sharp click of the action as I thumbed back the hammer. "I want Claude Belker, Jerome. That's where I started."

"Never heard of him."

"I'm going to count to three, Jerome, and then—"

There was movement at the doorway of the big refrigerator. Roger, I thought. He'd wriggled loose.

But then I saw against the glare from the lights on the loading dock a double silhouette, and a man's voice called my name: "Murdock?"

"Who is it?"

"Al Dugger. We met yesterday, at LAX. Don't shoot."

"Who's with you?"

Dugger didn't answer for a moment. Then I saw why. He had Roxanne. He was holding her by the hair, tilting her head back until her neck was all tight cords. A gun was in his other hand.

To my right I heard Jerome chuckling.

"Mister, you are dead."

214

20

The cold woke me.

My teeth were chattering and my ears burned and I remembered being this cold in Germany, when I was a young hotdog corporal in Uncle Sam's army. It was dark. I remembered being bruised by Jerome's meaty fists, but the icy cold had driven away my other pains. I tried to move and couldn't. My hands were manacled in front of me where Dugger had chained me to the wall.

The building had no windows. My chain gave me no slack. I pulled myself up, bracing my back against the wall. My hands were numb from the cold, but I knew the metal was cutting into them. Getting to my feet was no better because I had to stand bent over. When I tried to squat down, a muscle cramped in my leg. I did not know what time it was. And Dugger was out there, hurting Roxanne.

Dugger was working for Death, Inc. Maybe everyone

was. Maybe it was a great company, with wonderful perks. Maybe I could get a job there myself.

I straightened up again, and the chain seemed to move. My hands were icy and the inside of the fridge was dark, so I wasn't sure. Couldn't remember the goddamn room. Where was Roxanne?

Okay, you're a pro. Try to remember. Dugger had dragged you past the ice cream cylinders. There were dead people in those cylinders. You remember being pistol-whipped, cuffed, stepped on, and that's making you weak.

They made jokes about you. They called you "inventory." "Murdock on ice," they said.

I braced myself and tightened the chain. I thought it gave. I hoped it gave. Panting now, feeling the cold in my bones like a dark wheezing dullness, I tugged again. What was I cuffed to? Handles? Pipes? Stove bolts? Welds? How long had I been out?

I pulled again, feeling my wrists loose in their sockets. I grabbed the handle with my hands and pulled. Things were moving. I squatted down so I could use my legs. The cramped muscle tightened. I kept pulling, willing away the pain.

The legs were weak. I strained and nothing happened. I readjusted, cursing Dugger, cursing myself for sending Roxanne off. The cops weren't coming. Leon Book was home watching television. Webby Smith was out on the beach, toning his body for the Iron Man. I would never see them again. Murdock, R.I.P. The skin on my wrists burned. Was it heat? Or was it cold? There would be blood. Mine. I kept pulling. Even if I pulled away, then what?

My wrists moved again—I could not tell how far—and I heard something give. A creaking and a metallic tearing. I pumped the metal back and forth. It was loose now. My heart sang. I pumped and the metal tore, and then my hands were free above my head and something went clank on the floor and the momentum sent me sprawling into a hard and unforgiving wall.

I lay there for a moment, panting, and then I began to crawl, feeling my way along the wall, moving away from the cold coming from the blower. I had to get warm. Had to find a weapon. Had to find a light switch. Had to help Roxanne. Maybe I could drive the forklift through the wall. Cool idea. There was a strong whumpa-de-whump sound coming from the compressor.

I reached the door. It took me long moments of fumbling to find the light switch. When it clicked on, I had to wait with my eyes slitted against the brightness. I was not in the room with the forklift and the coffins shaped like cylinders. They had chained me to a wall bracket, which now lay on the floor, twisted out of shape. I guessed I was inside the fridge of Building #2.

Building #2 was the one with the bad compressor.

I opened the door and stumbled outside. The night air felt balmy. A brown Chevrolet was parked in front of the prefab office. There was no sign of my pickup. Had the repo man come at last? I wasn't thinking clearly. I fell down twice on the way to the rear of the building. The compressor was clunkier now. Grasping the shut-down valve sent pain through me. I gritted my teeth and turned the valve. For a couple of seconds, nothing happened. Then the compressor changed from its chug-a-lug rotation to a grinding groan, metal on metal, and I backed out of there.

With a deadly whoosh, the compressor exploded. Gas hissed out. You didn't need a Ph.D. in chemistry to know that stuff was poison. I sucked in a deep gulp of air and hobbled back along the wall to the parking lot, where I stopped at the corner. My brain hurt. I could not focus.

The raw stink of ammonia tainted the air. I started for the Chevrolet. Where was Roxanne?

The door to the prefab opened and Dugger stepped out onto the porch. He was holding a baby flame-thrower, made especially for the mercenary market.

It was a wonderful tool for torching thatched roof huts in Africa, burning up the homes of the innocent.

Dugger's coat was off and his dress shirt was unbuttoned and he had left his tie somewhere. His gut sagged down over his belt. The tails of the shirt were not tucked in. "You bastard, Murdock."

I looked around for a weapon and didn't see anything. The front gate was closed. No escape there. I edged toward the door of Building #1, with Dugger tracking me with the nozzle on the flame thrower.

"Where are your pals, Dugger?"

"Gone. I stayed behind, to entertain the lady. She's something, Murdock. A real cat, she is." He brandished the nozzle of the flame thrower. "Ever smell burning butt, Murdock?" And then he chuckled and pressed the trigger.

I back pedalled as he blasted me. The flames fell short, fanning out like water from a hose set on the spray control. I picked up a rock, but with my hands manacled I had to toss it overhand. It missed. I kept moving, keeping the distance between us. There was one white spotlight beaming down from Building #3. A sea breeze came up, shoving the toxic compressor smoke inland.

Dugger passed into shadow so I couldn't see his eyes. I backed up against a wall, tripped, and went to my knees. Dugger made an adjustment on the flame thrower and a bright tongue of flame sliced through the cold air, igniting the wall behind me. He stopped to make another adjustment and I headed for the fence. Maybe there was a hole I could crawl through.

218

"You know what they say about the thin ones, Murdock?"

"Up yours."

"The meat is sweet, they say, when it's closer to the bone."

"I'll kill you, Dugger."

He laughed, and I decided to rush him. I was going to burn anyway. Maybe I could jostle him off-balance. I leaned against the fence, trying to work up the last bit of energy. I felt courageous. I thought of that old movie about Joan of Arc, the fake flames that had made me sweat as a kid.

Burning is not a good way to die.

Dugger edged closer. His face was in shadow, but I could see the expression on his face. Smug, confident, earnest.

"You're my last detail, Murdock. The inventory's in a safe place. I roast your butt, then it's down to Mexico for a month of sun and señoritas."

Behind Dugger, a figure appeared on the porch of the prefab office.

It was Roxanne, naked from the waist up, wearing the jeans she had borrowed from me. She had something in her hand, a stick about eighteen inches long, and she was moving toward Dugger. Her hair looked mussed. The stick was cocked in the air like a baseball bat.

Keep him occupied.

"The cops have your name, Dugger. I told them who you were. They'll be after your fat ass."

Dugger chuckled. It was the sound of a man who has outsmarted a lot of people and who intends to go on doing it. "You and Halliburton, you're not so fucking smart. He thought he could squeeze the Big Guy for dough. Wanted a bundle, he did. Now he's dead. You thought you could close us down. Now you're dead."

"I thought you were the Big Guy, Dugger."

Dugger chuckled, and his face shook. I had tickled his vanity.

Roxanne was four long steps away when Dugger heard her. As he turned, I was up and running. With a horrible bloody shriek, Roxanne bounded forward, swinging her stick, catching Dugger on the shoulder. The stick, a rough redwood two-by-four, bounced off the shoulder and bonked him in the cheek, right under the eyeball. He was swinging the flame thrower up, but then he let go with one hand to feel his cheek, where Roxanne had whapped him, and before he got into action again, I hit him with a body block.

I had about enough force left in my frozen bones to punch through a wet paper sack. But I was lucky and caught him off-balance and that knocked him to his knees and Roxanne hit him again.

He dropped the flame thrower, which hit the asphalt surface with a clunk. Crying now, her eyes raging with tears, Roxanne slugged him a third time. This one caught him above the eye on the left side, drawing blood, and he went over in a soggy heap. Roxanne was crying my name and cursing him all in the same straggly sentence. She kept her stick going as he went down, pounding, pounding, lashing out, the stick tinged with blood now.

She jabbed the end of the stick at Dugger's gut, kept on poking him, like a cowboy digging a post-hole, the wood punishing his flesh. She wanted revenge. If I hadn't stopped her, she would have been jabbing at him still, paying him back.

"Easy," I said. "Easy."

"Oh, God!" she said. "He did some—"

The tears ran down her cheeks. She moaned, sagged down into my arms, throwing me off balance. I wanted out of there, in case Jerome and his pals came back.

"Oh, Matt," Roxanne moaned. "Oh, darling."

"Are you okay?"

There was a long moment while we clung to each other. "Yes," she said. "Now I am."

"Help me up. Find the goddam keys."

Dugger was out. The keys to the handcuffs were in his jacket pocket, along with his driver's license, car keys, a white handkerchief with a stitched monogram, A.F.D., and business cards from South Coast Life. There was a wad of hundreds in the wallet. I tucked those into my shirt pocket. Blood spots were drying on Dugger's bruised belly, where Roxanne had jabbed him. Maybe I should have let her keep poking.

Roxanne unlocked my cuffs. Her sweatshirt had been ripped off, so she threw Dugger's suit coat over her shoulders. I locked his hands with his own cuffs. And then I took a couple of turns through the prefab office.

The papers had been cleared out of the drawers. The computers were gone. The phones were out of service. No dial tone. The only thing left was Roger's nameplate, brass letters on a black field, and a cheap digital clock that said 9:47. We'd hit Viking Ice around 8:00. Almost two hours in that locker.

"I tried phoning," Roxanne said. "When he left me alone. The line was dead."

"Where was the hunk of wood?"

"In a closet. I was hunting for something . . . to cover myself. Then he went out holding that thing and I saw you and—"

I pressed the switch to open the gate and we went back outside.

The explosion of the compressor had set fire to Building #1, and Dugger's torch had ignited Building #2. Now, orange flames licked at the roof. A couple of minutes and the fire department would arrive.

"Where's the pickup?"

"I don't know. He grabbed the keys."

"Pricks."

Dugger was heavy. It took everything we had to bundle him into the Chevrolet. Blood had dried on his shirt front and he breathed noisily through his mouth. Roxanne was trembling now, her teeth chattering. "You okay to drive?"

She nodded, but did not speak.

With Roxanne at the wheel, we drove through the gate. Dugger's coat ballooned open in front. One strand of hair fell across her face. She drove too fast, a sign of nerves.

"Slow down, okay?"

"All right."

As we headed out of the labyrinth of streets, we heard the first siren. Roxanne drove south on Newport Boulevard to Coast Highway. Traffic coming across the Lido overpass was heavy for a Sunday evening. We drove past familiar spots—the Lido Spa, Thirty-One Flavors, the Kentucky Fried Chicken place—and I wondered if I would ever feel safe again.

Roxanne parked with a thump in my parking slot behind Wally's surf shop. Next door, at Leo's cafe, a light burned. I waited with Dugger in the car while she went into Leo's Café for a spare house key. Dugger moaned and shifted his weight. I studied him in the half-dark. He didn't seem to be waking up yet. Maybe he'd die. Tough shit.

Leo came out, looking strong and fit, and helped us up the stairs. My living room had an eerie feel. Was this nest safe? Roxanne went into the bathroom and closed the door. Leo made coffee. I could hear Roxanne throwing up, and then the sound of water running. Dugger opened one eye and stared at me and then the eye snapped shut. I stood up and started over to him, but stopped halfway when the shakes got me. I sagged to the sofa and asked Leo to phone Wally St. Moritz.

Roxanne came out, looking battered but determined. She wore one of my shirts and a heavy hooded sweat shirt. I gave Roxanne some arnica and then I took some and finally, after a delay, I popped five pellets into Dugger's mouth.

By the time Wally St. Moritz arrived, clucking like a mother hen, Dugger's eyes were open and he was staring around like a prisoner of the KGB.

If he didn't die, I could still have the pleasure of killing him.

‖‖‖‖21‖‖‖‖

We needed a change of clothes and a bath. We needed to shuck the experience at Viking Ice and turn Dugger over to the cops. But he knew things that I wanted to know.

And Wally St. Mortiz knew hypnosis.

We left Wally alone with Dugger for about five minutes, so he could take him under. Roxanne lay on the bed, staring at nothing, while Leo helped me work up some questions. My attention kept drifting. What was happening at Viking Ice? Where had Jerome and Company taken all those dead bodies, the frozen ones? How many more were there? Who did Dugger work for? Where was the eye of the octopus?

Wally came to the door to fetch us. He had on new tennis warm-ups, a green jacket and matching pants, with three stripes and an Adidas logo. "He's under," Wally said.

I handed him the questions.

"Good work, Matthew," Wally said as he read the questions. "Can I veer from the recommended scenario to pursue an issue that feels warmish?"

"Sure."

"He's pretty far under, and it's my voice he trusts. So if you have something urgent, give me the signal and I'll break off and we'll consult."

"Okay."

"How are you feeling? How is the lady?"

Roxanne came to the door. She had brushed her hair and washed her beautiful face. A bruise was forming under her left eye. There would be other bruises, some you could see, some you could not. She had changed into one of my shirts and a baggy pair of khakis.

"Well," Wally said. "You are feeling better, my dear."

Leo took one of my guns and went outside to stand guard. Roxanne sat in the easy chair, knees together. I lowered myself into a director's chair. Dugger was lying on his side on the sofa, his eyes closed. His head was battered, and he might need medical attention, but I knew if the cops got him, they'd never find out anything.

It was now or never.

He'd raped Roxanne. He'd tried to kill me. I'd given him arnica. He was a prick. I wanted him dead.

Wally pulled up a kitchen chair and began asking the questions. Leo started the tape recorder. Dugger answered in a calm voice:

Q: What is your name?

A: Al.

Q: What is your full name?

A: Alfred Franklin Dugger.

Q: Where were you born, Al?

225

A: Queens, New York.

Q: How old are you?

A: Forty-three.

Q: Are you married?

A: Not any more.

Q: Where are you employed?

A: I work for Excalibur.

Q: What do you do?

A: Enforcement and disposal.

Q: Who runs Excalibur, Al?

A: The Big Guy.

Q: What's the Big Guy's name?

A: No idea.

Q: Where does he live?

A: Europe.

Q: Where in Europe?

A: Not a clue.

Q: Have you ever seen the Big Guy?

A: Nope.

Q: Do you know a doctor named Ames?

A: Sure.

Q: Where did you meet him?

A: Company seminar.

Q: Where was the seminar?

A: Corona del Mar.

Q: Was it in a private home?

A: Yeah. We call it the Safe House.

Q: Where is the Safe House?

A: Corona Del Mar.

Q: What street?

A: Columbine. It's right on the ocean.

Q: Who lives in the house?

A: Jerome.

Q: The man with the white hair?

A: Yes.

Q: What is Jerome's last name?

A: Said it was Flanner.

Q: Is that his real name?

A: How the fuck should I know?

Q: Why was Mr. Mendez-Madrid killed, Al?

A: Who?

Q: Emiliano Mendez-Madrid. Why was he killed?

A: Oh, you mean The Laundryman.

Q: Yes.

A: It was a mistake.

Q: In what way?

A: They were taking him back.

Q: Back where?

A: Switzerland. Where the banks are.

Q: For what purpose?

A: He owed money. He tried to wiggle out of it. The Big Guy wanted him back so he could pay what he owed.

Q: How much did he owe?

A: I got no idea. Must have been a bundle.

Q: What did he launder?

A: He was a greenwasher. Money.

Q: Where did the money come from?

A: Mostly South America.

Q: Was it from drugs? The slave trade? What?

A: Eighty percent from drugs.

Q: Who killed Bruce Halliburton?

A: Some local guy. I never met him.

Q: Why did Halliburton have to die?

A: He was dumb. Tried a shakedown. Wanted two million bucks.

Q: Who ordered his death, the Big Guy?

A: I guess.

Q: Do you know the name Rudolfo Cantu?

A: Sure. Slick Rudolfo.

Q: Does he work for the Big Guy?

A: Nah. Cantu's an independent.

Q: And what is his business, exactly?

A: He runs coke up from Mexico, through Cocaine Alley.

Q: And what was his connection with Mr. Mendez-Madrid?

A: He was doing what a laundryman does. Washing the money.

Q: How was he doing that, Al?

A: Not my department.

Q: Where is Jerome taking the yogurt cartons?

A: We call them units.

Q: Where are they taking the units?

A: Another facility.

Q: What kind?

A: Aftermarket.

Q: Where is the facility, Al?

A: Irvine.

Q: Where in Irvine?

A: Peters Canyon.

Q: Is there a name?

A: Some kind of lab.

Q: Do you know the name?

A: Map-tel. Grap-tel. Something like that.

Q: What happens in the aftermarket, Al?

A: The old organ-swap meet.

Dugger's eyes blazed up and his face creased into a greasy grin and he started chuckling. The chuckle built into a laugh. Wally sat back and stared at Dugger for a long moment. Then he shook his head, looked over at us, and held a finger to his lips. When Dugger's laughter wound down, Wally asked a couple more questions:

Q: What were your orders about Murdock and the lady, Al?

A: Get rid of the bodies.

Q: How?

A: My choice.

Q: When and how were you supposed to contact Jerome?

A: Phone him from Mexico, in about a week.

Q: What were your plans for Mrs. Mendez-Madrid?

A: Take her to Mexico.

Q: And what then?

A: Have some laughs. Teach the bitch some obedience.

Q: And after that?

A: She's a looker. She'd bring a good price.

Q: Sell her, you mean?

A: Yeah.

Dugger grunted, his grin widening. "What a waste."

Wally asked a few more questions, going back over ground that he'd already covered, but then he stopped and motioned Roxanne and me to the bedroom. Leo stayed with Dugger.

"There's not much more there," he whispered. "He was a small man in a small job. He's never seen Mr. Big. His organization—Excalibur, was it?—probably uses the cell structure to stratify information access."

"Need to know?" I asked.

Wally nodded and the light flashed off his glasses. "Precisely. If we knew things in more depth, we might solicit deeper responses."

"It's not enough, Wally."

"I'm afraid that's all there is."

"I want Jerome." My voice was shaky. "I want the Big Guy."

Roxanne took my arm. "We're not doing anything tonight. That . . . person needs medical attention. We need medical attention. We need rest."

Wally nodded. "She's right, Matthew."

"What about him?" I nodded toward Dugger.

"Leo and I can take him to the police station. Phone your contact and tell him we're en route. What's the location of this Viking Ice?"

"Costa Mesa."

"The crime was committed there, so they have jurisdiction. When I last ran for the City Council, there was news of a triadic law enforcement relationship between Costa Mesa, Irvine, and Newport. Your prisoner is responding to the arnica. He'll live. Let the police take it from here."

I was tired and shaky. "Okay, Professor. Thanks."

He pressed Roxanne's hand in his, clucked once, and went off to take Dugger to jail.

"What a sweet man," Roxanne said as I closed and locked the door.

"On the tennis court he's a real killer."

With a shudder Roxanne came into my arms. "I never liked that word."

"Sorry."

"I don't think I'll ever play again."

"Why?"

"It seems so . . . frivolous. Now."

I pulled down the Winchester Defender from the gun rack and made sure it was loaded. The short barrel is just barely legal. It's very handy at close range. I gave Roxanne a Smith and Wesson .38 for the bathroom. She showered first, taking a long time under the spray. I rewound the Dugger tape and locked it in with the guns. I phoned Bongo Bodette and asked him to check on Jerome Flanner and the lab—Map-tel or Grap-tel—in Irvine. Then I phoned Leon Book at home and told him about the arrival of Al Dugger.

"Another alleged perp." Leon was yawning. "What's he done?"

"Not much. He started a fire at Viking Ice with a flame thrower. Assaulted a lady. Tried to kill me."

"What's this Viking Ice?"

"A frozen yogurt plant, over in Costa Mesa."

"That's out of my jurisdiction, Sherlock."

"Just book this guy, Leon. And call your look-alike in Costa Mesa."

"There's my other line, Sherlock. Got to rush."

"Bye, Leon."

Roxanne came out wearing heavy socks and a long terry cloth robe. "I still feel dirty," she said.

I nodded and went into the shower, where I stayed until the hot water ran tepid. My eyes streamed tears as I dried off. I blew my nose on a tissue. They had come close to getting me tonight, freezing me, burning me up. I'd had the drop on Jerome and Dugger had come up behind me. I stayed in the bathroom for five minutes, waiting for the shakes to subside.

Roxanne lay on her side in the fetal position. I climbed into bed, not touching her. She said nothing and was still.

"Are you all right?" I asked.

She shifted on the bed. "I will be."

I was exhausted, but could not sleep. I kept replaying the scene in my mind—the ice cream containers, the computer hookup to Europe, Dugger and the fire extinguisher, Jerome's crazy albino eyes, Roxanne going after Dugger with the stick of wood—and asking the big question: Excalibur had money. What were they going to buy?

I dozed off. Around midnight, I came spinning out of an ugly dream to find the sheet tangled around my feet. Roxanne was not in the bed. I found her in the kitchen, sipping a glass of red wine. "I didn't want to wake you," she said.

I touched her gently on the shoulder and she flinched.

"Sorry," she said, pulling away. "My nerves are shot."

I opened a beer and took it back to the bedroom, where I flipped on the television. Roxanne followed me after a moment. Before climbing into bed, she turned the dial to Channel Three, where a news team was pulling together a report about the situation at Viking Ice. We watched it without speaking.

There were some long-range shots of the parking lot at Viking Ice, where firemen in yellow jackets sprayed water on a building in flames. In another shot policemen were knotted around Bruce's Volvo. On the screen the scene receded to a safe distance, making you think the violence had happened to two other people. Alicia Concazar, an attractive anchor person with a movie star's smile and a probable annual income of $250,000, gave a cheery run-down of the alleged scenario in a wonderful Happy Talk style:

"Earlier this evening, fire broke out at Viking Ice, a frozen yogurt facility in the industrial district of Costa Mesa. Fire department units arriving on the scene discovered one abandoned vehicle, seen here on your screen in a cameo. Authorities are at this moment working to forge a connection between the vehicle and the blaze. Arson is suspected.

"Two of the four buildings burned to the foundation. Forensics investigators discovered blood, human tissue, and other signs of recent violence. A miniature flame thrower was seized at the scene. Police are checking the device for fingerprints. This weapon, from a Belgian manufacturer, is illegal. Channel Three's Donald Swearingen is on the scene in Costa Mesa and will keep us informed as these events unfold. Oh, here's something, just released. The vehicle was a 1988 Volvo Turbo, gray in color. The license plate number is being printed across the bottom of the screen. This vehicle was involved in a homicide on Friday, and police are now requesting that anyone with any information about the vehicle or its driver please call the number at . . ." Alicia paused to peer offscreen. "Do we have that number?" There was a long wait while someone answered. Alicia nodded, fixed her smile in place, and came back on. "We'll have that number for you after the break. Stay with us for more developments in Costa Mesa."

I turned down the volume again as an advertisement came on screen. It showed a calm suburban scene, with Mom and Dad and those two tow-headed kids biking along a residential street lined with leafy trees. Off to the right, looming up, was a red, white, and blue ranch-style family dwelling, five bedrooms, three baths, and a homey family room. An American flag flew proudly from the front yard, which was a perfect television green. The advertisement was for Heartland Mutual life insurance. "Stay safe with Heartland," the slogan said. It was a honey.

"Now what?" Roxanne said.

"Now we wait."

"Wait for what?"

"Maybe Bongo will turn something up."

"I'm afraid, Matt."

"So am I."

"What if it doesn't work?"

"That's the risk you take."

"You don't even have a plan."

"People have said that to me before."

Roxanne shivered and touched my arm. "I will never feel safe again. I will never feel clean."

I patted her shoulder, and she let go of my arm. "Takes time."

"A thousand years," she said, turning her back to me. "Two thousand."

The Winchester was on the floor, where I could reach it. I tossed and turned, trying to get comfortable for sleep. I kept the television on, with the volume turned down. There were no more Heartland commercials. The Heartland audience always sleeps safe and snug in its bed.

22

The phone jarred me awake. Roxanne stirred beside me. The bedside clock said 6:28. The caller was Leon Book, and his voice was angry.

"Okay, Sherlock. What's going on?"

"Who is this?"

"Leon Book. I want you down at the station with the phantom lady. You're both going to make a statement and fast."

"Statement about what?"

"What went down at Viking Ice."

"Hey, that's Costa Mesa. Not your territory, Leon."

"We're cooperating with the Costa Mesa PD to try and clean this mess up. That Volvo turned up."

"What Volvo?"

"Don't dummy up on me. The one your pal was driving. Halliburton, the insurance guy."

"I didn't notice any Volvo."

"They had it on television."

"I was watching *Casablanca*."

Leon shouted at me. "I want your goddamn ass down here, Murdock. I want a signed statement, everything you know, starting with the Belker business and that Volvo. I may lock you up with the goonies and the drunks and throw away the goddam key!"

"Okay, Leon. Okay."

"Eight hundred hours. Got that?"

"Gotcha."

"One other thing. Your pals Castelli and St. Moritz delivered a perp to us—Digger, no, Dugger—and he looks like he's been run over by a beer truck. He's signed a complaint against you for assault and battery."

"I told you about him last night. He set the fires. His prints should be on that flame-thrower."

"Eight o'clock!" He broke the connection.

I got out of bed and pulled on shorts and a T-shirt. Fog lay on the deserted beach like straggles of wispy gray hair. My ankles were cold. I turned on the burner under the tea kettle and went back to the bedroom and dressed. New socks, clean underwear. Maybe they would help me forget what had happened. The socks felt toasty. I put on a blue work shirt and my down vest. We were having what the natives call typical June weather, gray sky until noon, and then the molten California burn-off.

I was ready for some sun. After my time in the meat-locker, I would never be warm again.

While the water boiled, I ground beans for Murdock Blend. My formula changes with the availability of beans. Today I used one part Kenya, one part Viennese, and two parts Yuban. The Yuban beans were ripe with coffee oils.

I have seven coffee-makers. A lady friend told me I should throw them all away and update my lifestyle by using a Mr. Coffee maker, but she did not understand the depths of this particular ritual. Automatic screws it up.

I rinsed the white enamel pot and tucked in a filter paper. I measured out two mounded dollops of ground beans and filled the white cone with boiling water. Coffee aromas filled the room.

When the world blows apart, I turn to familiar ritual— shaving, bathing, making a pot of coffee, reading the sports pages. It helps. A little.

I filled two mugs with Murdock Blend and carried them into the bedroom. Roxanne was awake. She looked wonderful in the morning, rested, safe, dark hair caressing brown shoulders. The bruise on her cheek was turning green. The puffiness was almost gone. As I handed her the coffee, I wondered how the bruises were inside. She took a sip. "Hmm. Good."

"Murdock Blend," I said.

"You have so many talents. Who was on the phone?"

"Leon Book. He knows we're not dead. He wants a statement. He's inching toward a connection between Bruce and Viking Ice."

"Do we have a plan?"

"Leon said if we didn't show up, he'd send in the SWAT team."

"He sounds determined."

The phone rang and I picked it up. The caller was Rima Beaukirk, Bongo's pixie friend. She said Bongo said to read *The Orange County Tribune,* page one of the business section. There was a story about Golden Bear Savings and Loan.

"Thanks," I said.

"Oh, there was something else."

"Great."

"Those names you asked me to check on, Cantu, Rudolfo, and Flanner, Jerome?"

"Right."

"There was nothing on Flanner, Jerome. We ran the houses on Columbine, in Corona Mar. Owners of record don't include any Flanner. Bongo's working on a printout of them now, but some of it's not on computer."

"Thanks for trying."

"On the Cantu, Rudolfo, I penetrated an official police data base somewhere—Bongo figures it was Interpol, over in Europe—and there he was, Cantu, Rudolfo, right alongside of a ten-digit numerical code. He's the head of a syndicate with headquarters in Mexico. Bongo said the last three digits in the code meant drugs."

"What's the name of the syndicate?"

"It's called Los Primos. In English, that means 'the Cousins.'"

"Thanks, Rima. I owe you."

"Mr. Murdock?"

"Yes."

"Cousin Lucy June said I should ask could you carry me along sometime? On a case I mean? She said it was terrible exciting, what you do."

"Okay, Rima. It's a deal."

"Oh. And we're working on that old lab in Irvine. Nothing yet."

I thanked Rima again and walked across the quad and paid a quarter for a copy of my local newspaper. A note under the banner under the headline on the front page said circulation was 350,000 strong. I took out the business section and set the rest of the paper on top of the glassed-in sales box. The story was on page one, under the headline "British Conglomerate to Buy Local S & L."

I read the story.

The conglomerate was named Stonehenge, with headquarters in London. The local savings and loan was Golden Bear, Claude Belker's outfit. The offer had been made by representatives of Stonehenge—no names of the officers were given—and accepted by regulators from the Fed, who were working with a new management team and key executives from Golden Bear. Total assets of Golden Bear were estimated at $950 million. Regulators from the feds were pleased at the sale of Golden Bear because they were busy trying to salvage other financial institutions all over Southern California, and this was an optimistic beginning.

The story went to say that 277 area thrifts had been seized by regulators in the past eighteen months, putting Southern California in the lead across the country. The Golden Bear transaction, which had been underway since the death of company president Claude A. Belker, was scheduled for nine Monday morning, at the corporate offices in Newport Center.

Today was Monday. The time was 7:18.

The corporate offices were just up the road, on the outer perimeter of Fashion Island.

Within striking distance.

I walked slowly up the stairs and handed Roxanne the business section. Then I took out the Excalibur list from Bongo Bodette. Stonehenge, a financial corporation, with headquarters in London, was number 37 on Bongo's list.

Stonehenge was part of Excalibur. Like Viking Ice.

I refilled our cups. So this was what they did with the money.

I broke my promise to Leon.

We did not go directly to see him at the Newport Beach station.

At 7:55 Roxanne and I were sitting in Dugger's Chevrolet under a blooming bougainvillea at the far end of the parking lot outside the offices of Golden Bear Savings and Loan. There were three vehicles in the parking lot. While we waited, a brown van parked in the far corner. I could feel Roxanne getting tense. It resembled the van from Viking Ice.

Then the driver's door opened and a security guard climbed out. He wore a blue uniform and a gun on a Sam Browne belt. He walked to the building and used a key to let himself in.

"I am so nervous," Roxanne said.

At 8:22 a green BMW pulled into the lot and two men in business suits climbed out. Both had briefcases and shoes with a high polish. The haircuts had been done by the same barber. The two men walked up to the main door and waited for it to be unlocked. Then they disappeared inside. I checked the mini cassette recorder. It was a Sony, borrowed from Wally St. Moritz. Testing. Testing.

Roxanne kept reaching into her purse to touch the .32 she had borrowed from me. In my shoulder holster, I wore a Beretta automatic, a 9 millimeter with a silencer attached. There's a problem with conglomerates—you don't know who to shoot.

"Am I supposed to shoot this thing?"

"Only in self-defense."

"I should have had it last night."

"Correct."

"What's to become of us, Matt?"

"We're going to live happily ever after."

She poked me, gently. "You're a liar."

"Feeling the guilts again?"

She nodded. "A twinge."

"Don't keep kicking yourself."

"I just feel so stupid. To have missed so much, when there were so many clues."

"You were deep into your work. Forget it."

"The ostrich," Roxanne said. "She buried her head in books and refused to look up. I'll never make that mistake again."

"Sounds like a New Year's resolution."

"Maybe it is."

"So," I said, feeling the bruises from last night. "What's the Roxanne Mendez-Madrid plan?"

"The first step . . . is to change that name." Her voice had that gritty edge of determination. "Get rid of it."

"Change it to what?"

"My maiden name was Cooper. That will do."

At 8:31 a stretch limousine entered the parking lot, taking a long time to ease its rear whitewalls around the corner, slide across two parking slots, and aim its chromed nose at the entrance to Golden Bear. There was a long moment while nothing happened. Then the driver got out. It was Jerome, old White Hair. He wore a three-piece suit, dark gray, shiny shoes with tassles, and a clean white shirt. He walked around behind the limo.

I started the Chevy and rammed it into first and barreled across the lot in a tight circle. Jerome had the rear door half open. He heard us coming and reached inside his coat. I hit the brakes and cranked the wheel. The Chevy skidded sideways, tires squealing as the momentum threw the rear end around in a squealing arc, and came to a stop as it slammed Jerome against that side of the limo with a whump. My door was blocked.

"Climb out," I told Roxanne. "Keep your head down."

White-faced, she nodded and hustled out. The glass of my window shattered, but I heard no gunshot. Jerome had a silencer too.

The Beretta muzzle up, I hustled around the front of the Chevy. Jerome should have been dead, but there he was, red-faced and cursing as he tried to work his leg free. It was jammed between the Chevy and the limo.

There was still some fight left in Jerome as he swung the small automatic up in a nasty arc to fire at me. His fist was big and white, dwarfing the gun. I turned sideways to give him less to shoot at and felt something sting my left shoulder. I fired at his midsection, the Beretta spitting. Surprise glowed for an instant in his red-rimmed eyes. He brought his other hand up to steady his shooting arm, but then the weakness overcame him, and he sagged down between the two vehicles. He did not let go of the pistol. His next round slapped the asphalt.

Breathing hard now, wondering how badly I was hit, I worked my way to Jerome and planted the muzzle of the Beretta against his throat. His eyes fluttered one last time, blazing up in a final hopeless fury, and then the life sighed out of him.

A Peugeot station wagon drifted into the lot, sweeping past the limo to park in the loading zone near the door. The driver stepped out as I pushed away from Jerome and stood up. She was a young mom, a Newport Beach honey, coiffed and spiffy in her pink sweats. Every hair was in place. Her walk was wonderful. Trim little bottom, elegant wrists. She was away from the Peugeot, chin up, bright gaze fixed on the express window, when something in the scene tugged at her, bombing her perfect morning.

Blood oozed from my shoulder as I stood up. The blonde glanced our way. She could see me, the rear of Dugger's Chevy, the front end of the limo. Jerome was out of sight behind the Chevy. Roxanne was out of sight behind the limo.

"Yoo hoo?" she called, shading her eyes like a tourist. "Is everything . . . all right over there?"

I attempted a grin. "Just blocking out a scene for a movie shot. Everything's just fine, except we've got to do it again."

"A movie? You mean a film?"

"A film," I said.

"Matt!" Roxanne's voice, in a stage whisper. "Matt?"

I waved at Ms. Peugeot Perfect, who smiled and continued on her way to the express window.

On the other side of the limo Roxanne was gripping her gun in both hands, as instructed. The gun was trained on a man wearing a business suit. His hair was thinning. It had once been sandy, but now it was mostly gray. When he turned to look at me, the eyes gave him away.

The eyes were hateful, contemptuous, smug. He was up there. You were down here. He had seen it all and no longer cared. If you got in his way, there were procedures to move you aside. If he wasn't the Big Guy Dugger talked about, he was at least Number Two. To this man people were mere ants, following the whiff of sugar or grease, waiting to be poisoned or drowned or burnt up. A pale scar whispered along his right cheek.

"Jerome?" he asked, in slightly accented English. His voice sounded upper-crust, controlled, intelligent. He saw the Big Picture, and only that.

"Jerome-baby bought the farm." I nodded at Roxanne. "Good work, kid."

"Matt!" Roxanne said. "You're bleeding!"

I nodded. Pain blurred my environment, tilted the parking lot, dimming the sign at Golden Bear. The door to the limo stood open. I gestured Mr. Smooth inside.

"You drive," I said to Roxanne.

She opened the door and got in.

The man shrugged and ducked his head to enter the limo. I saw his hand brush his ankle, saw the wink of metal, and gave him a sharp rap on the back of his wrist with the Beretta. It caught him on that knobby little outside bone, where the nerves bunch up. Pain rose up in his eyes. He sucked in his breath and sat back against the cushions, the color draining from his face.

"Take the piece by the handle," I said. "Toss it on the floor."

He pulled the ankle-gun free and dropped it at our feet. It was a two-shot Derringer with a cute pearl handle. Looked like a 25 millimeter. The window was down between the driver and the rear seat. "Go down to PCH," I said to Roxanne. "Head north."

It was nervous time for a moment as she ground the starter, over and over, chunk-a-whunk, with nothing firing. Damn all diesels. Then it caught, and she backed up with a jerk, spinning the wheel, barely missing a Newport Beach mom in a Dodge Aerostar. I wondered what color sweats she'd be wearing.

As we swung past the entrance to Golden Bear, I saw Ms. Peugeot Perfect talking to the security guard, gesturing our way. His attention was on her. He was all teeth and smiles. If he made it past his pleasure with Ms. Perfect, he might think to call the cops. We had a couple minutes.

The limo was a Mercedes, designed with the Shah of Samarkand in mind. The seats were leather. There was a built-in bar and some fancy electronic gear.

"How far can you call on that?" I asked, pointing the muzzle of the Beretta.

"How wide is the known universe?" A thin smile from him.

Roxanne was rocketing along well past the speed limit. I told her to ease up. I brought out the Sony and pressed the record button to start the tape. The Big Guy didn't look worried.

"What's your name?"

"I have many names."

"Who are you today?"

"Surname, Ten Eyck. Given name, Stefan."

He handed me a business card. I let it drop on the seat.
"German?"

"Dutch. A Netherlander."

"Nice name, Stefan. Where's Claude Belker?"

The smile faded. "The Pyrenees, I should imagine.
Perhaps the Swiss Alps. Or the Black Forest area. He's an
inveterate hiker. He has a new identity. Reports are that
he is quite happy."

"Can you prove it?"

"I think you have broken a bone," Ten Eyck said. "My
wrist is most painful."

"Tough cookies."

Ten Eyck, or whatever his name was, took some time
crossing his legs and making sure his creases were
straight. "Jerome assured me you were taken care of, Mr.
Murdock. Both of you."

"Good help is hard to find."

He smiled thinly. "He had been with us for ten years.
Perhaps he was no longer—" Ten Eyck broke off his analysis, then indicated Roxanne, raising his eyebrows in appreciation. "I had not realized Señora Mendez-Madrid
was so attractive. A real beauty. I had not realized you
were so . . . tenacious. If you would sheathe your weapon
for a moment, I'm sure we three might reach an accom-
modation."

"Money, right? You want to buy us off, pack us up like
ice cream, and ship us off to the old holding facility."

"Not at all. I could offer you employment. Or retire-
ment with an annual income. I could offer various puri-
tan diversions. Or oriental delights."

He sold dreams, but delivered nightmares. "How about
lining up the people who killed Bruce Halliburton?"

He cut his eyes at me. "That, too, could be arranged."

"You got the world by the balls, don't you?" I shoved

the gun into his ribs, driving him back against the leather cushions, making him gasp from the sudden pain. "You prick."

He grasped the barrel of the Beretta, and our hands touched. My hand was cold as ice. His was warm and toasty. Who was under stress here, anyway?

"Please. You have every right to be angry, but I'm surprised you haven't tried to view it from . . . our perspective. You penetrated our perimeter, threatened our business. We do have procedures."

My laugh sounded forced, hollow, unreal. "Is that what killed Bruce Halliburton? Your goddam procedures?"

Ten Eyck sighed, heavily, a phony sound, with faked regret. "Halliburton compiled a list that could have been damaging. There were cash flow problems as payments slowed from his firm. He was about to inform other insurance companies. The industry is a ponderous one, all those actuaries, all those grubby little underwriters. Jerome handled it badly, I admit. If I had been on site, I would have reasoned with Halliburton."

"Reasoned how? With a baby flame-thrower?"

"I am not a barbarian. I try to suit the method to the man." He indicated Roxanne again. "Or to the woman. In the long run it's preferable."

"I should blow you away right here."

"I wish you would instruct our lovely chauffeuse to find us both some medical help. This wrist of mine feels broken. And your wound looks serious."

A wave of dizziness hit me again. I fought to stay conscious. "Stefan. Tell me about poor old Emiliano."

"What would you like to know?"

"Why was he killed?"

"An automobile accident. You were there."

"Okay. Why was Jerome after him?"

Ten Eyck sighed. "Mendez-Madrid stole some documents from us. He ran away. We searched for him for two months, finally located him here, in this country, as he was heading for California. He was disgruntled. He threatened to inform the authorities about our key holding facilities. He was out of control. Jerome was to bring him back."

"Then what?"

"After he cooled off, he would resume his chosen path."

I knew he was lying. "That's bullshit. He had money in a numbered account. You wanted that money."

"That fact was not in his dossier."

I shoved the Beretta deeper into his rib cage, forcing him back against the leather seat. Blood pumped heavily through my head. My eyes wanted to close. "The other lucky guys—Strich and Barrymore and the rest—did they lose control, too?"

Ten Eyck's smile was car salesman earnest. "Not at all. I am not personally acquainted with each case—last fiscal year our organization afforded a transit status for seven hundred plus clients—but reports about them are most favorable."

My mind was groggy. I tried to estimate Ten Eyck's take, seven hundred pigeons at $10 million apiece would come to—the road tilted as Roxanne zoomed around a truck. My mind refused to compute. A bundle of billions, I thought, fuzzily. Bundle me no bundles. "But you kept track of Belker and Mendez-Madrid?"

Ten Eyck nodded. "Belker owned a financial dukedom over which we wanted control. I took a personal interest in the Mendez-Madrid transit because it was unique."

"Because he didn't burn up or become fish-food?"

"You are astute, Mr. Murdock. Death by fire was on the drawing board when a double for Mendez-Madrid surfaced on a dingy side street in Houston. Plans were re-drawn for the simulated heart attack at the tennis club."

"Was Doc Ames in on it?"

"Of course."

"What happened to Doc Ames?"

"He was rotated."

"What does that mean?"

"He'll be working for us again. In some other location, under another identity. Physicians are handy for signing death certificates. In time, of course, they fall under suspicion and are rotated."

"What about Bobby Maclean?"

"Maclean's job was to restrain the distraught widow, to keep her from viewing the body, and then to identify the corpse. Had we known how resilient she was, we would have tried to bring her into the process.

"Thanks a lot," Roxanne said.

"De nada," he said, in fluid Spanish.

I prodded him with the gun muzzle. "What do you creeps want with Belker's S and L business?"

"Belker was a conduit for the funds from Mendez-Madrid, who received them from Cantu, a substantial narcotics merchant. Our scenario calls for doubling the business—the American press calls it greenwashing—in six months. Since Miami's increased vigilance, traffic has tripled in Southern California."

"A money laundromat, right here in peaceful Orange County."

"Laundromat. Very good. Very clever."

I wanted to kill him. "How did you locate these pigeons? What did you call them, clients?"

"Prospects." Ten Eyck coughed. "They were located through familiar channels. Financial statements, loan applications, credit reports. In this area we have access to documents prepared for Mr. Belker's bank and other

248

lending institutions. Across the country we follow similar patterns, targeting members of the local financial community for loan information. When necessary, our computers tap into the computers of credit reporting agencies."

"Like TRW?"

He nodded. "Whoever."

"Okay. You found rich pigeons who handled money. What then?"

"Hmm. That should be obvious. We look for five psychographic keynotes. First, a considerable debt-burden, ten million and up, enough to keep our clients agile making the monthly interest payment on loans outstanding. Second, and a direct extension of that debt-burden, a strong sense of claustrophobia, of being trapped by circumstance. As children, fifty-two percent of our clients suffered from asthma or related respiratory problems. Asthmatics, as I'm sure you know, live in constant fear of strangulation, suffocation. In stressful situations they cannot breathe."

I broke in. "Was Mendez-Madrid an asthmatic?"

"As a child, yes. He outgrew it. Or thought he did."

"Did you know, Rox?"

Her voice came from the front seat. "No. But it makes a lot of sense."

"The husband's little secret," Ten Eyck said. "Shall I continue?"

"Sure." The road swam past outside the window. My vision was wobbly. "Sure. Let's push on."

"Very well. Third, our prospects have to possess a deep drive for fantasy-realization, for transforming a dream into palpable reality. They are lost romantics, weary of life, eager for high adventure. We offer them escape, rebirth, new horizons, a fresh start. Fourth, each has an appreciation for design. Their escape routes are labyrinthine. Each route has its own inherent elegance."

"Tailored to fit the pigeon, of course?"

"Of course. Fifth, and most important, our clients are a secretive lot. In the mind is this secret room, a *camera obscura* where no one is admitted. There the dreams are. Only there does the dreamer really live. An interesting note—across the country we found that sixty-two percent of our prospects have done covert intelligence work during their military service. Some are heavy readers of spy fiction. Others—like Señor Mendez-Madrid—are merely secretive. Keeping secrets gives them fierce joy. The bigger the secret, the greater the joy."

"You did this stuff on computers?"

He shrugged, and the movement brought the pain into his eyes. "We have psychologists on staff. The principles are common knowledge, ignored by much of modern psychology. Our people use a combination of Jungian and Reichian techniques, with dashes of Freud—Oedipal drives, et cetera—as needed."

"Terrific little business, Ten Eyck. Washing dirty money, selling frozen corpses."

"Be realistic, Mr. Murdock. The substitutes are derelicts, street people, members of the great unwashed. Alive, they glut the cities, adding to the tax burden. Dead, they have purpose at last."

"You killed Bruce Halliburton."

"His death is regrettable. He was shrewd. He had connections. We could have used him."

"And you're telling me that all these pigeons are alive and well? Living it up in their own private Shangri-las?"

"Mendez-Madrid is dead, that's true. But if you telephone a certain number in Europe, you can speak to your Mr. Belker. Or any of the men on Halliburton's list."

"Give me the number for Belker."

He picked up the business card and brought out a gold fountain pen, uncapping it with difficulty, because of the bonk I'd given him on his wrist. He wrote a number on the back of the card and handed it to me. The printing was European, a seven with a horizontal line through the middle, a one that looked like a U.S. seven. I let it fall to the seat between us and gestured at the mini-cassette, which was still recording. "You're dead now, baby."

"Not if you work for us. You—" He glanced toward Roxanne, in the front seat. "—and the lady."

I stuck the Beretta in his ear. I had just enough strength left to splatter his brains all over the slick leather of the Mercedes. You had to hand it to Ten Eyck. He didn't shake or tremble. He didn't beg or blubber or start to cry. He placed his hands on his knees, a stoical gesture. He wasn't a big man—five-foot-ten or so—but the way he handled himself was impressive. Ten Eyck was a heavy hitter with a heart of stainless steel. "You won't kill me," he said.

"Why not?"

"Because, Mr. Murdock, for you honor is everything. For you there must be the weary and heroic face-off in the dusty street, the knightly joust on the dry medieval grass. For you, there must be—"

"Matt," Roxanne cut in. "There's a red light, coming up behind us."

I looked out the rear window. It was a police cruiser, light bar cranking, closing fast. This program was out of time. I poked Ten Eyck again with the Beretta. "These were sharp guys, Ten Eyck. They'd made a ton of money, fought off the competition, survived. Why did they fall for your spiel?"

"Spiel?"

"Yeah. What was the guarantee?"

"Guarantee?" His blue eyes held me for a moment. Then he smiled, shook his head, and looked out the window. "They were their own guarantee."

What the hell did that mean?

Outside, to our left, a khaki-uniformed cop leaned out the window of a blue and white, waving us to a stop. Dark glasses, tense hand on the wheel, an angry face.

"What should I do, Matt?"

"Pull over."

The limo skidded to a clumsy stop, and the cruiser angled into the shoulder, cutting us off. Two more police cruisers slid up behind us. The doors swung open, and the cops hunkered down behind them, using the metal for cover, gun barrels resting on the window frames. It was a crummy way to shoot. Someone talked through a bullhorn, ordering us to step out of the car. Ten Eyck plucked his card off the seat and tucked it into my shirt pocket. For that I rapped his wrist again.

He grunted.

I told Roxanne to roll down the window. She fumbled with the controls. Ten Eyck came to the rescue with instructions. There was a button on the driver's console on the seat, on the driver's right. The window slid down, letting in the salt-air smell from the beach. I made sure the safety was on and then I tossed the Beretta out the window. It went clunk on the shoulder. Ten Eyck's cute little derringer was next. Then Roxanne's revolver. Ten Eyck watched everything holding his wrist. He was unblinking now, calm as a Buddha.

He went out first. They ordered him to lock his hands behind his neck and assume the position. Roxanne followed. The sun was still lost behind a gray ceiling of June fog. It would be a muggy day in Murdock Country.

A jagged wave of dizziness hit me as I stepped out of the limo. I heard Ten Eyck say something to Roxanne in

French. I knew enough French to understand he was making her a job offer. She said something I couldn't hear. Ten Eyck, the smooth bastard, switched to Spanish.

Then the whirlies took me. My head went into a tailspin. A marsh bird made a wild, wild call. And the grayish Cal Trans tarmac rushed up to meet me as I fell.

IIIIII 23 IIIIII

Monks in ghostly white cassocks, roped at the waist, were loading the barge. In the gray and misty morning the narrow-hulled vessel sat low in the water, like a gondola in a musician's dream.

Gayla Jean Kirkwood boarded the barge with a cute little wiggle that brought sly smiles of appreciation from the assembled monks. She wore a sexy purple shorty robe, hip-length, and sexy silver slippers with four-inch heels. Her legs were stunning. Her coppery red hair glowed bright as the moon against the gloom of the barge.

There was a scattering of applause as she twirled, the hem of the shorty accenting the sweet curves of her naked bottom. Then a monk with a shaved head strode to a Gunga Din gong and took a long arced wind-up with a padded mallet. "Plong" went the mallet. The sound made my teeth chatter. Gayla Jean stared at something deep inside the barge. Her face turned white.

I shuffled forward one step. I wore my faded blue terry cloth bathrobe, but somewhere I had lost my slippers. My ankles felt the cold.

Philo Waddell boarded next. He weighed close to three hundred and wore white silk pajamas and a red smoking jacket. The barge tilted as Philo stepped on, and several people snickered. The gong sounded again. Philo turned to the crowd and held his arms out. "Come to me, O ye gates. Come hither to me."

"Come on, Daddy!" called Gayla Jean. "Quit blowing smoke. This is it, Daddy, the final call, so get your walrus ass on in here!"

The line shuffled forward. What was I doing here? Where was Jerome?

Butch Denning, Philo's bully-boy handmaiden, boarded the barge and the line shuffled forward. Agent Dorn of the INS followed. Then Ellis Dean and handsome Landis Mayhew, who had played tennis on the pro circuit. Then Mrs. Angela Mayhew, the Madame of Balboa. Then Jancey Sheridan, the cocky cowboy, followed by Bruce Halliburton. Bruce was still dressed in green, but now he wore his head.

The man directly ahead of me was Emiliano Mendez-Madrid, wearing a priest's severe black suit with the tight white collar. "Emmy," I said, "tell me what happened in Zurich."

Before he could answer, the gong sounded, the pace of the beat faster now, and he moved forward. The line shuffled closer to the barge. Panic rose in my throat. The pounding of the gong gave me a headache. With the lightfootedness of an athlete Emmy stepped on board.

"Hey, *amigo*," he said. "Watch out for my wife, you *cabron*. That one is a *bruja*, of a certainty I tell you."

The gong sounded, this time for me. A monk smiled at me. His face was a death's head. I woke up screaming.

                    *   *   *

They took me to the hospital on Monday. I stayed there, having bad dreams, until Thursday. Roxanne was there beside the bed every time I woke up. She told me Wally had given me arnica. I was healing fast.

On Thursday they wheeled me out to the parking lot and Wally drove me home in his Saab. Roxanne sat in the back seat, not saying much.

I kept seeing her, whispering with Ten Eyck, in Spanish.

On Friday I had enough strength to phone Bongo Bodette. He found the name of a research facility in a canyon over in Irvine. The firm was called Apptel Labs. I phoned Leon. It took them a day to put together a combined task force. On Saturday evening, around twilight, a fifty-four-man task force raided Apptel Labs.

The story made the front page. There were no photos, but an artist had drawn a sketch of the layout, with little indicator boxes to tell the reading public what went on inside.

Sixteen corpses were found in the refrigeration units at Apptel. Fifteen of the bodies were male; one was female. An investigation was underway to establish the identities of the corpses, but for now they were only numbers. From one to sixteen. An enterprising reporter, Natalie Green, had a statement from one police officer alleging that the bodies were undergoing reconstructive surgery. "Would you believe," he said, "they were getting their teeth fixed?"

The county coroner estimated the ages of the victims between forty-one and fifty-nine. Eight were Latino. Three were Asian. Three were labeled Anglo. So far, no Apptel employees had been located. The single vehicle at the scene was a medium-sized refrigerator truck, licensed in the state of Arizona.

The discovery of sixteen frozen bodies at a holding facility in peaceful Irvine blew the president and the Arabs and the Russians off page one of *The Los Angeles Times* and *The Orange County Tribune*. Reporters flew in from San Francisco, Sacramento, Dallas, St. Louis, Miami, Chicago, Pittsburgh, New York.

A week passed. I read the newspaper sitting on my deck above the quad near Punker's Strip. The dory fishermen were selling lots of fish. Girls in string bikinis paraded their sleek, oiled bodies like virgins from Tahiti. Jerome's bullet had torn a chunk of hide out of my left shoulder. When I showered, I wore a latex bandage. It only hurt when I laughed.

Roxanne had her money, $180,000 in cash, via registered mail, plus the $25,000 we had taken to Santa Fe. She had opened an account at Wells Fargo. The account was under her maiden name, Cooper.

Receiving that much money by mail restored my faith in the government and the U.S. Mail.

I, however, had not been so lucky. The check from my San Jose Cadillac dealer, the one with the wayward wife, had bounced. As a last resort I'd hired a collector in Northern California to squeeze what he could from that particular turnip. We would split what the collector recovered down the middle, fifty-fifty.

We paid one visit to Roxanne's house on Spyglass Hill to pack up her books and clothes and some records and a box of her favorite kitchen cookware and the trusty IBM computer. A Bekins truck took the furniture to a storage facility. As we were leaving, a real estate salesperson arrived in a Lincoln to show the house. "What a relief," Roxanne sighed.

Back at my place, Roxanne took over half my closet and two drawers in the dresser and one corner of my living room. Her desk was so clean you could eat off it. She spent two days cleaning my place, humming, sweating, exorcising her personal demons—Emmy and Rudolfo and Jerome and Dugger.

And maybe even Bruce.

As Roxanne cleaned, taking possession, she eyed the photos on my wall with less disdain and slightly more tolerance. We slept together. We shopped at El Rancho—steak and chicken and salad makings. We ate together at my kitchen table, washed dishes together, cooked. We did not make love. Most of all, we did not talk about what had happened that night with Dugger.

Dugger was in jail. The charges were rape, attempted murder, conspiracy to defraud, and arson. Roxanne and I were due to testify at his preliminary hearing, sometime in late August. The geek was in jail, trying to pin everything on Jerome. Jerome was dead. No one back in jolly old England had clamored to have his body returned home for a decent burial in the village churchyard.

A spokesman for the federal regulatory agency overseeing the buyout of Golden Bear expressed disappointment that the deal with Stonehenge had not gone through. Other buyers were being sought, the spokesman said, here and abroad.

In late June Sergeant Leon Book brought back my Ford pickup. It had been found in a supermarket parking lot in Northwood, a village in Irvine. I owed the police for fixing two flat tires. Leon also brought along Wally's mini-cassette recorder and the Ten Eyck tape.

"Nothing on there," Leon said, sitting down in a deck chair. "A few squeaks, is all. Nothing to back up your Great Golden Bear Greenwashing Machine theory. Too bad, Sherlock. That was a super story."

"I heard it, too, Sergeant," Roxanne said. "It was a conspiracy."

Leon shook his head. "The tape might have done it for us. Without it we're dead in the water."

"Goddam," I said.

"May not mean much," Leon said. "But my electronics guy found some wire coils inside the Mercedes that could have laid down a heavy magnetic field."

"He erased the tape?"

"A conjecture," Leon said. "A space age possibility. Remember we live in a Star Wars age. What is that wonderful smell?"

"Murdock Chili."

"Who cooked it?"

"We did."

Leon's expression brightened. I knew what he was after. "Want a taste?" I said.

"I'd love a taste."

"And I'd like my guns back."

"Sure," he said, nodding vigorously. "Anything."

"You're a charmer, Leon. A real charmer."

Over a bowl of Murdock Chili Leon told us what had happened to Ten Eyck. "Your guy gets taken to the station, where he makes one phone call. Twenty minutes later a call comes in from back East, from the State Department. The call bypasses me, my lieutenant, and the watch commander. In a couple of minutes word comes down to let this guy walk. An officer drives him to St. Boniface, where they work on his wrist bone. He says he's registered at the Bougaineville in Laguna, but when I call he's checked out."

After Leon left, I played the Ten Eyck tape, listening to every squeak and scratch. Nothing. That made me remember his business card. When I looked I couldn't find it.

In early July authorities came up with possible identities for four of the corpses found at Apptel Labs in Irvine. Two were Mexican nationals—José Confalon and Jaime Bienvenido—who had emigrated to this country by crossing the Rio Grande at night. Jose and Jaime had last been seen in May at a soup-kitchen in Houston.

The third man was Chin Lee, an Asian, last seen in San Francisco's Tenderloin, where he'd worked as a janitor for a topless bar that was now out of business.

The fourth man was Sam Treadle, last seen at a drug rehab center in the Soho district of New York City.

Identification was extremely difficult, the authorities said, when the fingerpads had been burnt away by a laser.

What's the price of a rich man's dream?

In the early mornings Roxanne ran along the beach. She'd roll out of bed at 5:30 or 6:00 and get dressed and head out, shimmering in the haze. She'd come home glistening with sweat and undress in the bathroom, out of my sight. I could hear the silken rustlings of cloth on flesh. I could hear the shower come on and the shower door close with a click as she stepped in. I remembered that night in Santa Fe with a certain pang of lustiness. My shoulder was healing. There was less tape, less pain. One day soon, I could run with her.

She wanted to take a trip north to Napa, to the wine country. She hadn't been there in awhile. She wanted to share it with me.

"I want us to go away," she said. "Together."

"I can't afford it," I said.

"My treat."

A trip north started making more sense one morning after a trip to the grocery store when we climbed the steps to the deck and found two reporters waiting for us.

There was a lady reporter with glasses, Natalie Green, from *The Orange County Tribune*. And there was a boy reporter with tousled blond hair and a surfer's smile. He was from *The Los Angeles Times*.

"Go away," I said.

"We'd like a statement, Mr. Murdock. On what you know about Apptel Labs and Viking Ice."

"Scoot," I said.

"Does that mean 'No Comment'?" the woman asked.

"It means scoot. Both of you. You're trespassing."

The guy with the surfer's smile tried to bluff me by jotting furiously in his little notebook. "Al Dugger's talking, Mr. Murdock. He places you both at Viking Ice the night of the fire. Rumor has it Mr. Mendez-Madrid was laundering money for the Mexican Mafia. Did you know a Robert Maclean?"

"No," I said.

"Hmm. A boat registered to Maclean is unaccounted for. Mexican authorities think it was lost at sea and Maclean with it."

"Buddy," I said, "it's a long way down those stairs."

"Is that a threat, Mr. Murdock?"

I got his arm in a hammerlock, forcing him to drop the notebook, and walked him to the stairs. He was stronger than he looked. Muscling him made me sweat. "You can go down your way, pal, or my way."

Behind us, the lady reporter said, "Oh, come on, Chick. Let's split."

She walked past me with venom in her eyes. I understood. Her job was gathering news. News sold papers. When papers sold, advertisers bought space to promote their goods and services in the crowded marketplace. When advertisers bought space, customers bought goods and services. It was the merry-go-round for a dying civilization, and I was screwing up the rotation. My job was cleaning up the gutters after the merry-go-round wheezed to a stop.

I stood at the top of the stairs and watched them walk away. The boy reporter's coat was rumpled.

Roxanne came up to me. "Feeling better?"

"Went a little crazy."

"For a moment there I thought you forgot who the bad guys were."

"My shoulder burns," I said. "Let's make some soup."

As we carried the groceries into the kitchen, we were both thinking the same thing—people were starting to tie things together. They were starting to follow the thread through the labyrinth, seeking the hated Minotaur.

But the Minotaur was in Europe, out of reach, smirking from a safe distance.

And we were here, within reach.

So while the soup simmered, I lay on my chaise lounge in the sun and watched life on the beach. My body was held together with Elmer's glue and old rubber bands. Roxanne came out bearing two cans of Bud. She had changed to shorts and a halter. The shorts were very short and cut down low so that her navel was exposed. The halter was only a suggestion of a halter. The bruise had faded from her cheek, but I kept looking for it, thinking of Dugger. Roxanne's body looked fuller than I remembered it, riper. Her dark shoulders had a fulsome mahogany roundness. A new sotfness made her arms exquisite. She stretched out, smiling to herself, a woman's smile.

"Señor like?"

"*Si.* This particular señor like *mucho.*"

"Señor, he is feeling some better?"

"I'll say."

"*Bueno.*"

I sipped the Bud. It tasted wonderful, going down. "I was thinking about those reporters."

"Oh?"

"A trip to Napa may be in order."

"I've always liked Napa."

Roxanne touched her beer can to mine, and we sat there drinking Bud and watching the beach. I think I dozed off. When I opened my eyes, her chaise was empty. I heard her moving around inside the house, a drawer opening, clink of glassware, pad of bare foot on good solid wood. Music pumped from my ancient stereo, one of Roxanne's records, Cuco Sanchez singing "Al Preso Numero Nueve." It is a rousing tune, thrummed to Cuco's magic guitar, about a prisoner whose name is only number nine. Numero Nueve.

"*Hola*, Señor. You. The Wounded One."

Through the screen door I could see only her outline. "That's me."

"Want to play something?"

"Sure. Football? Baseball? Tennis?"

"How about Catch?" The door opened and I saw a flash of bare brown arm as the blue halter sailed out to land on my knees. The screen door closed. My heart thudded heavily. Murdock was alive. I sat up, feeling slightly dizzy, and swung my legs over the edge.

"Is the Señor smiling?"

Before I could answer, the door opened, and the soft white shorts came floating out. I caught them in midair and went inside. No Roxanne in the living room. No Roxanne in the kitchen. I went to the bedroom door. No Roxanne. The bathroom door was closed. I opened it. Not there. The closet door was closed. When I opened it, there she was, smiling, wearing one of my blue shirts. She had not buttoned the shirt. My legs shook as I took her in my arms. She made me sit on the bed while she helped me off with the khaki shorts. She made me lie on my back while she snugged her shoulder blades together and slowly let the blue shirt fall away, like a model's drape in an artist's studio in a peaceful time long ago in another century. She grinned then and came into my arms and for awhile there I forgot about pain and dying.

Making love wiped the slate clean.

When we were finished, we lay quietly, letting the sweat dry, and shared another Bud while she told me about Dugger and that night at Viking Ice. "He slapped me around some—his wonderful way of letting a woman know he really cares—and then he tore my blouse off and unzipped in his special manly way. I was so angry then I could have killed him. But I pretended I liked being hurt and that really got Mister Dugger going. After that he was easy. I rushed him. 'Hurry, Al,' I said. 'Hurry, honey, I can't wait.' I suppose I moved rather . . . provocatively. I won't go into detail, but he—he lost it in what you might call a premature fashion."

"The dirty bastard."

"He's gone now."

"I should have killed him."

"No," she said. "I should have."

She took a long swig of beer and passed the can to me. Her face in the afternoon light had the stern look of a vengeful goddess, staring past me into a mystical space where I could not follow. I touched her, and she shuddered and snuggled back into my arms. I wondered how long she would stay here on the pier, in this house, with me.

24

In late July we took a trip north, a slow trip up Pacific Coast Highway to Santa Barbara and then up Highway 1 along the coast through Cambria and Big Sur. We spent three days in the wine country, drinking wine and making love. Roxanne wanted to buy a house and live there. I said okay, but I didn't mean it.

By early August she was back at work, but not on her translations. She was reading books on money, doing research on currency exchanges and the trade imbalance and the fall of the dollar. She went to lunch with James Wingo, one of Emmy's partners. She came back home with a long list of articles in obscure economic journals. She read everything she could on money-laundering. In bed she was intense and earthy. Learning about money excited her, made her skin hot. When Roxanne wasn't at UCI, using the library, she was with Rima Beaukirk, using Bongo's computers, or talking to Wally St. Moritz, probing his vast store of conceptual knowledge.

"What do you hope to find?" I asked.

"Knowledge that breeds experience," she said.

"What kind of experience?"

She looked up from the article she was reading, a piece in *Commonweal*. "The kind of experience that's the opposite of the kind of innocence that got me into trouble in the first place."

"From books?"

She nodded and crossed her trim ankles. "Yes. From books. They're all I know." And went back to her reading.

But something gnawed at me. "Maybe Ten Eyck could help."

"What?" Her voice was muffled from her deep concentration.

"Ten Eyck. You remember. Platinum marbles for eyes. His middle name was money."

"Hmm." She turned the page and made a notation on her notepad.

"What were you guys talking about, anyway?"

"Talking?" Her voice was far away. "To whom?"

"Yeah, talking. On the beach that day the cops rousted us. You and Ten Eyck were chatting away in Spanish. Whispering."

"I wasn't whispering, dear."

"Okay. Talking, then. What was the subject?"

"He asked me if I was afraid. I said, yes, I was." She looked up at me, a slight frown on her face. "What are you thinking?"

"I thought he might have offered you a job."

"Really, Matt. It's time for your siesta."

She went back to her reading. I walked out onto the deck. I felt restless, a hook, something, nagging at me. I spoke to her through the screen door. "I lost his business card."

266

"Hmm?"

"Ten Eyck's business card. He wrote a phone number on it, where I could contact Claude Belker. What a laugh. He tucked it into my shirt pocket, just before the cops came. When I looked, it wasn't there."

"Maybe the nurse threw it away. That cute one, with the red hair and the sweet twitchy bottom you admired so much."

"You never saw the card?"

"Please, Matt. I'm trying to get through this article."

By mid-August my shoulder was healed enough so that I started exercising again, taking off the slabs of weight I had put on during convalescence. Money arrived from San Jose—$845 from collector Roy Huggins, my half of the money recovered from the Cadillac dealer. I took a job working security for a preacher who thought some liberals were trying to kill him because he wanted to go into politics. He was down on Darwin, sex education, gays, AIDS, abortion, drugs, and the Soviet menace. He was a teetotaler. His wife was a known drunk. They had produced a whining but sexy-as-Satan teenage daughter named Jocelyn, who was flying high on coke, sleeping on the beach, and trying to nail anything with a zipper front.

I took the job with the preacher on Monday. Roxanne said she was glad I was working again.

On Tuesday the Channel Three Evening News ran a two-minute news squib called "Greenwashing: Orange County Style." Investigators had discovered a money-laundering operation in Orange County. Four men were named in connection with the money-laundering. The names were Strich, Belker, Barrymore, and Maclean. All four were deceased.

Tuesday night, our lovemaking was fierce.

On Wednesday Roxanne was gone.

The goodbye note was on the kitchen table, written precisely in her neat scholar's hand:

Darling Matt—

I must go away. I had to do it this way because I could not bear to say goodbye. What we had was so beautiful, so dear, and I shall treasure it always. I wish it could have gone on forever. Please don't try to find me. You are a hunter-tracker. For you finding me would be no problem. I shall find a place to be, and then I shall write. I promise. I hear the wolves, darling. I hear the wolves.

With all my love, R.

I read the note again, and then I crumpled it up and tossed it into the wastebasket and walked to the fridge and got a Bud. I drank seven Buds and took a shower, where I always get great ideas. When I got out, I phoned Bongo Bodette and asked him to punch into the airport computers. No problem, Bongo said. By the time I was dressed, Bongo had phoned back with a message. Roxanne had booked a United flight to JFK in New York and from there a Swissair flight to Zurich.

"What were she and Rima working on?"

"Shit. How should I know? Couple feisty females git their brains in gear, anything can happen."

He yelled for Rima, who came to the phone, to answer some questions in that slow bayou drawl. Yes, they had been tracing Stonehenge and Excalibur. Excalibur was a subsidiary of Camelot Industries, which had been taken over by a Dutch firm named Aardus, Ltd. The president of Aardus was a man named Rolf Arnhem, who had fought in the Resistance during World War II, when his age had been eleven or twelve. That would make Rolf about the same age as Ten Eyck. He was credited with eliminating at least two dozen Nazis and Dutch collaborators. Estimates of Rolf's net worth today ran as high as $40 billion, U.S. He spoke several languages, including English, and had never been married. Lately, Rolf's critics had been accusing him of gun-smuggling, drug-trafficking, selling secrets to the Soviets, and white slavery. No one had proved anything. Rolf was well-connected all over Europe.

My passport had three months before it expired. I booked a seat to Zurich, where I spent a week hunting for Roxanne, showing her photo to hotel people and restaurant maître d's. Bongo helped me locate twenty-two banks where Emmy might have kept his stash. Two of the banks looked like private homes, except for one thing: At the door a guard in a three-piece suit stopped you to ask for your bank I.D. number.

It rained on me in Zurich. I bought a cheap rain parka. The natives spoke excellent English. The dollar was weak against the franc. I gained three pounds on Swiss food and Swiss beer. I did not find Roxanne. After a week I gave up and came back home.

In November I was working on my deck, replacing a board that was rotting away, when a stranger came up the stairs. It was a guy in a business suit, gray, with a soft blue shirt and a striped tie, straight from the Ivy League. He wore dark glasses and carried a briefcase, new, with a gold monogram. His hair was sandy. His shoulders were wide, his movements controlled. A shiver went up my spine because for a moment there I thought it was the ghost of Bruce Halliburton.

"Mr. Murdock?"

"Yes."

"I'm Ken Trager. We spoke on the phone back in June, I believe it was. I represent Heartland Mutual Life." His firm handshake guaranteed him a lifetime spot in the old boy network. His suit was impeccable.

"What can I do for you?"

Trager smiled and removed the dark glasses. "I've been authorized to offer you work."

"A job?"

"Yes, sir." His voice was too hearty, too packed with the confidence of the earnest jock. He handed me an embossed business card, with two phone numbers in Los Angeles. "Kenneth J. Trager," the card read. "Heartland Mutual Life."

"How about a beer?"

"Sorry. I'm in training. Have you any Perrier?"

I got him a Pepsi.

Kenny apologized for dropping in unannounced, as it were. He was down in Orange County on business and had a few moments, so he thought he'd stop by. He asked what my rate was, and I told him. He said okay, fine, wonderful. I smelled money. Money always brightened the day. He sipped his Pepsi and opened up his attaché case, which was full of manila folders. Jackets, they call them in the insurance trade. The folder he handed me was labeled "Mendez-Madrid, E., et al." I waited before opening the folder.

"Terrible thing," he said, "about Bruce Halliburton."

"Yeah."

"He was a super investigator. I learned a ton from him."

"What's it all about, Trager?"

He reached over and opened the folder he'd given me. On top was a list of names. The first name was Strich, Albert J. The last name was Ames, Sylvan, M.D. It was Bruce Halliburton's list, expanded slightly. Bruce's list had been handwritten. Trager's list was from a computer printer. Very official.

"Have you ever seen this list?"

"Where would I have seen it?"

"Bruce Halliburton was working on it. He might have shown it to you."

"He didn't."

Trager cleared his throat and gave me the Heartland spiel:

"It has come to our attention that certain individuals have taken out large amounts of life insurance with the clear intent to defraud. Our stake in this matter is over one hundred million dollars in payouts, so you can understand how time is of the essence." He leaned forward, his big wide hands on his big jock's knees. "We're still not sure how it was done, but we feel certain that deaths were staged, that bodies other than those of the insured were switched into place."

"Pretty fancy planning."

"Well, we're onto them now. Agents in the field are tightening up on policy writing. There are new standards in effect. When an individual requests more than a million in coverage, Heartland investigates. We do not intend to finance their escape."

"Good thinking."

"Thank you." He snapped his neon smile at me and plucked another file folder from his case. "And here is where you come in."

It was a thin file on Bobby Maclean, the guy who'd identified Emmy down in the hospital morgue on that sunny Sunday last March. In the file was a photo of Maclean launching his campaign for the Newport Beach mayor's job. He was waving at the camera and grinning like a politician. His wife, a blonde with a starlet's chest, stood beside him, also smiling. The caption underneath identified him as a Southern California financier. There was a copy of Maclean's military service record. He'd been in Vietnam, attached first to a PRU—Provisional Recon Unit—and then to the CIA, where he'd done some drug-busting in the Golden Triangle. There was another photo showing him in safari clothes, a hunting rifle in one hand, and an animal's horn in the other. The caption said: "Californian bags first rhino." Accompanying documents listed his debt-load at $14 million, his personal financial wealth at $21 million. Maclean's house in Big Canyon had an estimated value of $3.7 million. His business—Maclean Financial, Ltd., in Newport Center—had a value of $10 million.

The last document was a tally of insurance policies with a total value from six companies of $17 million. The bite on Heartland was for $6.5 million.

"This man was reported drowned off the Baja coast in June," Trager said. "We have a copy of the Mexican death certificate. But we have reason to believe he's alive and hiding out."

"Where?"

"Mexico."

"Mexico is a big place."

"One policy has been paid. We're holding up payment on the others. He owes us two-point-two million. We'd like you to find him. Your usual rates."

"It might take years."

"We have leads that might narrow your search."

I shook my head. I was tired. If I found Maclean—which was the long shot of the century—I'd pound him to a pulp. "Sorry. I don't want the job."

There was a pause. A gull swooped down, heading toward the beach, where an old guy in white trousers was opening a sack of bread scraps.

"How well did you get to know the widow? Mrs. Roxanne Cooper Mendez-Madrid?"

I thought of Roxanne at her computer, Roxanne undressing, Roxanne in bed, dark hair, dark skin, her body outlined by the sheet, waiting for me. "I did some work for her. Why?"

Trager smirked and handed me a photo. It was a four-by-six shot of a big blond man negotiating a purchase with a street vendor in a crowded market somewhere south of the border. The man wore baggy trousers, boat shoes, and a Mexican shirt. A woman was with him, holding his arm, leaning a hip into him. She had dark hair, shoulder-length, and a trim figure. Her face was not visible.

"The man is Maclean," Trager said. "The woman has been identified as Mrs. Mendez-Madrid, the grieving widow."

My heart hammered like a snare drum. I wanted to hit Trager. My hands shook as I studied the photo. I cleared my throat. "You think Maclean is down there with the Mendez woman?"

Trager's smirk broadened. "The scenario does have a certain logic. They were tennis friends, thrown together at the local club. Maclean and Mendez-Madrid were in the financial industry. The widow was awfully attractive and her . . . ah . . . footwork so far has been remarkable. Did you know Bruce was seeing her shortly before he died?"

I shook my head and handed back his folder. "Nope."

"I thought Bruce might have mentioned her. When this kitten came to light—" He tapped the grainy photo with one finger. "—I suddenly understood why he'd been spending his weekends out of town."

Kenny leaned toward me, putting his jaw within easy reach. "We could sweeten the pot for you. I'm authorized to offer five percent of recovered value, on top of expenses, of course."

Five percent of $2.2 million is $110,000. Could she

really be down there with Maclean? My voice was an angry cave-man growl. "Let me think about it."

"Very well. I must tell you, we've other operatives in mind. My superiors have quite a lot to lose. The underwriters are extremely concerned that these holes are plugged, and time, as they say, is of the essence."

"I'll bet."

He snapped the briefcase closed and stood up. "Any questions before I go?"

My mind felt like pegboard. All those little holes. The little holes filled with little pegs. Stuff hanging on the pegs, inside my mind, inside the holes, spinning away. Roxanne's white dress. Roxanne's bracelet. Roxanne's computer. Roxanne's white panties, running gear, tank top, running shoes. My stomach felt sick. "Not right now."

Before he left, Ken Trager looked with a critical eye at my repair efforts. "It's real great, being able to work with tools. Those repair types charge an arm and a leg before they even start to work."

I felt like throwing him off the deck. He shook my hand and walked down the stairs, grinning like he'd just hit the big homer to win the World Series. I sat there awhile, running my finger along the sharp edge of the manila folder, thinking back to those days in August, the white beach heat, Cuco Sanchez on the stereo, Roxanne smiling at me, beckoning, the salty tang of her skin beneath my tongue.

And then I called Zeke Torres, an army buddy, who had a network in Mexico.

||||||| 25 |||||||

It took Zeke and me and Zeke's relatives ten days to find Bobby Maclean. He was hiding out in Bufadora, a tiny village on the western coast of the Baja Peninsula. Bufadora sits on a spit of land that juts out from the coast about fifteen miles southwest of Enseñada.

We drove into Bufadora at siesta time on a chilly November Sunday. The road corkscrewed down from a bare brown hill, where nothing grew except dust and rocks and scruffy, stunted cactus. There was one main street lined with cheap shops. At the end of the street, around a corner and behind a marble shrine, was La Bufadora, the blowhole, a narrow cleft in the black sea-cliffs. When the tide chugged up through the cleft, the bottom pressure blew the water up a couple hundred feet, like a whale spouting.

"Lunar power," Zeke said. "That crazy Mexican moon."

Bobby Maclean was not at the blowhole with the other tourists. He was taking a siesta in a small house on the edge of a rocky cliff at the southern edge of the village. We studied the house through field glasses—among his other jobs Zeke was a trader in Army surplus—and saw a small U-shaped structure with a red tiled roof, white-washed walls, and bright blue Mexican shutters. Three dogs slept in the patio. We bought three pounds of hamburger at the local *carniceria*. We doctored it with a dose of sleeping powder and fed it to the dogs. We waited five minutes, until the dogs were snoozing, and then we went inside.

The main room looked out across a balcony to the sea. A piece of the railing on the balcony was broken, in need of repair. The kitchen was to the right, the bedrooms to the left. The place smelled—marijuana smoke, unwashed dishes, dead dreams. Bobby Maclean lay sprawled in sleep in a big four-poster in the master bedroom. A dark-skinned girl—black hair and perky brown breasts—lay curled on one corner of the bed. Her eyes opened in fear as she came awake and saw us. Except for a silver ankle chain she was naked.

Maclean was a big man, a once-muscled guy who was on his way to fat city. His blond hair was thinning, and his skin was red from too much tropical sun. He wore an Errol Flynn mustache. I figured his weight at 280.

We woke Maclean up and got him into a chair with his hands cuffed behind him. His breath stank of alcohol. While Zeke questioned the lady—her name was Guillermina—I searched the house. There were guns in the closet—an Army-issue .45, a Beretta 9 millimeter, a Mannlicher, and a Winchester pump shotgun. There was no sign of Roxanne. Most of the clothes belonged to Maclean, and the flashy female stuff was not Roxanne's style.

I heaved a sigh of relief.

Trager's photo had lied.

There was Tecate beer in the gas-powered fridge. I liberated two cold cans and walked back to the big room, where Maclean, hands locked behind him, sweated in his underwear. The girl now wore an acid wash miniskirt and a red silk blouse. Maclean's puffy eyes tracked the Tecate I handed to Zeke.

"Okay, Maclean. Ready to ride?"

"Ride where?"

"Back to the States. Back to California to face the music and pay the piper."

"I've been to the States."

"No place like the States. You can insure your fat ass for a lot of money, then buy a body to die in your place, and live the rest of your life in beautiful Bufadora."

He grunted. He was about my age, but life had caught up to him, and he looked old and beaten down. His gut was flabby, his big arms soft. Tiny blood vessels reddened his cheeks and nose. In college he'd probably been a BMOC, class prexy, fraternity cocksman, and hotdog on the Dean's List. Those days were a memory. "Who are you?" he growled. "What do you want?"

"Murdock's my name. I've been hired to bring you back. You and the insurance money."

"I don't have it, friend."

"Where is it?"

"GAF. Greater Atlanta Futures. We're cut off, friend. We're broke in a foreign land." He shifted in his chair. "I've got a small stash here, pesos and Eagles and some Swiss francs. You want it, take it. If I'm careful, it'll last three months."

I asked some questions, probing and poking at his story. He was good at rapping, good at pumping forth empty words. Ten minutes of his talk, and you needed wings to hover above the bullshit. We weren't getting anywhere.

Outside the wind whipped the waves, and it started to

rain. I sat back with a sigh and finished my second beer. Maclean watched me thirstily as I drank. The girl sat on the couch, her feet tucked under her, not saying anything. The downpour gave me an idea. I motioned to Zeke. We walked Maclean out to the deck, where we handcuffed him to a heavy wooden chaise. A Montgomery Ward's thermometer, vintage 1950, said the temperature was 37 degrees. He wore only his boxer shorts. Goose bumps peppered his wet, freckled shoulders.

"Bastard!" he said. "You can't leave me here."

"Bobby Maclean," I said, "the drowned rat."

While Maclean shivered in the rain, Zeke talked to the girl in Spanish, and I closed my eyes and tried to doze off. No luck. I was considering another beer when Maclean called out in a choked voice from the rain-washed deck. He was ready.

We took off the cuffs and wrapped him in blankets and let him pull on wool socks. The girl gave him hot tea. He shivered and sneezed. "Brandy," he said. "For the love of God."

"Talk first," I said. "Tell the truth. Then you get a brandy."

He let out a defeated sigh. "Okay, friend. You got me. Anything you want to know. Just name it."

"What I asked before, Maclean. How did they work it with you and Emiliano and the boys from the poker club?"

"Hell," he said, wheezing. "It started as a joke, a kid's fantasy for boy's night out. We'd meet once a week, play some poker, watch a porn flick, maybe waltz in a couple of beach chicks for bedroom rugby. Then one night in August, we were watching a video of *Behind the Green Door* when Bud Strich announces he's found his escape hatch. I remember Bud's eyes. They were very bright, glittery. I remember thinking how drunk he was. 'By October,' Bud said. 'I'll be gone from this life. Departed, as it were, out from under my tearful burden and latched tight onto Paradise.' We were pretty buzzed so we didn't take him seriously. I remember joking with Bud: 'You're going through the green door, right?' 'No,' he said. 'This is no joke. I've found a way out. In October look for me in Paris, at the Deux Magots.' Bud's big dream was to be a chef with an international reputation. His hobby was cooking."

Maclean rolled his meaty shoulders and adjusted the striped blanket. "I didn't think much about it at the time. Most of the guys I knew wanted out. As a group we had a combined book value of a hundred and fifty million personal wealth alone, and we had the debt-loads to match, real bone-crushers, and not much ready cash. We were all leveraged to the max, so on Thursdays there was a lot of talk about chucking everything—the wives, the kids, the houses, the cars, the club memberships, the three-martini lunches, the eighty-hour weeks—and starting over. Friday morning everyone got back to the treadmill. Wendy Barrymore, our scholar, called it the curse of Sisyphus."

"So what happened?"

"This guy shows up. Living proof, you might say. A walking bona fide."

"Who was he?"

"I'd like that brandy now."

"First, the story." I drank a long swallow of Tecate, letting him watch my throat work. When I was finished, I wiped my lips with the back of my hand and grinned at Maclean. "Go on. Who was he?"

"His passport said he was Max Delon, a citizen of Portugal."

"Delon sounds French."

"The guy spoke French."

"He was the contact, right? This guy Delon?"

"Yeah, right."

"What did he look like? What kind of guy was he?"

"He dressed Banana Republic—the bush pants and the matching jacket with the flap pockets, the Stewart Granger hat. His face was sunburned and chiseled. He had steely blue eyes and wore his hair long in back. We gave him a drink, and he showed us a videotape of Africa—I'd been there, hunting, so I knew the country— with him knee-high in sawgrass while he tracked down a wounded water buffalo. There were close-ups of his face, sighting his gun, so we knew it was Delon all right. When the tape was over, he brought out some pictures and said, 'The videotape was after. These are before.' He passed the snapshots around. They showed some corporate Mr. Milktoast getting into a station wagon, wearing a suit, posing with his family, the wife, the two-point-two kids. The fellow in the photos was pasty-faced, overworked, out of shape. Looking at those snaps, it was hard to believe the same man was sitting in the room, playing Great White Hunter."

"But you bought it, right?"

"Hell, we grilled him. Where had he lived? Winnetka, he said. What kind of job? Insurance, he said. He'd been a successful broker. Did he ever see his family? His wife was happily remarried, he said. His kids were off to college. Did he miss them? Not much. They were part of another life, another lifetime. It was clear he was having a helluva lot of fun. He said he'd been up to his ass in debt but had found a way out. You could smell the envy in the room."

"And you believed this stuff?"

"I was sceptical. So were some of the guys. But Delon wasn't selling anything. Not then, anyway. We finish our questions. Delon leaves with Bud, and we don't hear anything more from him. Three weeks later, Bud dies in a car accident, a real flamer down in San Juan Capistrano. There wasn't much left of Bud because the fire had been so hot. I was shocked. Bud had been a good pal, and I missed him. Then at the funeral this guy Delon shows up. He takes me aside and tells me that's not Bud in the closed coffin. I've had a few, and I get mad. We go outside. He says if he can come back to the poker group, he'll have a surprise for us. I say okay. That Thursday he walks in and shakes hands all around and then picks up the telephone. He calls Zurich. It's late September and Bud has been dead for eight days. The call goes through and Delon hands it to me. I get on the phone and talk to Bud Strich for a couple of minutes. You better believe I was surprised. Bud's not dead. He's in fucking Zurich. There's a girl with him—a real knockout, he says—and he's having a ball. 'Bobby,' Bud says. 'I haven't felt this good since I was seventeen! I feel ten years younger, no, make that twenty.' In a week or so, when his money came through, Bud would be going to Paris to enroll in a cooking school. The goddam world thinks he's dead while Bud's starting a new life."

"The money was from insurance?"

"Yeah. The way Delon explained, it would be paid to a beneficiary, then split up three ways. A third for the family. A third for the organization. A third for the dearly departed."

"Did everyone talk to Strich?"

"Yeah. Sure. We all did. One by one."

"Emmy Mendez-Madrid? Did he talk?"

"Sure. Emmy stayed on a long time, asking questions. Anyway, when the phone call is over, Delon gives us his sales pitch. He's selling escape, a new life. 'If you're fed up,' he says, 'if you're over-burdened by this cage you call a life, you have a chance to buy your way out.' I have to admit the setup sounds pretty sweet. Delon's organization will provide escape for each of us. In return we sign over our death benefits. They handle the details—a corpse trucked in from Houston or San Francisco or wherever, the local doc to sign the death certificate, transportation to Europe to the safe house—and when we get there, we stick around as their guests until the money comes through."

"Who had Swiss accounts?"

"Just Emmy."

"Okay. Go on."

"There's not much more. Bud Strich went off to his cooking school. That was September. We tot up our insurance, and Delon puts us in touch with an insurance weenie named Robertson. We take physicals and beef up our coverage. In October Roy Bennett takes the plunge. Roy was older and already insured for a bundle. I remember his dream—he wanted to sail the seven seas and bang island girls, like that guy in *Mutiny on the Bounty*. Freddy Logan went in November, Rip Marlowe in—"

It was Bruce's list, rich men with greedy little-boy dreams. "Did you talk to them?"

"Just to my pals. Freddy Logan. Wendy Barrymore."

"What about Belker? Mendez-Madrid?"

He stared at me. "Belker was a loner, kept to himself. But I talked to Emmy."

"How was he?"

"Just great." There was a pause. Then he said: "At first." Maclean sighed, and a tear ran down his cheek. It was not a tear of sadness, but rather one of lost hope and endless frustration.

"He warned you off, didn't he? Emmy blew the whistle on them."

Maclean nodded. "Okay. I know where you're going with this. I talked to Emmy when he first went over, back in March. Things were great. Then he calls again, in June."

"What did he say?"

"The message was garbled, a lot of static, you know, like he was in a phone booth on the side of a mountain road in Spain. I knew it was Spain, because the operator said the call originated from a Pamplona exchange. Anyway, he said there had been a snafu at the other end and that some people were after him. He needed a place to stay when he got back. He said he had some money stashed. I asked him what had gone wrong, and he said they were thieves, after his Swiss account stash. He warned me not to go through with it. I waited around for him a day or so, and when he didn't show, I headed out on the boat."

"Where is it now?"

"Off the coast, south of here, three fathoms deep."

"Who filed your claim?"

"Who do you think? GAF. Greater Atlanta Futures."

"Did you trace the money?"

"Huh. I went to Atlanta. It was a phony address. Didn't find anyone or anything."

I walked to the fridge for another Tecate. The brandy bottle was on the cabinet. It was Pedro Domecq. Feeling weary from all the crap, I carried the brandy back into the big room, where the rain streaked down the long windows. Maclean poured his own brandy, rattling the bottle against the glass, and gulped it down.

I took a different angle of attack. "When you signed over your life insurance, what line did Delon feed you about the substitute bodies?"

"Take it easy, Dad. He had a list of dead people. A computerized list. It had sex, age, height, weight, and holding facility. No name or race, nothing like that. He called them units, part of the inventory. He was all business. The inventory was urban, he said, street people, derelicts, flotsam."

"Where from?" I broke in.

"Metro areas. Houston, New York, L.A., Chicago. Street spotters would locate a dead person and call Delon's people instead of the cops. They'd use ambulance pickups, to avoid bureaucratic fuss. In private, he told me my replacement was from the Tenderloin in San Francisco."

"That's the term? Replacement?"

"Sure. It was a business. Replacement. Units. Inventory. So what?"

Anger flared. I came close to losing control. "I saw your goddam inventory, Maclean. I saw stiffs in ice cream containers waiting to be shipped off somewhere. I saw your goddam replacements!"

He glared up at me. "People die every day, Dad. They die on the freeway and on the streets. They freeze, they starve. They die in bed, in wars, in jail. Life's a goddam war, so don't get righteous with me for trying to win one stinking battle!"

I grabbed his wrist and spun him around and jammed his arm behind him. The brandy glass shattered on the orange pavers. The blanket slid off his shoulders. I forced his arm upward until he groaned. "Jesus, Maclean. If they couldn't find the right double, what's to keep them from knocking off someone?"

"People die, goddamit. They up and fucking die!"

I wanted to break his arm, hurt him, give him some real pain, shake him out of his middle-class tree. There was one surge of strength, one short attempt to fight back, the old survival urge rising, and then he gave up, surrendered, fatty muscles going slack. He was sweating again, wheezing with fear. I walked him out to the deck, into the cold, got him down on his knees, then prone on his belly. I levered him through the broken place in the railing, his chest and shoulders pushed out into space. "You were after Roxanne."

"Huh," he grunted. "Who wasn't?"

I forced him farther over. The rock face fell away from us in a black and gray pattern washed with salty sea spray. Maclean was scum, a barnacle, a sorry parasite. I was ready to drop him. "Run through it."

He wheezed again, gasping for air. His body was slick with sweat. "You want time and temperature, pal?"

I bent down, my knee in his back, pressing forward, until we were both close to going over. "Three seconds. One. Two."

"Okay. Okay. It happened at the club. I knew Emmy was banging every gash in sight and I'd had the hots for his lady ever since I first saw her. I mean, she was class, right? So I propositioned her, just testing the water, okay? Hell, it's not against the law. The way she dressed, the way she walked, that brown skin, those incredible tits, she looked ripe. I gave her the old goose and gander spiel."

I tightened my hold. "Then what?"

"Turned me down. Flat."

I grabbed his ear and jerked his head back. Rich guys, playing games, killing people, selling corpses so they could live out a crappy little fantasy. "But you kept on trying, right?"

"Sure. But nothing happened."

"And that's why you hung around for Emmy's escape, right? That's why you cooperated? So you could be handy for the grieving widow?"

"Okay. Sure. Delon told me what to do in the hospital, walked me through it. This was a new pattern they were trying out, the heart attack in public, the morgue, so they needed more actors on the scene. The doc showed. Rox insisted on going down to the morgue. Christ, I had the hots so bad even her trembling turned me on. Then the morgue guy pulls the sheet back, and Roxanne's eyes go wide and she faints, right in my arms."

"Then what?"

"We take her home. We stay with her. A couple of days later I make my pitch, but it's no go. She was cool, man, the original ice lady. Wouldn't let me get to first base."

The world tilted on me as I realized how close to death we were. My eyes watered. My breath came in staccato bursts. He was a bug, an insect, so why not kill him? He was scum on the bathtub, slime in the sewer. I could let him drop and give the girl some money and no one would know.

Except me.

Maclean wasn't worth it.

I braced myself and heaved him back away from the edge. Zeke Torres stood six feet away, ready to grab me if I fell. I grinned at him and he grinned back, relaxing, and then I stood up and sat against the wall, hearing the sea wind, shaking.

No matter what people did to each other, the world kept on turning. Night would come to Bufadora and then the dawn and then another night, on and on, turning, turning, turning.

Maclean crawled away from the edge to lie near the wall about ten feet from me, his chest heaving.

"What was Emmy's dream, Maclean?"

His short laugh turned into a cough. "Ski instructor. Feeling up the chicks. Goosing all those butts in tight ski pants."

"Did you have asthma as a kid?"

"Yeah." He looked at me, sharply. "But I outgrew it."

I thought of Ten Eyck, Mr. Smooth, and his profile of

asthmatic entrepreneurs dreaming of escape. "What was your dream, Maclean?"

"Up yours." He sat up, slowly.

"What was it? Come on. Cook? Casanova? Mountain climber? Big game hunter? Mercenary? What?"

He flipped me the finger. It was his dream. He'd paid for it, and now he wasn't sharing with anyone.

It was time to go. I stood up and left him there, on the windy deck, resting his head on his knees.

Before we left, I made sure Maclean's guns were unloaded. I pitched his ammo into the water, and then Zeke and I walked out to the Land Rover. The girl, Guillermina, followed us as far as the patio. She had eyes for Zeke.

Maclean appeared at the door, holding the Winchester pump like a club. He'd been handcuffed, soaked, chilled to the bone, and humiliated. His secret had been poked at and he was ready for revenge.

"I thought you were taking me back," Maclean said.

"Couldn't stand the smell, Maclean."

He took two steps, then stopped, coughed, and leaned against the adobe wall. "She left you, too, didn't she? Left you high and dry, whistling to yourself. She's good at that."

I turned and walked away from him. The rain had stopped and there were tiny puddles in the hollows of the rock driveway. I reached the Land Rover and opened the door and climbed in beside Zeke. Maclean shouted something, but I could not make it out.

"El Señor Loco," Zeke said, going into low gear.

I didn't know whether he meant Maclean or me.

Zeke made his turn and we left Bobby Maclean standing at the edge of the patio, leaning against the wall, shouting into the Bufadoran breeze.

*   *   *

It took us four hours to cross the border at Tijuana, so I reached home about midnight. Wally had saved my mail in a box just inside the front door. My answering machine bristled with calls. Four sales types assured me I could safely shelter my income with an umbrella policy, multiple instruments, telephone transfers, earn more interest, pie in the sky, yadda yadda. One of the four was an agent for Heartland. Two people wanted to consult about some serious detecting. A sexy voice from the bank, identifying herself as my personal banker, wanted to lend me money to refinance my house. Three reporters wanted to talk to me about greenwashing in Orange County. So did two investigators from the post office. Leon Book wanted me to come down to the station to make a statement for some feds. He did not say what the topic was. The last call was from Trager, who wanted to know how I was doing. *"Cherchezing la femme"* was the way Kenny phrased it.

I opened a Bud and unfroze some soup—Minestone à la Murdock—and got to work sorting the mail. There were bills, ads, slick flyers, coupons of hope and promise that assured me the great consumer carousel was still pumping along. I had not won the Reader's Digest super sweeps. I had not won a trip to Hawaii.

Roxanne's letter was near the bottom in a fat brown envelope. There was no return address, but the stamp was from Mexico, dated November 7, the day I'd left on my manhunt. It had been mailed from Mexico City:

Dearest Matt—

I have landed at last, in a small village in the mountains near X——. The house is beautiful. It has a patio and a lean-to garage and a lovely kitchen and a sunny place for me to work. I have a maid named Alicia and a gardener named Tomas and I have found this wonderful Doctor Montoya who does an advanced version of natural childbirth. He says I have the body—the hips and pelvis—for effortless child-bearing. It's a wonderful feeling. I am so happy. I glow. I glow. I glow.

A child, you say?

I can see your face, hear your voice. Questions. Stern macho queries. You want to know why you were not told. I wanted to tell you. Very much. But I was afraid to spoil what we had, that glorious time overlooking your beach. You were healing. I felt the world closing in, the wolves, darling, the howling wolves. It broke my heart to leave like that.

You were right for me. I was right for you. You are so gentle. When he hired you, Bruce told me you were a killer, nothing more. "Dial 'M' for Murdock," he said, with heavy irony. How wrong he was! You nurtured me, brought me back to life, got me all blooming with child. How does it feel to be a father, darling? Are you smiling? Are there tears in your eyes?

I turned the page.

My belly did not begin to show until the past week, but somehow Alicia knew much earlier, as if by a sixth sense of sisterhood. She is the mother of five herself and offers much advice for child-rearing in this dusty, primitive place. As I walked to the market yesterday, two women called good morning in a different and wonderful way. Their smiles said they knew I was with child. By now the village knows. In the mornings I sit at my desk and translate Ocampo. In the afternoons I do volunteer work at Doctor Montoya's clinic in the town of X——where they need so much. Homeopathy helps, magically. Thank Wally for me.

So darling, do you prefer a girl or a boy? If you were here, we could argue. Then we could make love. I miss you, Señor. I will raise our child to be strong and true. And when the time comes, I will come back to see you, and bring the child to its father.

How are you? How is dear Wally? I must rush now to get this in the post. It is time for my drive through the mountains to the clinica. I miss you, Señor, with all my bursting heart. All my love.

Roxanne.

I stared at the letter. My hands shook.

It took awhile for my eyes to get dry. I reread Roxanne's letter, and then I switched from Bud to Mondavi red and went out to the deck, to the beach and the November night wind. Winter had come to California, short gray days, rain on the highways, tourists deserting the beach, gulls going hungry. Parking on the quad was no problem. From now on to get a tan, you'd have to work at it indoors in a mirrored booth with phony sunrays. Thanksgiving was coming. Then Christmas. Then a new year. The earth whirled on, and I was having trouble accepting the idea of birthing a child.

Father Murdock.

If I found her, I could ask her about her flight to Zurich. I could ask her about Emmy's secret Swiss account. I could ask her about Bobby Maclean. I could stir things up, punish myself, really feel betrayed.

One thing was certain, Roxanne had left just in time. Ken Trager would not give up. The newshounds and law enforcement types were poking into the case again. And Roxanne had committed a fraud by identifying her husband in the gray-green morgue in the basement of St. Boniface. If they caught her, they would work her over good. And I didn't want her hurt.

Not now. Not ever.

Emmy was dead. Bruce was dead. Jerome was dead. Maclean was finished. Dugger was in jail. The poker club would not be assembling for Thursday fun, ever again. Belker would not be united with Sheena. Ten Eyck was back at work. Roxanne was alive. So was I. Roxanne was pregnant. So was I.

Enough killing. Enough hate. Enough blood.

I drank a swallow of Mondavi and then I walked inside and tasted the soup and then I phoned Ken Trager in Los Angeles and told him to take his Heartland money and go to hell.

||||||| Epilogue |||||||

LAGUNA BEACH—One person is dead and three remain on the injured list as the result of a three-vehicle collision Friday evening on Laguna Canyon Road, the California Highway Patrol reported.

The accident occurred at 11:43 P.M. when a sedan driven by a Newport Beach man veered across the divider stripe, colliding with a light truck. A third vehicle was unable to brake in time, crashing into the wreckage. The driver of vehicle number three was arrested on suspicion of drunk driving.

The dead man has been identified as William Sheldon, forty-eight, of Newport Beach. Sheldon, well-known in the community for his work with the homeless, was the founder and president of The Money Tree, a home mortgage organization based in Newport Beach. Sheldon's body was greatly disfigured by the fire, which resulted from gasoline igniting.

"When I arrived," said CHP officer Randy Thurgood,

"it was hotter than hell. You couldn't get within twenty feet of the blaze. Lucky for those other people they were thrown free."

Sheldon is survived by his wife Wanda, twenty-eight, who suffered contusions and shock. Chris Jobs of Anaheim was reported in satisfactory condition after his light truck was struck when Sheldon's Cadillac Biarritz veered into his lane.

"It was the first fog of winter," Jobs said. "I was poking along, feeling my way, like, when I see these headlights ramming up into me. I yank the wheel, but nowhere near in time."

A spokesman for the City of Laguna Beach reaffirmed the city's earlier position, asking the state for traffic signals and a lowered speed limit along this stretch of the highway.

"This is a horrible thing to happen at Christmas," the City spokesman said.

A spokesman for the state road authority could not be reached for comment.

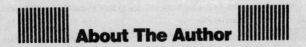

About The Author

Robert J. Ray was born in Amarillo, Texas, earned a doctorate in English at the University of Texas in Austin, taught English for thirteen years and tennis for five years, and now lives in Irvine, California. He teaches fiction writing at Chapman College in Orange and at UCI-Extension. Mr. Ray has written two previous novels in his Matt Murdock mystery series: *Bloody Murdock* and *Murdock for Hire*. He is the author of three other novels, *The Heart of the Game*, *Cage of Mirrors*, and *The Hit Man Cometh*. He is currently completing the next Matt Murdock novel.

FREE FROM DELL

with purchase plus postage and handling

Congratulations! You have just purchased one or more
titles featured in Dell's Mystery 1990 Promotion. Our goal
is to provide you with quality reading and entertainment, so
we are pleased to extend to you a limited offer to receive a
selected Dell mystery title(s) *free* (plus $1.00 postage and
handling per title) for each mystery title purchased. Please
read and follow all instructions carefully to avoid delays in
your order.

1) Fill in your name and address on the coupon printed below. No facsimiles or
   copies of the coupon allowed.

2) The Dell Mystery books are the only books featured in Dell's Mystery 1990
   Promotion. No other Dell titles are eligible for this offer.

3) Enclose your original cash register receipt with the price of the book(s)
   circled plus $1.00 **per book** for postage and handling, payable in check or
   money order to: Dell Mystery 1990 Offer. Please do not send cash in the
   mail.
   Canadian customers: Enclose your original cash register receipt with the
   price of the book(s) circled plus $1.00 **per book** for postage and handling in
   U.S. funds.

4) This offer is only in effect until April 29, 1991. Free Dell Mystery requests
   postmarked after April 22, 1991 will not be honored, but your check for
   postage and handling will be returned.

5) Please allow 6-8 weeks for processing. Void where taxed or prohibited.

Mail to: Dell Mystery 1990 Offer
       P.O. Box 2081
       Young America, MN 55399-2081

NAME_____

ADDRESS_____

CITY_____STATE_____ZIP_____

BOOKS PURCHASED AT_____

AGE_____

(Continued)

Book(s) purchased:_____

_____

_____

I understand I may choose one free book for each Dell Mystery book purchased (plus applicable postage and handling). Please send me the following:

(Write the number of copies of each title selected next to that title.)

☐ **BLOOD SHOT**
Sara Paretsky
V.I. Warshawski is back—this time a missing person assignment turns into a murder investigation that puts her more than knee-deep in a deadly mixture of big business corruption and chemical waste.

☐ **FIRE LAKE**
Jonathan Valin
In this Harry Stoner mystery, the Cincinnati private eye enters the seamy and dangerous world of drugs when a figure from his past involves him in a plot that forces him to come to terms with himself.

☐ **THE HIT MAN COMETH**
Robert J. Ray
When a professional hit man who has his sights set on a TV evangelist wounds Detective Branko's partner instead, Newport Beach's hottest detective finds himself with a list of suspects that is as bizarre as it is long.

☐ **THE NANTUCKET DIET MURDERS**
Virginia Rich
A handsome new diet doctor has won over Nantucket's richest widows with his weight-loss secrets—and very personal attention. But when murder becomes part of the menu, Mrs. Potter stirs the pot to come up with a clever culinary killer.

☐ **A NOVENA FOR MURDER**
Sister Carol Anne O'Marie
"Move over, Miss Marple, here comes supersleuth Sister Mary Helen, a nun with an unusual habit of solving murders."
—San Francisco Sunday Examiner & Chronicle

☐ **SHATTERED MOON**
Kate Green
When a young woman gets involved with the L.A.P.D. and a missing person case, her most precious gift—her healing vision—becomes her most dangerous enemy, filling every moment with mounting menace. . . and turning the secrets of her past murderously against her.

☐ **TOO CLOSE TO THE EDGE**
Susan Dunlap
Jill Smith, a street-smart, savvy detective, finds herself trapped within a murder victim's intricate network of perilous connections.

☐ **A NICE CLASS OF CORPSE**
Simon Brett
When the sixty-seven-year-old Mrs. Pargeter checks into a seaside hotel for some peace and quiet, what she finds instead is a corpse in the lobby and a murder to snoop into on the dark side of the upper crust.

☐ **POLITICAL SUICIDE**
Robert Barnard
A member of Parliament meets an untimely—and suspicious—demise.

☐ **THE OLD FOX DECEIV'D**
Martha Grimes
When the body of a mysterious woman is found murdered, Inspector Richard Jury of Scotland Yard finds himself tracking a very foxy killer.

☐ **DEATH OF A PERFECT MOTHER**
Robert Barnard
Everyone had a motive to kill her. . . so Chief Inspector Dominic McHale finds himself stumped on his very first homicide case—puzzled by a lengthy list of suspects and a very clever killer.

☐ **THE DIRTY DUCK**
Martha Grimes
In addition to the murders being staged nightly at the Royal Shakespeare Theatre, a real one has been committed not too far away, and the killer has left a fragment of Elizabethan verse behind as a clue.

TOTAL NUMBER OF FREE BOOKS SELECTED _____ X $1.00
= $_____ (Amount Enclosed)

Dell has other great books in print by these authors. If you enjoy them, check your local book outlets for other titles.